THE WOMAN AND THE APE

PETER HØEG was born in 1957 and followed various callings – dancer, actor, fencer, sailor, mountaineer – before he turned seriously to writing. After publishing his first novel, *The History of Danish Dreams*, in 1988 ("a vaultingly ambitious and hugely accomplished first novel" in the opinion of Peter Whittaker, *New Statesman & Society*), and a volume of short stories, he went on to write an innovative crime novel, *Miss Smilla's Feeling for Snow*, which assured him an international reputation. The variety of his talent was amply demonstrated with his subsequent novel, *Borderliners*, a remarkable study of children which caused controversy within Denmark and beyond.

BARBARA HAVELAND, a Scot married to a Norwegian, and resident in Denmark, has translated Peter Høeg's *Borderliners* and his first novel *The History of Danish Dreams*. She is also translator of Solvej Balle's *According to the Law*.

By the same author in English translation

THE HISTORY OF DANISH DREAMS
MISS SMILLA'S FEELING FOR SNOW
BORDERLINERS

Peter Høeg

THE WOMAN
& THE APE

Translated from the Danish
by Barbara Haveland

THE HARVILL PRESS
LONDON

First published in Denmark
with the title *Kvinden og Aben*
by Munksgaard/Rosinante, Copenhagen, 1996

First published in an export edition in 1996 by
The Harvill Press,
84 Thornhill Road,
London N1 1RD

First published in Great Britain by
The Harvill Press, in 1997

3 5 7 9 10 8 6 4 2

© Fonden "Lolwe", 1996
English translation © Munksgaard/Rosinante, 1996

Peter Høeg asserts the moral right to be
identified as the author of this work

A CIP catalogue record for this book is
available from the British Library

ISBN 1 86046 254 5 (hbk)
ISBN 1 86046 255 3 (pbk)

Designed and typeset in Sabon at
Libanus Press, Marlborough, Wiltshire

Printed and bound in Great Britain by Butler & Tanner Ltd
at Selwood Printing, Burgess Hill

THE WOMAN AND THE APE

An ape was approaching London. It sat on a bench in the open cockpit of a sailing boat, on the lee side, all hunched up with its eyes closed and a blanket round its shoulders. Even in that position it made the man sitting across from it seem smaller than he actually was.

The man was presently going by the name of Bally, and there were just two things in this life he still had any time for: the moment when he arrived in a big city and the moment he left it again. Which was why now he got to his feet, crossed to the rail and stood there looking towards the city, and in so doing made the first and last mistake of the voyage.

His absent-mindedness transmitted itself to his crew. The helmsman switched over to autopilot, the deck hand worked his way aft from the foredeck, both gravitating towards the rail. For the first time in five days the three men stood idle, lost in the sight of the electric lights of suburbia dancing like fireflies past the boat and fading away astern.

The wind had risen during the night. The Thames was now overlaid with fluted bands of white foam and the boat, besides having the wind dead aft and a billowing mainsail, also had a large foresail hoisted. Carrying this much sail was verging on recklessness, but Bally had been hoping to make it in while it was yet dark.

He was not going to manage it, he could see that now. There was a change in the air, with the first light of this spring morning spreading like a grey pelt across the buildings. Reminded of the ape, Bally turned around.

It had opened its eyes and leaned forward. One hand rested on the little switch on the dashboard for adjusting the autopilot.

Bally had always brought up on deck the animals he sailed with because it lessened the risk of their dying of seasickness, and this strategy had never brought him anything but good results. They had been attached to lifelines, wrapped in blankets and given one milligram per kilo of body weight of an effective neuroleptic twice daily. Well cushioned and with no clear sense of their surroundings, they had dozed the voyage away.

This procedure would now, he thought to himself with the speed at which thought is occasionally possible within a span of time too short to allow for any physical reaction, have apparently to be altered.

Lagging – though only minutely so – behind the ape's movement, the autopilot turned the bow of the boat a few fatal degrees out of the wind. It pitched awkwardly on the choppy water. Then it gybed.

At that instant, the ape was looking directly at the three men.

Many years before this, Bally had discovered that life consisted of a series of repetitions, each one savouring of less than its predecessor – an overall distastefulness in which man himself was but one more repetition. He was also well aware that the reason he had sought, throughout his life, such close contact with animals had to do with the fact that amidst this instinctive loathing there was a kick to be got out of having power over automatons of a lower order than oneself. This notion of universal vapidity was now being challenged. The ape's movements were purposeful and studied, but that was not the worst of it. The worst thing, the thing which, though it lasted only for a fraction of a second, was to make itself felt throughout the rest of Bally's life, was what he saw in its eyes.

For this he had no words – for this, at that point, no-one had any words. But it was in a way the opposite of automatic.

The vessel's mast was 55 feet tall, her mainsail had an area of more than 480 square feet, so the swing when it came was quicker than the eye could follow. All that the three men had time to register was a slight list and a crack like a gunshot as the boom snapped two steel shrouds on the port side. Then they were swept into the Thames.

With a screech of overtaxed bearings the autopilot adjusted to the new tack and corrected course accordingly. At her own speed of

6

twelve knots plus two knots from the incoming tide the boat carried on towards London, now with the ape as her sole passenger.

Fifteen minutes later the first call to the boat went out over the short-wave radio. This and the two subsequent calls went unanswered, and after that there were no more.

But behind the smoked glass of an observation window in a cabin near Deptford Ferry Road an officer of the River Police put down a microphone and lifted a pair of binoculars. Slowly but intently the city's immune system was being activated to detect a breach of regulations.

Seaward of Tower Bridge, at the marina by the Pool of London, St Katharine's Yacht Club has a café. Here, during the summer months, breakfast is served on an open-air terrace between the Thames and St Katharine's Dock and on this morning, even at such an early hour, some dozen guests were already seated there.

The Pool is said to be the only point at which the Thames is blue. It is here that the royal yachts anchor. From here legations to London sail out to have lunch on their national training ships. Here, one September day in 1866, 100,000 people watched the famous race for the finish between the two tea clippers the *Taeping* and the *Ariel*.

Something of the expectancy of that earlier time was now aroused on the Yacht Club terrace at the sight of *The Ark*. Everyone there recognized the boat as an Ocean 71, built at Poole, a speedy but nevertheless classic English ketch. And by its casual approach and rash spread of canvas they could tell that this was a skipper of the old school, a traditionalist, heading into port under sail alone. A few minutes later, over the gilded dolphins on the bow, they caught a glimpse of the man himself wearing neither oilskins nor sunglasses, not even a cap. Just a sober grey overcoat. A hush fell over the terrace, everyone knew what was going to happen next because they had heard how the real pros did it, dropping anchor at the last minute, every inch of canvas brought down with a clatter and the boat gliding smoothly and neatly round the chain and into the quayside. As *The Ark* approached the pier they prepared to applaud, a few already had their hands in the air, but by then it was too late. With an apocalyptic screech of splintering timber the ketch ploughed into the outermost of the moored yachts, sliced it in half and sparked off a domino-style chain reaction along a serried rank of mahogany and rosewood hulls.

None of the breakfasters came to their senses fast enough to see how the grey overcoat leapt from the cockpit and across a foundering hull and then disappeared – swiftly, if haltingly – around the side of a building. But two others did. In the sluice-gate control room a lock keeper employed by Taylor Woodrow, the company which owns and runs St Katharine's Dock, laid down his binoculars and lifted a telephone. And on the east side of the dock, Johnny broke into a run.

2

What Johnny was running towards was a van, parked beside the marina facing Wapping industrial estate. In this he had tracked *The Ark* from the pre-arranged rendezvous at the pier by Amsterdam Road on the Isle of Dogs and from there to the Pool of London.

This van was Johnny's only home and sole possession and yet it was never locked, not even now. Instead, on the door was the transfer of a sign showing the silhouette of a dog and some words in very small lettering. This sign was not there for decoration. In the bunk behind the driver's seat lay a hundred-pound Dobermann called Samson who had been for five years one of the champion dogs in the illegal ring of dog fights held in Britain's immigrant communities. Johnny had bought him when he was starting to lose and was therefore about to be put down and it had taken him a year to ease him off life as a sports star on a strict diet with a drastically increased lung capacity and stroke volume and make him both his watchdog and his best – and only – friend.

Johnny had two names, the second of which was every bit as important if not more so than his given name. It was Golf Zulu India One Three Foxtrot Whisky, his radio ham international call signal. On the dashboard in front of him was his radio transmitter and now, as he started the engine with one hand, with the other he tuned the receiver to the Metropolitan Police waveband in time to catch the tail end of the first vague description of the man in the grey overcoat and the order to seal off the harbour area.

Johnny's face – as he drove up to East Smithfield Road and over

Tower Bridge – was set. In the three years he had been working for Bally he had never seen him make a single mistake. In bewilderment his thoughts flitted back and forth between the road, *The Ark*, the river police, the crash, the immediate future and the limping fugitive in the grey overcoat.

"Would you," he said to the dog behind him, "have said that Bally's arms reach all the way to the ground when he stands up?"

Samson made no reply. But he stirred, affected by his master's unease.

Johnny had spent the past ten years of his life endeavouring to make himself invulnerable and he had almost succeeded. He had his work, with the van, and his home, again the van. He was mobile and dependent on no-one. At his back he had Samson and via his radio transmitter he was in touch with ethereal friends throughout the civilized world. And yet here he sat behind the wheel, shaking. Because there was one chink in his armour which he had never succeeded in covering up: Johnny gambled on animals.

His was an anonymous, an almost invisible, weakness in a world where everything is a gamble. Bally was the first to detect something in Johnny's obsession beyond the dreams of winning and it was because of what he had seen there that he had taken him on.

Johnny did not play to win. He always placed the lowest possible bet and with a peculiar blindness in this betting, never knowing who the favourites might be and never giving or taking a tip. He gambled because of something he could not quite put his finger on but which had to do with being near the animals when they exploded into life. At the sight of six greyhounds all lunging as one after the mechanical hare, at the crack of the racing pigeon's wings as it takes to the air, at the Derby, at the trotting track, at Sedgefield or Pontefract races, at cockfights in the Indonesian quarter, something inexpressible happened to Johnny.

Bally had never said where his cargo came from, nor where it ended up and their partnership had lasted this long – despite Johnny's awareness, from the outset, of the scale of the risk involved – because Bally had brought him very close to that mysterious goal for which he longed.

For Bally he had carried, behind him in the trailer section hooked up to his sleeping quarters, a Javanese rhinoceros with skin as cracked and hard as iron, but of a strangely gentle and querulous nature. He had carried two okapi; carried a saltwater crocodile measuring a record 32 feet in length in a crate that jutted out 15 feet behind the truck. He had carried fifteen poisonous Amazonian frogs, blinking and perfect, like fifteen tiny cobalt-blue gems. He had carried eight rare giant angelfish in two 1,000-gallon tanks. A half-grown elephant. Two Himalayan snow leopards with tails longer than their bodies. He had carried South American black saki monkeys and emperor tamarins. And on one unforgettable occasion, a family of tarsiers with two young, which had swivelled their heads around through 180° and stared up at him from their box with their great eyes as though begging him to drive carefully.

He had not let them down, not them nor any other creature. He had transported them with infinite tenderness and patience. He had adjusted the heating for them, fed and watered them, separated them if they fought. And the journey itself, which he knew to be a dreadful experience for the animals – hours and hours of disorienting darkness in a mobile prison – had been smooth as a caress. Not one of Bally's animals had ever died while being transported by Johnny.

During those hours on the road in the van, with some powerful or wondrous but always fragile creature in the back, gliding over the bumps in the tarmac, Johnny had felt almost happy.

Now it was over, he was quite sure that something irrevocable had occurred, that he would never again drive a consignment for Bally. That was why he was shaking.

Behind him the dog gave a hacking cough and Johnny stretched back a hand to give it a reassuring pat. Then he frowned. Dobermanns have dense, short-haired coats. What he felt under his fingers was a shaggy Rya rug.

Ahead of him the lights at the crossroads with David Street, below the railway bridge, changed to amber. He brought the van to a halt and looked in the rear-view mirror.

The first thing the people sitting in the cars behind the van saw was the driver's door flying open. They saw Johnny jump out and then begin to run away from the vehicle as fast as his legs could carry him. Next they saw him stop in his tracks, turn round and walk back. They saw him open the door and peer into the cab. They could not tell what he was looking for, but in his face when he saw that it was empty they read disappointment, surprise and yearning. They saw him drive the truck in to the kerb and as they drove past him a number of them saw that he was wearing earphones and holding something that might have been a street map. A few also managed to read the whole of the legend under the picture of the dog on the van door. It said: *This vehicle is guarded by a Dobermann. Fuck with it and find out.*

3

Some distance to the south and east, the railway lines split. One branch continues, running on granite supports, along a spur narrow as an animal track and high as a migratory route, through Peckham Rye to the fashionable suburb of Dulwich.

In Dulwich, at the foot of the railway embankment stands a row of eighteenth-century town houses with large back gardens. In one of these gardens, on the steps of the house – now, in what were still the early hours – a man lay, eyeing the ape through a telescope sight mounted on a hunting rifle.

It was a Holland & Holland rifle with a hair trigger and it was loaded with a 230-grain bullet that could have slain an elephant, no bother. All that had kept the ape alive up to this point was the absence of a very slight touch of the man's index finger.

On the barbed-wire fence that marked the boundary between the bottom of the garden and the railway spur hung a sign bearing the words NO TRESPASSING and citing in true British style the law of Aggravated Trespass, and the man knew it made no difference that the ape could not read. He had the law on his side, and behind him – barricaded in on the second floor – he had his family to protect. And in his heart burned the old love of the chase.

But even though he had had the ape in his sights for forty-five minutes he had not yet pulled the trigger. And, what was worse, he knew now that he never would. Each time his finger had curled around the trigger the animal had made some move, a tiny, microscopic shift in position or a turn of its head that – for the first time in his life – had evoked in the man the overpowering feeling that were he to shoot this animal he would be committing murder.

Twenty minutes earlier, in desperation, he had got his wife to look up some telephone numbers and make several calls, and now he was waiting, waiting and hoping. Then the doorbell rang.

He had been expecting a commando unit, or, at the very least, a couple of armed men. Instead, the new arrival whom his wife ushered out onto the steps was a woman in her late thirties wearing a long dress and a hat.

The ape was sitting propped up against a tree, its chin sunk onto its chest. The woman walked right up to it. The man waited ten paces off. He held the rifle at the ready but it was the woman and not the ape on whom his eyes were pinned.

Ever since – in his twenties – he had begun to earn money, he had been able to buy whatever he wanted – most recently this town house and the address that went with it – and it was his experience and his belief, generally speaking, that everything had a price tag. He had come across very few exceptions to this rule and had always felt both intrigued and puzzled when confronted by something for which no price had as yet been set. In the woman facing him he saw something he did not understood, a courage which he sensed eschewed the usual haggling.

"How come you didn't shoot it?" she said.

The man realized that, even though she had never met him before, she recognized that under other circumstances he would cheerfully have paid out ten thousand pounds and travelled halfway round the world for a chance, in different surroundings, of shooting an animal such as the one that had just shown up in his own garden free of charge. In vain he tried to come up with a plausible answer only to find himself driven by the awkwardness of the situation to a new and unfamiliar honesty.

"I couldn't," he said.

Two men in brown coats came out onto the steps.

"We'll take it with us," said the woman. " Will you give us a hand?"

The man looked at her blankly. The animal was as tall as a man and broader. And it was a long, long time since he had done any manual labour.

He had been under the impression that the woman was already standing upright. But now, without any visible change in her stance, she grew an inch taller.

"It's dying," she said. "Would you be so kind as to help lift it."

The man bent down and grabbed hold.

From his window, a little later, he watched the ape being driven away in a black car that put him in mind of a funeral cortège. He came to the conclusion that probably it would die and with that he dismissed the thought. But for a long while afterwards he was bothered by pain in the small of his back from having lifted too heavy a weight and the unreal sensation of having lived through a dream.

The car was no hearse. It was an animal ambulance belonging to the Holland Park Veterinary Clinic and the man who made the first cursory examination of the ape, as it lay on the ambulance cot was Dr Alexander Bower, proprietor of that institution.

"Will it live?" asked the woman.

"We have to get it into the clinic."

An indiscernible nod from the woman sanctioned the implicit costs entailed by the ape's admission.

" I would rather it wasn't registered," she said.

The ambulance stopped, the woman climbed out. Halfway through the door she turned.

"If it lives," she said, "I'll see that you're well rewarded."

This promise prompted in the doctor a little schoolboy bow.

"But if it dies you might as well fill one of your own syringes right there and then and put yourself to sleep."

4

In South Hill Park, by Hampstead Heath, outside the door of one of the vast rooms of a mansion that lay, hidden away, inside a garden as big as a park, Madelene Burden took a last swig from the water carafe in her hand, straightened the topknot into which her hair was drawn, pushed open the door and walked into the light.

"How do I look?" she asked.

Adam, her husband, drew himself up and viewed the spectacle.

"Enchanting," he said.

Had he been closer he would have been able to catch a whiff of something else apart from this enchanting vision, namely the reek of ethyl alcohol exuding from his wife's pores and from the carafe. But he was standing in the middle of the room and at that distance the illusion held.

With the exception of one large surgical lamp all of the furniture in the room had been pushed back against the walls and Madelene embarked upon an erratic progress along sofas, occasional tables and wing chairs.

"Is there going to be dancing?" she asked.

Adam Burden was fond of encapsulating any significant and complex phenomenon in a single, telling expression. For Madelene, when he met her in Denmark, he had come up with the word "dewy". That had been just over a year and a half ago. At the time it had seemed to him to sum her up perfectly. Since then he had occasionally, as now, felt a twinge of doubt.

There was a knock at the door, their housekeeper opened it and stepped aside.

Out of the darkness and silence there came first footsteps and then a flash of white. Two men wheeled a hospital trolley into the room. They were followed by Alexander Bower. Finally Andrea Burden, Adam's sister, came in and closed the door.

The porters pushed the trolley into the middle of the room. It was covered with a thin blue sheet under which Madelene could discern the outline of a body. Only the deceased's head lay uncovered and as yet in shadow.

Andrea Burden trundled the surgical lamp over to the body, lowered the head and switched on. The porters removed the blue sheet.

The lamp blanked out the rest of the room. For a moment, within its golden sphere, the only thing that existed was the ape.

Like moths Adam and Madelene were drawn towards the creature. Just for an instant Madelene forgot her tight skirt and high heels. She teetered dangerously, as though on stilts, regained her balance and positioned herself alongside the trolley.

She could hear the animal's breathing, thick with mucus, drugged. Behind her in the darkness she was aware of her husband circling around the light. Silence reigned in the room. But somewhere in that silence a secret dialogue had struck up.

"Let's hear it."

"We pick it up day before yesterday. In a garden in Dulwich. The owner looked in the Yellow Pages under animal protection societies and just worked his way down the list. Eventually he gets through to Miss Burden who calls me. There's been considerable blood loss, dehydration, it's suffering from delayed shock. General condition is critical. I operate as soon as it's admitted to the clinic."

With his forefinger the doctor traced a white bandage running round the animal's shoulder and upper arm.

"After administering a transfusion I remove forty pieces of number five shot from the area around the right scapula. The shot was fired from forty yards, wounding superficially but causing pain and loss of blood. I sew up two gashes, in the medial and lateral gastrocnemius. Bite marks, possibly a dog."

He pointed to two dressings below the ape's knee.

"We took a fair amount of rust out of four vertical tears in the abdominal area. Where they back onto the railway embankment most of the houses have had barbed wire put up. Reinforced here and there by electric fencing."

He turned the palms of the ape's hands towards the light to reveal burns salve glistening like chalk.

"It had come across the viaduct, seen the gardens and tried to climb down. The sides are sheer, concrete and granite, so it fell. Partially torn ligaments on both ankles."

He placed a hand on the ape's chest.

"London has etched a map of itself on this one," he said.

"How did it get to Southwark?" Adam asked.

"The Met and the River Police had cordoned off St Katharine's Dock that day."

"But that's on the other side of the river."

The doctor motioned with his hand, the two porters rolled the ape onto its side. The bite mark was long, narrow, deep, every tooth having left a gouge that had either been stitched up or sealed by pus. The hair around the wound had been shaved, exposing a third of the back. The skin was black and blue from bruising. Madelene turned her back and began the journey back to the water carafe.

"A van left the area just before it was cordoned off. It has not been found. But they did find the Dobermann which would appear to have been in the van. The ape must have had its back half-turned to it when it climbed in."

Once more there was silence. Madelene located the table; under cover of the darkness she took a drink from the carafe.

"So," said Adam Burden, "everyone is now looking for a large ape covered in bite marks?"

"Everyone is looking for the skipper of a boat," said the doctor. "A yacht rammed into the dock. There's been no mention of any animal."

Madelene felt how Adam became still, how – out of a range of unspoken options – he had reached a decision she did not understand.

"It can stay here," he said. "Wheel it down to the garden room."

The porters drew the trolley out of the light.

Madelene's field of vision and her mental radius were now

narrower and shorter than the room itself, and dwindling by the minute. She sensed rather than saw the meeting breaking up.

"But Mrs Clapham baked some pastries," she said. "Cream horns. Oh well, I can always eat them with the baboon. When it wakes up."

A door closed. Madelene had no idea whether she was alone. She tried to drink, and failed. Then she rested her head on the table top. To Adam Burden, who had remained standing next to the surgical lamp, her heavy snores sounded exactly like the ape's.

Each morning Madelene was resurrected. This resurrection occurred in front of her mirror and took between thirty and forty-five minutes. While it was under way, she was totally absorbed; during that space of time, with uncompromising thoroughness, she did the one thing she knew herself to be truly good at: she re-created the myth which said that Madelene looks gorgeous.

The face which greeted her when she sat down at the dressing table was, in her own opinion, a dull face. Not a faded face nor yet a face in decay – Madelene *was* only thirty years old. But it was – in her eyes – a pale, nondescript face which looked as if it might at any moment disappear, not in some blazing inferno but simply because, being so drably mediocre, it might easily have merged with its surroundings.

To this surface she now applied a mask, which was at one and the same time sensual and reticent. Having first cleansed her face with skin tonic to create an oil-free base of tightly closed pores, she then used a silk-matte foundation to erase the past ten years of her life. The face in the mirror before her might now, in all its smooth neutrality, have been twenty, even perhaps fifteen or twelve years old.

With a concealing stick she eradicated the microscopic lines around the eyes along with the gradually acquired scepticism of a lifetime. She used a fine brush to raise her eyebrows into the permanent wonder of youth.

It is in the dark areas of our faces that age and weariness reside. Her eyes she enlarged with a pale eye shadow that followed the line of her eyebrow before carefully outlining them with liquid eyeliner. They were now wide, clear and uncritically receptive. She then touched up her cheeks with a delicate golden terracotta blush, accentuated the curve of her mouth with a lip brush and enhanced the fullness of the lips with a natural gloss. Last of all, with a sickly yet widening red dot at the mouth of each tear duct she erased her iron constitution. Her face seemed now childish, radiant and very slightly peaky; so skilfully and subtly reconstructed that only an expert could have told that cosmetics had been used.

Madelene had learned the art of making up from her mother. Not by asking questions or being given any direct answers – it was too touchy a subject for that – but by watching her.

Madelene's mother's life had been one long succession of panic-stricken but more often than not successful attempts at beautification. First and foremost, the beautification of the family's stylish and hectic day-to-day life in Vedbæk, north of Copenhagen, where it was not only the dinner service that was made of porcelain, where the very atmosphere was crystalline and under constant threat of shattering and no voice was ever raised above a whisper for fear of setting off an avalanche of glass. But also, and in more exacting fashion, at the receptions held by the family trust, at which the unresolved tragedies of certain families were thrown together with the calamities of other families and individuals to form an elegantly turned out, graciously served-up version of a modern-day hell on earth here, at the end of the twentieth century. On such occasions Madelene's mother managed to organize a repast that served as a form of social first-aid, she could bid a warm welcome to one and all! in a voice that sealed off emptiness as effectively as Polyfilla. Not only that but, despite the force of both internal and external circumstances, she always looked wonderful. She could emerge from seeing to things in the kitchen enveloped in a cloud of steam and, when the air cleared, there she would be, *décolletée*, looking attractive, hospitable, attentive and girlish, to the point where even Madelene's father's features would momentarily soften into an expression of unmitigated pride of possession.

Around the turn of the century, by dint of a suicidal concerted effort, Madelene's father's family had pulled themselves out of medieval poverty and paid for Madelene's great-grandfather to study engineering. His two sons also went on to become engineers and – in the nineteen-twenties – uncommonly well-off. In a very low-key, Danish fashion and with a distinct, inherited memory of the starvation and cholera epidemics of the previous century the two brothers had used this sudden wealth to entrench their position. They invested and reinvested, bought land, bred and made provision for their offspring so that by now they were not so much a family as a clan – large, unremarkable, unobtrusive and exercising a direct influence on Danish foreign policy.

The family fortune had been founded on the building of byres, an aspect of the empire which Madelene's father had kept up. There was no talk here, though, of half-timbered cottages down some leafy country lane, as seen in Danish Tourist Board brochures, rather four-storey, totally mechanized industrial plants for the manufacture of domestic animals. Madelene's father hated any kind of publicity and he had succeeded in remaining a stranger to all but a select few. These few could, however, detect his personal thumbprint on Denmark's annual production figures – as quoted in the country's *Statistical Yearbook* – of 20,650,000 pigs and 813,000 head of beef and veal cattle.

As is so often the case with people who attempt in their terror to put some distance between themselves and their poverty-stricken past, Madelene's father only respected people who had made their fortunes or who happened to be pioneering men of science and, until she ran away with Adam, Madelene had had to put up with her father referring to her – even, or perhaps especially, in her presence – as: "Madelene, who is nothing really." True, she had been treated to a token education, but she and everyone else had always known that the only thing that really mattered was that one day she would take her place by the right man's side; and in order to assume that place it was not enough to be heiress to a fortune, one also had to look good and looking good meant work, even now, this morning.

Madelene had never found the courage to stand up to her parents. With some defiance, but unable to see any alternative, she had travelled down the smoothed and well-trodden paths marked out for her. But she had dreamt agonizingly, aimlessly, passionately of the chance of another kind of life. Into this dream stepped Adam Burden – a man, an amiable, attentive and not altogether harmless man, on the way up, and Madelene climbed aboard, at once the princess swept up behind the prince on his white charger and a castaway, all at sea and three parts drowned, clutching at the lifebelt that suddenly hoves in view.

Madelene had had 529 days of marriage and each one had begun like this, in front of the mirror, just as what came next also followed a set pattern.

She would now get up and go down to the kitchen for a chat with Clapham's wife about the housekeeping. Thence she would proceed to the terrace to exchange a few words with Clapham himself. After that she would either go up to the West End to do some shopping, or play tennis, or go riding on the Heath. She would then go for a walk with a woman friend and be home by five to welcome Adam home at seven.

Anyone whose days are all the same and free from want inhabits eternity of a sort and that was how Madelene looked upon her life. As though she had wished for, sought and found eternity.

She slipped into a short, pleated skirt and approved her reflection in the mirror. She looked like the oldest daughter of the family on her way to an early tennis lesson. Then she left the room.

In the doorway, as always, she paused for a moment.

Madelene had two rooms, a bedroom and a dressing room, which she left as an animal leaves its territory, tentatively and warily. The routine which lay ahead of her was familiar right down to the last detail. Even so it was not without its terrors.

She herself had organized the decoration of the two rooms she was now leaving behind. She never knew where she found the courage to insist on their pale wooden floors, clean-lined furniture and white walls. To her they represented the only piece of Denmark left to her. Over that threshold the British Commonwealth began.

Adam Burden's parents had died when he was in his twenties, but Madelene had heard his father's voice. One evening Adam had played her a recording from the BBC series *Tales from the Dark Continent* on which an assured and nonchalant speaker had described, warmly, wittily and with never an um or an er, the grand old days in India and

26

British East Africa, and to Madelene it had seemed as though the house in which she lived was talking.

This house had been built by Adam's parents on their return to England in the mid-fifties. They had built it as a memorial to their life by the Indian Ocean and named it Mombasa Manor. It was an L-shaped building with a tiled roof and vast parklike gardens planted with tropical trees and shrubs. In its rooms lion skins were spread on wall-to-wall carpets and spears and shields hung next to the fire-places, and Madelene knew that other people thought she led a very grand life, intriguingly exotic and much to be envied. She also knew that she was, ostensibly, the mistress of this house.

Nevertheless every morning, this one included, she was momen-tarily brought to a halt in her doorway, checked by an instinctive sense of dread embodied in the thought that, since the Empire had subju-gated everything else of an alien nature might it not also devour her?

The pause was brief, this morning as on every other. Madelene gave her head a shake, it was a crazy idea, she drove herself on. And as on all other mornings, as she walked along the corridors, down the staircases and through the rooms she left her fear behind her, a little of it in each place.

Clapham had a standard greeting for her. Whenever Madelene stepped on to the terrace he would stand up, doff his cap, present her with a flower and offer her a cup of coffee.

He always made this offer in a whisper. The coffee was a token of their fraternization, the alliance – in a world that had never known anything coarser than Darjeeling first flush – between her, the foreigner, and him, the worker.

Madelene trusted him up to a point. Like her, he was a part of the surroundings – and, like her, he was not one with them.

She walked through the door. Clapham clicked his heels together and handed her a lilac blossom. Smiling at him over the flower, she waited for his line. But it never came.

"Mr Burden called," he said. "He's coming home early. To work."

Madelene put down the flower, grabbed hold of the chair and eased herself down into it. Adam had never worked at home before.

She was not sure that he had ever spoken of his work at home. She had had the feeling that it was his intent – and one that he had only ever declared to himself – not to so much as think about it once inside the walls of the park.

"Work," she repeated. "On what?"

Clapham's face closed, becoming that of a stranger.

"That you would have to ask Mr Burden, Madam."

Madelene looked away. Clapham had not called her "Madam" since they had first been introduced.

He put down his cup and stood up.

"Duty calls," he said.

And he turned his back on her.

From the games pavilion, just below the terrace, Madelene fetched a racket – the last part of her disguise.

The tennis court lay on the other side of the house and it was in this direction that she set out with a lively spring in her step, but she did not go all the way there. The momentum and optimism in her gait lasted only as far as the corner which, once rounded, hid her from view. From that point on her movements became stealthy and feline. Leaving the gravel path she passed through a doorway in the gable end of the house's other wing, and straight in to the potting shed.

The room was warm and humid as a rainforest, half the roof was glazed, flowerpots and hotbeds held thousands of cuttings, water lilies in bloom floated in a huge freshwater tank. Madelene caught sight of her own reflection in the door of a stainless steel cabinet and smiled reassuringly at herself. Then she did as she always did.

She took a pipette from a wire shelf, a Pyrex flask from a cupboard, a small measuring glass from a drying rack. She removed the rubber cork from a demijohn packed in excelsior and drew off 280 millilitres of 99.6% proof alcohol for hospital and laboratory use. She then topped up the flask with distilled water from a plastic container. The resulting liquid was 55% proof. She knocked back the first half glass.

In her alcoholism, as in everything else, Madelene was pretty much on her own. She had no-one to advise her, no companion and no experience. She was in the process of discovering alcohol, as a lone traveller explores a new continent. She did not know why she did it, nor did she want to know. But she sensed that 55% was the optimum. At 55%, just before the first rush, as the volatile vapour was absorbed into the mucous membrane of the throat, the destruction of the mouth cells brought on an exquisite burning sensation. This burn was essential. In it there was clarity; in it Madelene discerned something of the spirit of abuse: the intense, all-consuming urge to self-destruct.

This was followed by the first wave of inebriation. She located herself in the cabinet door. Slowly, in the void within her, a hot pulsating spirit flame flared up. From having been nothing she was rapidly becoming something.

Mombasa Manor was hers, the park was hers, the world was hers. And she looked great. Not a fault to be found anywhere. She toasted herself, congratulated herself. Then she took a drink.

She swung a stylized backhand at the stainless-steel surroundings. A queen had a need for and a right to some space. She drew the racket back over her shoulder and arched her body in a perfect dummy smash at the door in front of her. The door into the garden room. She put down the racket. The recollection of the ape struck her with the same force as the alcohol. She turned the door handle and went inside.

Mombasa Manor had been built with African rather than British conditions in mind: African wages for the servants, the African climate and the social round of the British colonial administration. When it proved too large, too expensive and too cold for London the entire side wing – with the exception of Clapham's flat on the first floor and the workshops along the gable end – had been sealed off. Madelene had been through the room she now went into on only a handful of occasions. She recalled heavy tasselled curtains, plastic sheeting covering the carpets, bags around the chandeliers, dustsheets over the furniture and a heavy scent of something that was gone and would never come again.

The room was now in use.

It was a large room – more a small hall really – extending, by means of a conservatory of glass and white-painted steel, for fifteen feet into the park. The entrance to the conservatory had now been blocked by a metal grille. A tropical thicket of ferns, hardwoods and low bamboo had sprung up in front of this grille. And around the vegetation, splitting the room from floor to ceiling for two-thirds of its width, ran a glass partition. At the spot where Madelene entered the room the glass ran up against the wall. On the other side it came up against a white metal barrier topped by white bars that reached to the ceiling.

Next to the thicket grew a climbing tree of the type found in children's playgrounds. Next to the tree lay two tractor tyres. Next to the tyres stood a wheelbarrow filled with fruit and vegetables. Next to the wheelbarrow sat the ape.

With some effort Madelene succeeded in coming up with a sketchy log of the past two days. The ape had arrived the day before yesterday. She had spent yesterday in bed with her carafe and that dreadful migraine. The bulk of the set-up in front of her must have been erected inside a day.

The ape was asleep, sitting on its haunches with its back against the wall.

Access to the cage could be gained through a door in the metal wall. Pinned to this door were feeding and temperature charts and a vaccination checklist. There were two latches on the door. Madelene lifted both and stepped inside.

As soon as she crossed the raised doorsill she became aware of a subtle burning under her skin, as though her nervous system were overheating. The same sensation as she experienced when the ethanol seared the epithelium of her throat and mouth. That faint, almost lighthearted, call of the longing to go under.

She closed the door behind her.

"How do I look?" she said.

At the sound of her voice the ape opened its eyes. Madelene crossed over to the animal one pace at a time until they were about ten feet apart, sat down on one of the tractor tyres and placed the flask and glass at her feet.

The crossing of this boundary had rendered her all but sober. From a gentle, stupefying warmth radiating from her stomach she had moved into a state of crystal-clear hypersensitivity. She could hear them both breathing, her own breath coming twice as fast as the animal's. She filled the glass and drank.

"Cheers," she said.

There was a fleeting instant of pleasure in knowing that one could not be understood. Then she met the ape's gaze.

It was open, incalculable.

Madelene was overcome by a sneaking sense of unease, rather as though she had sat on an ant hill. She shifted position and still the ape kept its eyes on her. She had the feeling that she was being unmasked, spied on, scrutinized, as though it saw right through her, saw her naked, devoid of make-up and, worse still, saw her pathetic inner self, her insecurity, her worthlessness.

Flustered, she started to get to her feet. It occurred to her that she too was an ape for, while she might well be able to leave this cage, and this house, she would not get very far before running up against the financial, social and marital barriers that circumscribed *her* life.

Her hands were frozen, shaking. She had spilled some of her drink onto her wrist and the chill of the liquid evaporating had turned it to ice. Up she got.

"Sorry," she said.

There was a peach dangling just in front of her. She followed the line of the branch on which it grew back to the trunk – the ape's arm. It had handed her a peach.

Very slowly and gingerly she took the sun-kissed, ripe and downy fruit from the grey hand. Then she inched her way backwards.

"Thanks," she said. "As a matter of fact I did forget to eat anything this morning."

2

Madelene's bed measured six feet square, the bedclothes were of pink satin. To her it was both cocoon and kingdom and the only place where she could, on occasion, feel absolutely safe. Now she sat herself in the centre of it, legs crossed, with the carafe in one hand and a large medicine glass in the other.

Madelene liked to imagine that she inhabited a new age, one that had been ushered in by two more or less simultaneous events which had conspired to cancel out the past: her marriage and her discovery of Vitamin B.

Where her marriage made it possible for her to escape from Denmark and her family, the big 15-milligram B1 tablets, available over the counter from any chemist, had provided her with an ally in the battle against hangovers and helped her to carry on, apparently unaffected, no matter how much she had drunk.

Now she had the jitters, and no notion of why this should be. She poured the contents of the carafe over these feelings like some soothing balm and so as nevertheless to maintain a clear head for what lay in store, for every swig she took two tablets and washed them down with half a glass of water.

What lay ahead was, like everything else in Madelene's life, something that recurred at regular intervals, in this case once a week. But where she evidenced a blithe disregard for being on time for other appointments, this one she approached full of expectation.

The person she was going to meet was already present in the room in the form of a dog-eared bus-pass photograph propped up against the framed portrait of Adam on her bedside table. The face was that of a pale, freckled woman. Her name was Susan and she was the only friend Madelene had ever had.

When she was ten years old Madelene was enrolled at the English School to the north of Copenhagen, an international boarding school and one of the last all-girl schools in the country. It was run by the sisters of an Anglican nursing order and attended by the daughters of British businessmen and diplomats and the daughters of Danish parents who wanted their children out of the way and could afford to bring the wish to pass in an academically defensible manner. Her first three years at the school seemed to Madelene to be a period of deathly hibernation, surrounded by teachers so distant as to be quite unreachable and by classmates who looked upon one another not as individuals but as representatives of that grey uniformity of which all were a part.

In her fourth year at the school a natural catastrophe occurred. Within just a few months sexuality broke out among all thirty girls in Madelene's class.

The class had always been worryingly quiet, in recent years this silence had deepened and the sisters had made the mistake of confusing restraint with apathy. In actual fact, this stasis was an illusion. From the outset the girls had constituted a fluid which time had saturated with expectant, hormonal menace. Into this saturation there now fell a microscopic, never to be identified, particle and around this sliver of the magic mirror the fluid crystallized. And then it exploded.

The catastrophe took a number of forms. None of the girls had known where they were bound and for some the change came as an incurable shock. On their bodies, which had until then been slender and boyish, swelled tumorous cushions of fat which held them back on the sports field, squeezed them out of their clothes and their familiar framework and exposed them to vitriolic masculine lust. Others were engulfed by the forces building up inside them. From a shy and tranquil childhood they were thrown – and threw themselves – straight into disproportionate, promiscuous prurience, first verbally then physically.

It was like the end of a journey. They were like thirty lemmings all reaching the sea at once. And here they foundered in their convulsive attempts to cling to the world of childhood. If, that is, they did not throw themselves into the water and drown.

In the midst of this chaos Madelene and Susan caught sight of each other after years of unwittingly being an arm's length apart. They looked at one another, briefly and thoughtfully, and found that amid the general immersion they were both staying afloat. At that instant and without a word being said, they knew they had both come to a secret understanding with the forces now shattering the world around them.

In tackling what was happening to their pupils the sisters had recourse not only to training and experience but also to a modicum of resolute brutality. But the force inherent in such synchronism caught them off-guard and it took them the best part of two years to regain control. After that time, however, after a succession of abortions and instances of venereal disease and two successful suicide attempts and, in the end, open mutiny followed by the last, definitive purge, they were left – on the face of it, at least – with nineteen well-adjusted, docile girls. Among them Susan and Madelene.

They had two more years at the school before disaster struck and during that time they went for the most part unnoticed. The people around them did not understand them and anything incomprehensible invariably remains invisible.

What they found in each other was a wantonness which, so far as their classmates and the sisters were concerned, went beyond the recordable range of the senses and into another, inaccessible dimension. They came to maturity like a couple of cubs. Bypassing the panic that struck their contemporaries, they quietly and undramatically grew towards an intense and certain knowledge of how it feels when it tickles. For most of the girls in the group to which they had belonged the journey ended here. For Madelene and Susan this was where the real journey began.

They were never in any doubt as to where it would lead them. Deep down in their neurological fundament they understood that what awaited them at the other end was a man. For whom as yet they had no name, face or even a body, but whose nature they understood with instinctive assurance.

On this journey they helped one another. When the final grand expulsion left whole sections of the school deserted, they were given a four-bedded room to themselves and from this room they ventured out onto the high seas. The bed they shared was their ship and the waters were first blue, then pink and finally dark-red, and of the same delightful temperature as bath water.

During those two years they slept very little at night, nor was there any need to. Their love was like a game – leisurely, untouched by desperation and, for the most part, aimless. What they were trying to do was to surf for as long as possible over the torrid surface that spread beneath them.

They never spoke of what they got up to, not to others, not to each other, and not even to themselves. They knew that the fewer words employed the naughtier it becomes. No-one ever saw one of them lay a finger on the other, in the life they shared with the rest of the school there was nothing to suggest that they were anything but very good schoolfellows, buddies and vaguely overlooked, quiet, fair-to-middling pupils at a good school. But alongside this sphere there lay another. And in that one a look, a flicker of a nostril, the way in which the tip of a tongue moistened the bow of the upper lip was enough to send a shaft of fire shooting from the inner thighs to the roots of the hair and on up into the blue sky.

Around this private, vivid, sensual orgy their everyday lives showed up, not surprisingly, in tones of charcoal-grey wretchedness. They were surrounded by teachers whom they feared, by an over-whelming feeling of insecurity, and by schoolfriends who were in much the same situation as themselves – having been handed over, at their fathers' expense, to insensitive women supervising a ludicrous curriculum.

Under these conditions the girls' friendship flourished, and it was there that they learned to love their bed.

At the end of those two years Susan found her first lover outside the school. She was caught out, given a warning, caught again and expelled, after which she was packed off back to London by her father – the British ambassador to Copenhagen – and, consequently, sucked out of Madelene's life.

Twelve years were to pass before they met again, in London. During those twelve years they had not been in touch with one another at all and yet the bond between them had never been severed. Just as they had, at the school, spent whole days each in their own corner of the bed, never exchanging a word, like fox cubs curled up and resting, safe in the knowledge of the other's presence in the room so, throughout their twelve-year separation, they had sensed the whereabouts of the other. At that moment when they stood face to face once more Madelene saw beyond Susan's two children and her husband and the nanny and Susan saw through Madelene's make-up and the reek of alcohol and what they saw was that behind the guises they assumed some parts of the world they had shared remained intact.

Since then, every Tuesday afternoon while Susan's children attended Danish lessons at the Danish Church, they had gone for a walk together in Regent's Park. Where people will usually endeavour to reduce the gulf that separates them, one from another, through conversation, these two had once and for all accepted the differences between them and their walk was taken gently, lingeringly and often in silence.

But not today. Today Madelene arrived late and immediately started talking.

"You're on the board of the Royal Society for the Protection of Animals, aren't you," she said.

Susan had to think for a minute. She was on the board of all sorts of charitable organizations. To please her husband, to embellish her idleness and to have plenty of excuses for not being where she was expected to be.

"Then you must know Adam's sister, Andrea?"

Susan shook her head.

"The Animal Welfare Foundation," she said.

"What's the difference?"

Susan fell silent. People interested her. First and foremost – besides Madelene and her own children – certain men. And farther out on the periphery of her awareness, the rest of the human race. For animals she felt a profound lack of interest.

36

And yet this question had conjured up, in her mind, an animal association. She remembered how she had always thought of Madelene as a cat, as loudly purring, electrified velvet or a sudden ball of fury with five flick knives on each hand. Now, within and behind her friend's urgent and vehement questioning, she glimpsed a number of other animals, less elegant but more stubborn: a sheep, a donkey, perhaps a cow.

"It's something to do with money," she said. "The Animal Welfare Foundation has something to do with money."

Between the two friends there existed an agreement which had never been voiced but of which both were aware, namely that while Susan told Madelene everything, Madelene told Susan a good deal, but never more than that. Now Susan waited respectfully. But Madelene's face remained blank and withdrawn.

They headed towards the church, arm in arm. A tall, freckle-faced woman in whose abdomen the sperm of three different men were vainly trying to come to terms. And a gazelle of a girl with a working blood-alcohol level that would never have passed a breathalyser test who stayed on her feet and relatively lucid thanks only to the support of her friend, Vitamin B and her own curiosity.

3

The number of men whom Madelene had known, while too small to be statistically quantifiable, had been large enough for her to deduce certain general rules of behaviour. The most important of these was her discovery of the fact that the content and course of any love affair is revealed within the events of the first twenty-four hours.

Adam had called on her father on official business. He had met her at a party and, taking his time as he always did with anything that mattered to him, he had begun to work his way through the crowd towards her. His whole being contained, even then, in that one action. In his body resided his cricket, his javelin throwing and a veritable succession of physical victories over other males; in his hide the requisite arrogance and essential resources and in his voice when he reached her a richness possessed only by those with a roar that comes from the gut, together with the kind of polish acquired only at the most expensive private schools and universities. Around him, like a mane or an aura, hung an awareness of having practically no natural enemies.

The rest of that first day served to confirm this impression, adding to it the observation that he seemed considerate and very, very interested.

In the course of those twenty-four hours, during which time they never left one another's side, Adam Burden did not laugh once.

Not because he had no sense of humour. He possessed deep reserves of a fine-honed, intellectual brand of sarcasm that might be triggered at any moment, especially if he felt professionally threatened. If anyone else were to question his knowledge, thereby encroaching on the cornerstone of his self-esteem, he could turn lethally witty. But at no point in the 529 days of their marriage nor – presumably – at any time prior to it, nor – in all likelihood – at any time thereafter had it occurred or would it occur to Adam Burden that there might be anything funny about him. What his first move towards Madelene had shown and what all of his subsequent moves had confirmed was that he had all the monumental self-importance of the big beasts of prey and of the great dictators.

Not that Madelene looked for humour in her marriage. Laughter comes as an extra, a luxury item, and Madelene knew that Adam had saved her from certain familial ruin. For anyone who has survived by the skin of their teeth, the daily gratification of basic needs is a miracle and that is how Madelene viewed her marriage: as a daily, reciprocal and miraculous gratification of basic needs.

This mutual meeting of needs usually commenced at 7 p.m. when Adam came home. But today he turned up two hours earlier, Madelene met him at the door at 5 p.m. Ten minutes later they were taking tea in the library.

The library was Adam Burden's den. It had all the murkiness, the snugness of a den, as well as its smell – a subtle whiff of Adam, of the tropical jungles from which the wood for the furniture had come and the leather of the book bindings.

It also provided the restorative refuge of a den. By the time Adam arrived home his face was white with exhaustion. But the minute he sank into one of the armchairs in that room and put away his diary he began to revive. While one small fraction of his awareness drank tea and chatted, the rest of him was absorbing the security of his surroundings and the woman sitting across from him.

Madelene was alert to the fact that during these ostensibly undemanding three-quarters of an hour she administered a large feminine blood transfusion to the man in the chair opposite her.

Little by little during the course of this, Adam Burden dropped his defences, becoming a weaker character than usual. Never before had Madelene taken advantage of this weakness to speak of anything of importance and now when she did so the question was thrown in casually, desultorily, one single element in a host of insignificant associations.

"And the ape?" she said.

Through half-closed, indifferent eyes Adam watched the question float past, like an insect, like steam from a teacup.

"It's in the garden room," he said. "Just for the time being."

"What kind of ape is it?"

There was silence. The borderland between them lay as yet unexplored. But Madelene sensed that she was on the brink of the demarcation zone.

"Some sort of dwarf chimpanzee."

"What's so special about it?"

Adam's face lay in shadow. Now, in this shadow, two yellow lights gleamed – as though some big cat were staring out at Madelene from the gloom.

"When a wild animal escapes from captivity it will either blunder around in panic or it will look for a place to hide. Animals are incapable of adjusting to unexpected freedom. The interesting thing about this one is that it got as far as it did."

Madelene bowed her head. A gesture of acceptance, of submission almost. Adam had not lied, that she knew. But he had divulged as little as possible of the truth. Behind his bone-china cup he curled himself around his prize with animal alertness.

She raised her face and smiled at him, the reassuring smile of a nurse. Then she poured tea for him, put sugar in his cup and stirred for a count of thirty, the exact number of stirs required to ensure the complete dissolution of the coarse, molasses-heavy tropical cane-sugar crystals.

That night she waited for Adam in his bedroom. It was two in the morning before he came up. But when he saw her on the bed his tiredness and tight-lipped exasperation were swept away with a smile, and he began to undress.

Adam's diary consisted of a little grey book to which he had, as people under great pressure of work often do, committed his memory. It was diary and memo pad rolled into one, in it he made a note of everything from the most minor of errands to the most serious of obligations and without it he could not remember a thing. It was a weapon of self-defence, like the tea in the library, like his silence on the subject of his work.

Madelene had never looked inside this book before, she had never wanted to look inside it, it had seemed to her both too trivial and too sacrosanct. But on this night she did take a look. When Adam went to the bathroom she swung her legs over the side of the bed and lifted the book from his bedside table.

She had already abandoned any thought of deciphering the main entries, Adam's notes were as cryptic and elliptical as bird footprints in the sand. Instead she concentrated on the loose sheets tucked in between the pages of the diary.

There were five of these, a little larger than A4 size, held together by a paper clip and tucked in at that day's date. The first three pages were covered in an illegible scrawl, the last two had been drawn on.

The drawings were of the ape. First some full-length sketches of the animal – in profile and face on – not in any detail, merely capturing the posture and the relative length of the limbs.

Beneath these several drawings of the animal's nostrils had been made one after the other, from different angles. Then came the hands, reproduced without hair or fingernails, leaving nothing but the outlines, resting on the animal's knees just as they had rested when she had been sitting facing it.

The last half-page was impossible to make out. It showed a map, a group of islands shaped like two parabolas turned back-to-back, like a double-sided, inverted Polynesian atoll. This had been sketched out something like a dozen times, then again from the side, the islands seeming to rise up out of the water – some smooth, others rugged, or square, like circular towers, like planks of wood.

From the bathroom came the sound of Adam soaping his cheeks. She tore a blank white sheet from the back of the diary. Using her eyeliner she copied out one of the maps, the only one where an attempt had been made at a working drawing and one which Adam had also underlined. She drew it both from above and from the side, quickly and accurately. Anyone who has spent all of their adult life drawing on a face will find paper an accommodating medium.

Just as she was weighing up the relative heights of the islands above the surface of the water, just as she heard Adam patting his cheeks with after-shave she realized what she had been copying. She had been drawing the creature's teeth. She opened the drawer and replaced the diary.

In the drawer lay a strip of grey plastic. Some hazy recollection told her this was what the ape had been wearing round its wrist when it was lying on the stretcher. She picked it up. It was the type of thing used in hospitals to identify corpses and the newborn. The band bore the word *Erasmus*.

When Adam walked through the door she was lying back against the pillows.

Now, as always, she was grateful for his careful preparations and his fastidiousness in lovemaking. She experienced just one brief moment of secret, inner distraction before turning all her attention to him. She thought of the exasperated look on his face and came to the conclusion that whatever he had been looking for, the ape had not given it away. It had not given anything away. Except to her. To her it had given a peach.

4

Madelene woke up early and, as always, alone. She had never spent a whole night next to her husband. However passionate and intimate their lovemaking might have been there came a time, often just before dawn, when Adam would turn in his sleep and brush against her and, registering the closeness of another human being, would be gripped by a kind of desperation. Asleep but determined he would get out of bed, gather up his bedclothes and retreat to the next room to bed down there. Madelene had never asked him why. Ten years in advance of other women of her age she had learned that there is no point in discussing matters that cannot be altered.

Usually she woke up to the feeling that the bed was an uninhabited island onto which she had been washed during the night and only when she had made it to the mirror was the sense of impending doom dispelled. This morning was different. She awoke with the impression that she was floating. Without turning her head she stretched out her hand and located, under her clothes, the torn-out sheet with its drawing of an archipelago named Erasmus. Clutching this, she put on a kimono, returned to her own room and sat down at her dressing table.

And here something strange happened. She got her colouring wrong.

Under normal circumstances Madelene could hit upon her pale, youthful base colour with unerring accuracy. But this morning when she looked up from the brush and the section of her face reflected in the concave make-up mirror in front of her she saw that she was way off the mark. While her face was indeed wrinkle-free it was still as colourlessly neutral as it had been ten minutes before.

She reached for the cleanser, then stayed her hand. She took a closer look at herself. She drew a line the width of a finger below each eye with the eyeliner, then gently rubbed this away, transforming it into a dark hollow, into five years of wear and tear. She took a lipstick and applied a hard, wide, "proper madam" mouth. She put on a pair of sunglasses. A scarf over her hair. She stood up. Tried affecting a slight stoop. She had quite forgotten herself. For the first since she had in a dim and distant past shed a child's delight in grown-up clothes, for the first since then Madelene made herself look older than she was.

She positioned herself over by the window and felt the wind against her new disguise. She saw Clapham. He cut a rose from the bush next to the gate, let in a delivery van, turned away a grey man in a white car, walked back to the house. She was seized by the thought of the daily routine. She recalled that Adam was working at home that day, in the garden room, with the ape.

It was a disturbing thought. Madelene's was not only an emotional, legal and physical marriage. It was also a territorial one. Prior to this, until the end of the working day, she had always known there was no risk of her bumping into her husband on her reserve.

She dealt with her unease in her usual fashion. She retrieved her carafe from beneath the bed and standing by the window she took the first little drink of the morning.

Her daring increased. She unearthed a thin duster coat and put it on, leaving it unbelted, shapeless as a sack. She found a pair of battered platform sandals. She looked at herself in the mirror. Her own mother would not have recognized her. Or at any rate would not have wanted to recognize her.

Into a little black bag she popped all the things a woman has need of: keys, money, lipstick, eyeliner, handkerchief, a drawing of an ape's teeth and a little plastic flask of alcohol. Then she left her rooms, swiftly, stealthily and without the usual pause in the doorway.

She went down the back stairs, through the kitchen garden and out through a narrow gate in the wall. It was the first time in a long while that she had gone anywhere on foot with no tinted car window coming between her and the outside world. She revelled in the sunlight, the sounds, the sharpness of the colours. She relished the anonymity of her new mask. She passed a truck with a picture of a dog on its door, the man inside the truck not sparing her a glance. She passed a maid walking Kasimir, the neighbour's Borzoi, the girl and the dog looking at her with no sign of recognition. She walked past a white car in which sat the grey man whom Clapham had turned away, the man staring in the direction of Mombasa Manor and right through her. She came to an underground station and headed downwards.

On the platform she took fright.

Madelene had grown up in a singular and sheltered environment, in the domain of the well-to-do. For the greater part of her life she had to some extent been kept clear of ordinary people, between her and the general public there had been filters, big houses, special schools, nannies and chauffeurs. Now, in the underground, she was brought face to face with the brutality of London, like a woman throwing herself out of her covered jeep in the middle of a game reserve to carry on alone and on foot.

Madelene was of course acquainted with tragedy, death, nausea and self-hate – every human being carries these things with them from birth. But she had had no practice in understanding overt misery, no words to explain it. The shell within which she had circulated had been very much of a linguistic nature. Not long after they met Adam had presented her with a number of Debrett's publications, smiling as he showed her how here, in the twentieth century, you had a publishing house issuing – under the thinnest veneer of self-irony – textbooks on the preservation of a feudalistic class supremacy. And Madelene had learned her lesson well. After only a year and a half she was speaking a slightly Latinized upper-class English with not a trace of an accent. But she lacked any kind of personal association with such words as bleeding gums, hunger, hard chancre, Wormwood Scrubs, knuckle-dusters, corns, the dole, foot drop, fractured skulls or tinnitus. In the train she sat tensed, still and watchful, shielded from the impressions that assaulted her only by what she sipped from her little flask.

She had no sense of time or space. Only when she had by instinct changed trains, got off, climbed up, gone round corners, dodged predatory animals and beggars, avoided being trampled underfoot and – finding herself in front of a long, low concrete building – realized that she had made it, did it transpire that she had had any goal in mind. That she had been guided by a spatial law which was struggling to re-establish a balance. She had moved in the opposite direction from Adam. He had stayed at home, she had been led to where he ought to have been. She was standing outside the Institute of Animal Behavioural Research, one of the research departments attached to the London Zoological Gardens. An institute of which Adam was director.

On Madelene's first visit to London Adam had taken her across to one of the Mombasa Manor outhouses, closed the door behind them and left her to stand there for a moment surrounded by the darkness and the stench of moths, formalin and barely suppressed decay. Then he had switched on a dazzling electric light and recited his professional credo.

The shed was chock-a-block with his parents' hunting trophies. With tusks, lion skins, shark jaws, bird-of-paradise plumage, rhino horns, antlers, roebuck heads, python skins, whalebones, a stuffed and mounted gorilla head and the skins of two Komodo dragons grafted, by the new dermatoplasty method, onto life-size models. Adam had steered her over to a picture of his father and mother standing arm in arm atop a mountain formed by the bodies of six elephants. In soft and measured tones he had explained how his parents' object had been to shoot, collect and exhibit – a task they had fulfilled with panache. But the world had changed, now was the time to study, present and preserve and he had said this with the gravity that comes from knowing that one's family traces its ancestry back seven hundred years, that one has had splendid forebears and that one is oneself even better. Then he had told her about London Zoo.

"It's the oldest zoo in the world," he had said, "once it was the best in the world and it can be again. But, for that, expansion is necessary. This is already underway, you've heard about it, but it's going to be more far-reaching than anyone imagines. Andrea and I are both involved in it."

He had run his fingers over a row of photographs and stopped at one of the Last Night of the Proms showing Edward Elgar on the podium.

"A charity concert," he said, "for London Zoo."

His fingers had drummed a tattoo across the British upper-class animal lovers. When he next spoke, Madelene could tell that he had forgotten her, that he was talking to his own class and its ghosts.

"They did the work. Their children don't lift a finger, they have control of a monopoly. When London Zoo was founded it was their own private property. These days it's all we can do to cover the day-to-day running costs. They've lulled themselves to sleep but they're going to wake up to discover that it's too late."

This speech, which Madelene had remembered even though she did not understand a word of it, lay one and a half years in the past. Since then she had visited the Institute once, had been given a tour of the construction site and attended a dinner where the top table seating plan had been arranged in strict pecking order, where she and Adam as the director and his lady-wife had sat at the head, a dinner which she had only got through because she had been drinking before she got there and had continued to drink heavily throughout the evening.

Now, for the first time, she walked through the glass doors unaccompanied.

A woman darted out to a desk and barred her way, nippy as a terrier. For a split-second Madelene was ready to turn and run. Then she remembered that today she was someone other than herself.

"I'm from the Meat Marketing Board Dental Research Centre," she said. "We have an inquiry regarding the arrangement of an animal's teeth."

The receptionist backed away. Behind her sunglasses Madelene understood her perfectly. They had both had too brief a schooling. They were surrounded by people who were cleverer than they and liked to flaunt their cleverness. And the words "research centre" and "inquiry" acted upon them both like a command that could not be ignored.

47

The woman made a telephone call then yelped out a name and a floor. No sooner had Madelene taken her first few steps towards the elevator than the woman had forgotten all about her, with the watchdog's instant indifference to anyone who has received its master's seal of approval.

The man who invited Madelene to take a seat at a large desk wore his white coat like a cloak and it was by this way of carrying himself that Madelene recognized him. He had been seated a little – but only a little – further down the top table from Adam and herself.

She placed the eyeliner sketch in front of him.

"We have a problem," she said. "We've been given this and they can't put a name to it so they've sent me to you . . ."

"Why me?"

Madelene rapidly and judiciously assessed this doctor's most prominent feature to be his vanity.

"Back at the Centre they say you're the best," she said.

"Do they indeed? Don't tell me they still remember my root-canal job on Roberto?"

"Not a day goes by without its being mentioned."

" It was the right tusk, I had to use two gallons of chloramine just to clean it out."

"The stuff of legend long since," said Madelene.

The veterinary odontologist picked up her drawing, glanced at it and let it drop.

"I will not be made a fool of," he said.

Madelene removed her sunglasses and leaned towards him.

"It was sent to the Centre," she said, "and they can't make head or tail of it."

Suspicion niggled at the doctor.

"You're not by any chance a vet yourself, are you? Or a dentist?"

Madelene smiled, warmly and dumbly.

"Office dogsbody," she said.

The doctor relaxed.

"Of course one cannot be certain," he said. "Not with such a poor drawing."

His fingers drummed the sheet of paper.

"Molars, small molars, conical canines, incisors and diastema. All of which points to a chimpanzee."

"But?" said Madelene.

"I could go along with there being four teeth too many. One extra small molar on each side. We're always coming across mutations. Even though evolution is tending towards fewer teeth. At a pinch I could even let the front teeth pass. But why the chiselled edges, like knife blades, rather than masticatory surfaces? And the dental arch, that's going too far, wouldn't you agree?"

Madelene nodded.

"That kind of curvature would be inconceivable in an ape, it's humanoid. I'll tell you one thing: you've been taken for a ride. Somebody has taken advantage of your ignorance. You've been sent the dental chart of a non-existent creature."

Madelene sat back in her chair, took out her little bottle and sipped.

"Medicine," she said, "asthma, I have all these allergies."

Slowly she got to her feet.

"Is any record kept of animals that have been stolen or kidnapped?"

"Newsletters. All zoos of any standing exchange a daily newsletter. Every theft is put on record."

The doctor was starting to tense into the attitude in which she had found him.

"Doctor," she said. "What would you say if, even so, you were faced with an animal with just this set of teeth?"

"I would point out that there had to be some mistake."

"And what if it was actually lying there with its mouth open and teeth like the set in that diagram?"

The brow above the desk creased, reluctant to budge, annoyed at being forced off its empirical pedestal.

"Until it was proved otherwise I would most certainly assume that it was a hoax."

Madelene smoothed her skirt and smiled a wide, gummy smile.

"Doctor," she said. "How many teeth has a human being?"

"Thirty-two."

"Well I'm going to go back to the Centre and have a look at my teeth, just to make sure *they* are no hoax."

The doctor looked away.

"You can borrow a mirror from the toilet here. But there's no need. I have already remarked on your dentition and occlusion. Quite normal."

Out in the corridor Madelene stood for a while tuning in to the building. It had Adam's dynamism, it was young, intensely businesslike, ambitiously efficient. It was a place where anyone with no good reason for being there might easily feel in the way. In an attempt to stifle this feeling she took a drink from the bottle. As she was wiping away her tears she noticed Adam's name and title above her head. She had come to a halt outside his office.

She put on her sunglasses and walked in.

She stepped into the secretary's office. A woman on a swivel chair whirled round to confront her.

Madelene had met Adam's secretary five or six times and now she was struck by a fleeting sense of being in free-fall. Then she filled out her role from within.

"I have an appointment with Adam Burden," she said.

The secretary smiled – a pleasant, impersonal, pliant smile, as much as to say there was absolutely no way Madelene could have an appointment since, if she had, it would have been made through her, which was not the case, so there was no oversight on her part, but this she could afford to gloss over.

"I'm afraid Mr Burden is attending a lengthy and important meeting in town," she said.

"Is he somewhere where I could reach him by phone?"

The woman's face turned cold. Her civility, rationed from the start, had run out. "I'm afraid that is quite out of the question. What was the name?"

Madelene stared at the woman in front of her in fascination. At the impeccability of her dress, her dismissive air of authority. Adam had once said that a great leader saw to it that the people around him never made mistakes. This women looked incapable of making a mistake. Then she remembered Adam's dawn retreats, how he could not bear anyone close to him, the doors he erected between himself and the outside world. The woman facing her was just such a barrier. She leaned forwards.

"I came to find out where he got to last night," she whispered.

The secretary tried to get away by pushing her chair backwards, Madelene followed her, closing in and closing in until the woman could see her own reflection cracking in the sunglasses and breathe the ethanol.

"And in the Meat Market no less," Madelene went on. " What d'you think of that?"

The secretary's back was pressed right up against her word processor, all avenues of escape cut off. She had gripped the arm of her chair.

"You tell him," said Madelene, "that he'd better have one helluva good excuse, because otherwise I'm going to call his wife."

On the desk the woman's hand lighted on a slip of yellow paper with a note in Adam's handwriting. She held it out.

"Perhaps you would like to ring him yourself and tell him," she said.

Madelene took the slip of paper and backed off.

"Four hours," she said. "Surrounded by frozen chickens and organic sausage skins. You just tell him that."

Even in such a tight spot the secretary could still summon up the strength for one last sally.

"And who shall I say called?"

"Priscilla," she said. "Priscilla from the Meat Marketing Board Research Centre."

And she closed the door behind her.

Back in the corridor she stopped and gazed blindly into space. Madelene entertained many different feelings for her husband, not all of them unmixed. But her confidence in him had always been absolute. There were sides of Adam and of his life which she could not fathom. But she had always felt sure that, in time, she would get to the bottom of and learn to accept most of them. Now she found herself faced with the first downright lie of her marriage. Adam, she knew, was at home in the conservatory. But he had left a note for his secretary that said *"Earp. Vet. Inst."*

Madelene took a sip from her bottle. Then she made her way back along the corridor.

The veterinary odontologist was sitting just as she had left him. Madelene laid Adam's note in front of him.

"Doctor," she said, "there was one question I forgot to ask. The Centre is considering doing some work with this institution. Can you tell me anything, in the strictest confidence, about this place?"

The doctor looked out of the window, across the covered construction site that was soon to become the New London Regent's Park Zoological Garden.

"I've more than enough to do just keeping people here up to scratch," he said.

"I was so hoping you could help," said Madelene. "You're renowned for your contacts."

The doctor glanced at the paper then reverted to looking out of the window.

"Drop it. Never heard of it. It's not in London at any rate."

Madelene stood her ground. The doctor reached behind and brought out a hefty-looking reference book.

"The *Who's Who* of the veterinary world. Provides a list of all vets and veterinary colleges in the country. Comprehensive, but full of intolerable printing errors."

He looked something up, closed the book and put it back on its shelf.

"You've been conned again. There is no such institution by that name in Britain."

He regarded Madelene over his bifocals.

"Everywhere you go it's the same story. We're up to our eyes in inefficiency and incompetence. And a nice, polite girl like you, too."

Madelene made a tentative attempt to let go of the desk, to see whether she could stand unaided.

"Thank you very, very much, doctor," she said slowly. "And that comes both from me and from the Research Centre."

Madelene walked across London for what might have been an hour before taking a taxi, stepping out as carefully and circumspectly as her condition would allow.

It was not herself she was endeavouring to protect, nor was it the thought that she had practised one piece of deception and herself been witness to another that occupied her mind. What she was guarding was a new sense of inner worth. For the first time for as long as she could remember she had stepped out and to one side of herself and become another person. She was no longer just Madelene. On the fringes of her own being she glimpsed the silhouette of another woman who was also herself. It was this other person she was shielding as she made her way across London.

In her rooms again she removed her face with a flannel and lay down on her back on the bed. She had been gone from Mombasa Manor with no explanation given and no-one had noticed a thing. But elsewhere in the city three people had encountered a strange woman, different from Madelene and yet one and the same: Priscilla from the Meat Marketing Board Research Centre.

5

When she woke it was midnight by the clock. The warmth in the room was heavy and humid, she groped about beneath the bed, her carafe was empty. She pulled on a dressing-gown, the fabric hurting where it touched, and stuck the carafe into one deep pocket. Dizzy and weak, she embarked upon her journey to the source of the Nile.

The house tried to bar her way with its darkness, its menacing shadows, the sense of human breathing. The courtyard slabs burned the soles of her bare feet and the sky was black. But there was a bit of a nip in the air. She walked across the gravel and turned the handle of the door into the potting shed. It was locked.

Her first reaction was to freeze in the face of this new and unfamiliar secretiveness. The outer perimeter of Mombasa Manor came under the aegis of the same security firm as the other houses in the road. But as a rule the house doors were never locked. Then she smiled. Like all expedition leaders of foresight, on this her solitary journey she too had laid down her caches.

The potting shed's large freshwater tank passed through the wall into a trough and in this trough stood row upon row of jars containing water specimens. Madelene shut her eyes, felt among the water plants and the goldfish and pulled out a jar, apparently no different from all the rest. She unscrewed the lid, took a cautious sip and let out her breath. No chance of any tadpoles developing in this liquid. It was crystal-clear, 55% proof ethyl alcohol.

She settled herself on the rim of the stone trough. Above her the clouds parted and the Milky Way came into view. From the basin came a murmur reminiscent of the fountains and canals of Copenhagen.

She toasted herself. She was having a lovely time, what a delightful, cosy Danish-style evening this was, the perfect end to a perfect day.

She thought of the ape. Of how lonely it must be feeling now, with no little helpers to sweeten its loneliness. Had anyone ever heard of an animal taking a drink? No. On the other hand no-one had ever heard of Erasmus' tight dental arch either. And it was never too late to learn to drink, was it? Not when they could teach chimps sign language.

Madelene lay down in the trough. On her knees, with the jar held well above any risk of dilution, she crawled through into the potting shed. She crossed the threshold of the garden room and switched on the light. The windows were masked by inky black-out curtains. The cage looked just as she remembered it. But the ape was gone.

She stayed where she was, beside the glass partition, until she was quite certain. Then she unlatched the door and stepped inside.

It is at the very moment of realizing that we are bereft, when the loss bleeds and the awareness of it has not yet begun to coagulate, that the significance of what has been lost strikes us most forcefully. Advancing further into the empty cage Madelene understood that she was going to miss the ape.

She had never had a pet. Without envy, without desiring anything of the kind for herself, she had observed her friends' Shetland ponies, golden retrievers and hamsters and right from the start she had known that the horse between the legs, the puppy against the bosom and the guinea pig in the bed were substitutes for something else. In silence and feeling nothing but pity, she had time and again witnessed the collapse of a sentimental illusion, with an animal outgrowing its cuddly puppy stage to become large and tediously horny – at which point it would be banished from the girlish bedroom to an outdoor run, there to develop – as a quite logical consequence of its isolation – a psychopathic savagery which would culminate in its biting the postman and costing the family 50,000 Danish kroner in damages, plus 700 kroner to have it put down.

Now, standing in the cage, she saw that where *those* animals were supposed to put one in mind of something else – of children, of parents, of dolls, of men – *this* ape in its stoic helplessness had put her in mind of herself.

Desolation washed over her. She drank from the specimen jar, in a ritual gesture of farewell, a funeral toast, like an exclusive little wake for a departed friend. As she drank she wandered slowly across the cage and thus she arrived at the only spot in the room from which the ape was visible.

She parted the branches. It looked at first as though the plants had twined around one another to form a bed beneath the animal, then she saw that it was lying on a woven cradle. Without snapping or forcing them it had drawn branches and leaves together and plaited them into a hammock. The side of this hammock facing the glass was hidden by a screen of greyish-brown, withered greenery which merged with the animal's fur, making it impossible to see the structure from the outside. At the only spot in the room where the vegetation formed a thicket capable of concealing it the ape appeared to be hovering, around shoulder-height, in a masterly piece of camouflage.

Madelene seated herself on a branch.

"You're even more invisible than you might think," she said. "You don't exist at all."

She pointed at the ape's teeth.

"Like the bumblebee. It can't fly, it's been proved. But it doesn't know that. So it does it anyway."

She drank a toast to the bumblebee.

"Would you mind opening your mouth?"

She opened her own mouth wide to demonstrate.

The ape's lips parted hesitantly, then its mouth opened.

Madelene saw the reddish-white maw, the powerful gums, a palate ridged as a sea-bed, the glint of spittle under the tongue. She saw the two small molars on each side, the chiselled edges of the front teeth, the cone-shaped daggers of the canines, the tightly-curved, humanoid dental arch. She saw the original of Adam's faithfully reproduced dental chart. But all of this she saw in passing, as it were, as one small part of something far more important.

At the moment when the ape opened its mouth it was not only its dental chart that was humanoid. For an instant its whole face seemed human, and not only human in the abstract sense but as human as her own face. And at that instant it imitated her movements, not like

56

some sort of caricature because there is always something unreal about a caricature, in the grossness of it. No, its imitation of her was perfectly true to life.

This impression lasted for a fraction of a second, it was like gazing down onto the surface of some fluid, pure alcohol for example, when all at once the surface becomes absolutely still and then you see your own reflection, and beyond it an abyss, and you feel yourself being sucked down into the abyss and there is a flash of not knowing whether the reflection is, in fact, the real you.

Then the thought was blotted out, the animal sat back and Madelene pulled the carafe from her pocket. Using both hands, she filled it from the jar, took a swig, and had to put it down in order to catch her breath. She would have lifted it again. Except that she could not, because some sort of plank had been placed on top of it. Her eye ran the length of the plank and met the ape's eye. It had put its hand over the glass.

Madelene backed away.

"No," she said, "you're probably right."

Leaves and creepers dropped back into place in her wake, like waters converging. Soon only the ape's eyes were visible, then the thicket closed up and the animal was gone.

6

Madelene and Adam had been married for six months when Andrea Burden gave a party at her home in Mayfair, the ostensible purpose of which was to welcome Madelene to the family. One minute after getting there Madelene had tried to make a run for it, but Adam had held her back.

Present had been twenty or so members of the family, a cross-section of the present and up-coming British élite – men who had been fitted for their first dress suit at the age of five and women who had had servants to do their bidding from the cradle. And in Andrea Burden's company each one of them, regardless of age – from the youngest teenager to seventy-year-old Sir Toby, the government adviser on veterinary matters – had been as jumpy as a shoal of minnows sensing the shadow of the pike.

Drenched in champagne the party had swum through a succession of rooms all opening off one another to end up in a dining-room that looked for all the world like a gilded well, lit only by candelabra that were reflected over and over again in the burnished precious metals of the dinner service and with so many oil paintings on the walls that the wallpaper was visible only at those patches where a painting had been taken down and a small white card from Lloyd's stating to which special exhibition the picture was on loan hung in its place.

In this room Andrea Burden had made a speech in which she had thanked everyone there – none of whom Madelene had laid eyes on before – for their support in setting up a *development corporation* – a term which Madelene was here hearing for the first time – for

Primrose Hill, Albert Terrace and Gloucester Gate – places which lay Madelene knew not where. So Madelene did not, in fact, understand one word of the verbal side of this welcome, but while Andrea was speaking she kept her eyes on her and what she saw was that Adam's sister was neither a buxom queen bee nor a wiry, indefatigable she-spider but that she was slender, smooth, angelic and deadly and that one of her objectives in gathering all of these people together was to smite as many as possible at one blow. This blow was delivered by her speech and when it came to an end the company remained prostrate. Her guests had listened to it sitting bolt upright, eyes fixed on the tablecloth, with no hope of fleeing, transfixed by a blood-tie of the sort which, beneath the seeming chaos on the surface, binds an ant hill together through rigorous discipline. Afterwards dessert was indeed served and a feeble conversation was even struck up and Madelene sensed that these guests must have felt the lash before now and developed a high pain threshold. But the company as a whole was still reeling and one by one couples slipped away, seen to the door and kissed on the cheek by Andrea Burden, who graciously accepted their transparent excuses.

When only Adam and Madelene were left the hostess sank into a capacious armchair across from them and eyed Madelene's wine-glassful of cognac.

"She doesn't scare that easily, does she?" she said to Adam.

Madelene realized then that Adam's sister was driven by motives more complex than common or garden malice. She had felt a twinge of curiosity, an urge to get to the bottom of the other woman.

Not long afterwards Andrea Burden had shown them to the door. They had gone down just three of the front steps when she came after them.

"I'm sorry to have to tell you this, Adam, but they've been checking up in the kitchen, there's a fork missing."

Adam pulled up short and stared wordlessly into the night.

"You two are, of course, above suspicion. I just thought I should mention it. It is C. J. Vander after all."

"I'll send you a replacement," said Adam, tight-lipped.

Then he and Madelene had leant on one another – she reduced to a spineless jelly by drink and he rigid with suppressed fury – and together they had stalked off into the night.

Since then Madelene had seen Andrea Burden only briefly and in passing, until three days earlier when Andrea had come with the ape. Now she was on her way to see her again. For the second day running she was on the underground, heading this time towards Aldgate and struggling, as she sat there, to reconstruct her ambiguous picture of Adam's sister.

Madelene had begun that day by changing her life.

She had woken up two hours earlier than usual, after a short but deep sleep, to the conviction that the past two days had been a bad dream, a hallucination, and that she was now going to make a fresh start. Even before she was fully awake she had perceived that the true meaning of life lay in love, that from now on she was going to live for Adam, unselfishly, following her mother's example, maybe even give up drinking. And after a brief, concentrated effort in front of the mirror she hurried down to the kitchen, still in her dressing-gown, to persuade Mrs Clapham to let her do the honours for Adam herself.

She made his tea, and toast. She walked down to the garage with him and once the car had turned the corner and driven out of sight she had a sudden urge to run, through the kitchen garden, out through the little door in the wall and out onto the pavement. There she would stand and wave, stunning and unexpected, as he drove past. She heard the buzz of the automatic gates and her hands were already in the air when it dawned on her that Adam's Aston Martin was retreating into the distance, that for the first morning ever he had turned right instead of left.

Right was the wrong way, eastwards, in the opposite direction to Regent's Park and the Institute. To begin with Madelene just stood there. Then she whipped off her slippers and took off.

She rounded the corner in time to catch a last glimpse of the car's rear end. She was still waving and shouting when a car pulled away from the kerb a few yards ahead of her and just as it occurred to Madelene that this was the same white car driven by the same grey man whom Clapham had turned away and whom she had seen again later, a truck with a picture of a dog on its door swung out and drove after the white car that was following Adam, and neither of the drivers in the two pursuing cars noticed Madelene, who was left standing there forlornly with no-one to wave to, witness to a pattern she could not make out.

Back in her room, on her bed, with trembling hands she fished out her carafe, glanced fearfully about her like a deer on a river bank then knocked back two half-glassfuls in quick succession.

She immediately grew calmer. Ordinarily, alcohol sparked off a funfair inside Madelene, complete with a roller coaster where, having once climbed onto it, there was no way of predicting in which direction you were likely to be catapulted. This time, however, she was not catapulted anywhere, this time the liquid immersed her in mellow, voluptuous sentimentality. She thought of Adam, of his iron will, his drive. She started to cry. Her tears watered the rose-pink satin and up sprung the desire for a grand reconciliation. She had to see him right away. She had to have him now, physically, inside her. Anywhere, in his office if necessary.

She grabbed the telephone and dialled his direct line, her longing for the sound of his voice so powerful that she had no chance to be surprised when the secretary answered.

"May I speak to Adam?" she said.

From the woman's voice and her reply Madelene gathered three things. That the secretary believed she was speaking to Priscilla, that she had already given up any idea of resistance and that Adam had managed both to fool the world once again *and* to cover his tracks.

"Mr Burden is working at home," she said. "Can I take a message?"

Madelene leaned back against the wall. Had she been alone the conversation would have stopped there. But she was not alone. The secretary had summoned up a spirit, one which was now materializing. Priscilla took the receiver out of Madelene's hand.

"Write this down," she said. "Your body means more to me than all the streaky back in Smithfield Market."

Then she replaced the receiver and got up.

She walked out into the corridor, down the stairs and through the house, not with any particular end in view but because she was too shaken to sit still. In the doorway to the terrace stood Clapham.

"Might I offer you a steaming-hot cup of freshly brewed mocha?" he said.

Madelene took the rose he held out to her.

"So long as it's strong," she said.

It was strong, black and thick as oil paint and as she drank it Madelene's eyes rested thoughtfully on Clapham. He seemed to be in good form, relaxed; everything was as normal. From his laid-back vantage point he could discharge his duty while exercising the control of an authoritative butler over the woman who was his superior in name only.

He thought they were alone on the terrace as always. Only Madelene detected the shadow of the other woman falling across the table.

"The car you turned away yesterday, I don't know whether that might have been any of my business?"

Clapham drained his cup and set it down, bottom-up, in a definitive tradesman's gesture.

"Duty calls," he said.

Madelene's eyes clouded over. Right at this minute, more than ever before, she needed him to have remained in his seat. For him to have laid his head – metaphorically speaking – in her lap and shown her kindness and just a smidgen of respect. But instead here he was joining up with the caravan which had broken camp that morning leaving her all alone in the British Sahara.

"Sit down!" she said.

Clapham froze.

"You dare to get up when I am talking to you."

The man bowed his head. He felt the sting, but could not see from which direction the blows had come. Madelene herself could hardly have said. Priscilla alone knew that the tone of voice she was now brandishing over Clapham's head came from Adam. That it was his master's voice the man in front of her was obeying.

"The white car, Clapham?"

"The veterinary authorities."

Neither of the two women had ever heard of such a body, but they understood they were riding a wave which might break at any minute and that there was no time to look back.

"On what business?"

"To see Mr Burden."

"And you said?"

"That Mr Burden was not at home."

Madelene paused, allowing the situation to build up to the final question.

"Where is Mr Burden?"

Clapham's frame seized up. Slowly Madelene and Priscilla got to their feet.

"Where is Mr Burden?"

"Aldgate. The Animal Welfare Foundation."

Madelene followed her action through and Clapham ducked as though he really were expecting a blow.

But Madelene did not strike him. Gently she patted the uncooperative, unsympathetic, uncomprehending figure before her on the head.

"Thanks for the coffee," she said.

7

You find them on the drab fringes of every European city: little offices where elderly ladies volunteer their time to discreet societies dedicated to pleading, genteelly, and quite inconspicuously, the case for the preservation of the hedgehog or the gillyflower or the water shrew. And it was in such surroundings that Madelene had envisaged finding Andrea Burden. That, however, was not what she found.

The lobby on the thirteenth floor of the House of the Animals at Aldgate was not drab but actively grey and, standing before the polished tombstone on which the floor directory had been inscribed, Madelene began to suspect what was brought home to her in no uncertain terms once she had been let in by two steel-grey security guards – who then sent for a man in a grey suit – and had embarked on a long trek after said suit: That the Animal Welfare Foundation was not housed in one office or one section of some open-plan office floor, but that this organization occupied a floating continent which took up an entire floor of the most expensive chunk of real estate in the world.

At journey's end sat two secretaries in a room as vast as the antechamber of a mausoleum. By now, under other circumstances, Madelene might well have felt overwhelmed by the weight of such surroundings. But not today. During the twenty minutes she had spent in the underground she had found some comfort. Not just in what she had drunk, but also, and more especially, in a clear certitude as to her errand.

She had reviewed her previous meetings with Adam's sister, even though this severely taxed her powers of recall – she was by no means sober now and had been anything but sober then. This exercise had nevertheless had a calming effect on her, since she had eventually come to the conclusion that behind Andrea Burden's frosty demeanour there beat a warm and human heart. And if there was anything Madelene needed right now it was solace and human kindness. In Andrea's presence she would confront Adam, the other woman acting as a fond but firm intermediary, and everything would turn out just fine. Where Madelene had boarded the train like an animal fleeing from a forest fire that has finally reached its own lair, she arrived at her destination like a lost chick seeking shelter under the mother hen's wing.

And there was in fact something rather maternal about Andrea Burden's smile as she entered the outer office, a warmth in the kiss she planted on Madelene's cheek, a protective air to the way in which she shepherded her into her office and closed the door behind them.

Then, softly, standing just inside the door, she delivered the first straight right to the chin.

"Madelene darling," she said. "What can I offer you this early in the day? A large gin?"

Alcohol was Madelene's most intimate secret, a deep-seated chamber of her heart, awash with liquid, which she could have sworn she had succeeded in hiding from the outside world. Until now.

In the gulf of suspended reality that now opened up, it occurred to Madelene that the one way above all in which animals differ from human beings is in the consistency of their thought processes. The most terrifying thing about the permanent uncertainty from which she herself suffered was its volatility. There were days when she mistrusted her body, others when she feared for her sanity, and still others when she lost faith in her marriage, her hair, her financial situation, her actions, her smell, her senses. The possibilities were endless. Whenever she thought that she had now arrived at an albeit lengthy but at long last definitive index of all the forms adopted by her self-hate, up it would pop in some hitherto unseen guise.

The face before her represented the antithesis of this inner imbalance. Andrea Burden eyed her with the cold, appraising curiosity of a reptile.

The room was empty, there was no sign of Adam. As things now stood, that was all for the best. Madelene sank down onto a chair.

"I just wanted to see this place," she said.

"A workplace must seem quite stimulating. To someone who doesn't actually do anything."

Madelene knew her time was up. She would find herself an elephants' graveyard to which she could drag herself off and die. If only she had the strength to get up out of the chair.

"A little drink would be lovely," she said.

A glass was placed in front of her.

"This place, why does it look the way it does?" she asked.

"The endangered species and the most popular pet animals attract very large sums of money. We distribute these funds."

"It looks like a crypt."

"Death is a great confidence inspirer. All banks are designed to look like burial vaults."

"Where's Adam?"

Andrea Burden made no reply. She had walked round behind the chair, Madelene could feel her hands on the chair back.

"You must see the view," she said. "Before you go."

The chair lurched under Madelene. The other woman had turned her and the chair round in a semi-circle.

Madelene closed her eyes, smarting from the gin and surprised by the force of this manoeuvre. Then she opened them.

Three of the office walls were of plate glass. Beneath and beyond them stretched London, remote and unreal.

Andrea Burden had remained standing like a nurse behind a patient in a wheelchair.

"What are you thinking?" she asked.

London was not a city. Madelene could see that now. For a city has an end. There was no limit to the irregular, rippling expanse of stone below her. Even at the point where the curve of the earth formed the horizon, buildings reared up, out on the visible bounds of the universe.

She could see that it was too vast for just one sort of weather. Around them, over St Katharine's Dock and the Thames, the sun was shining. The sky over the new City was cloudy and grey. To the east, over Docklands, it was raining. And on the south side of the river hung a yellow curtain of industrial fumes.

"How can anyone bear to live here?" she said.

"We adapt. Even to an existence such as this. The ability to adapt is the mark of a human being."

Andrea Burden stepped into the light, alongside the chair.

"20,500 chickens per day," she said. "To feed London. 5,800 pigs. 1,520 head of beef. 6,000 sheep. According to the Meat and Livestock Commission. Each day the city consumes two million kilos of animal protein. London could be regarded as a monstrous machine for the processing of domestic animals. That, however, is not how I see it. Because the slaughterhouses are only one small part of the story. If we look beyond basic sustenance the first group we come to are the working animals. In Greater London there are at least 5,000 watch-dogs registered with security firms. At least 5,000 horses in service as drays and hacks. 4,000 racehorses belonging to fifty different stables, 2,000 police and cavalry mounts, 3,000 greyhounds, 3,000 homing pigeons. Then there are the animals that satisfy other needs. The Office for National Statistics estimates that down below us there are a million dogs, one and a half million cats, five million cagebirds – breed unspecified, two million small rodents – guinea pigs and the like, and a number of reptiles and fish at which we can only hazard a guess. Not forgetting those animals in scientific research laboratories – private and public – and pharmaceutical plants, the livestock kept on city farms, at the veterinary colleges and so on. A group which, in the Greater London area, is reckoned to amount to ten million animals, ranging in size from shrews to musk oxen. And all of this, all of these twenty million-plus living creatures are not even the half of it. The other half are what might be termed the animal lumpenproletariat of the city. The stray dogs, the wild cats, that band of semi-wild animals which strive to adapt to the city biotope: foxes, pigeons, house mice, seagulls, rats, insects. And we haven't even begun to talk about the zoos and aquaria."

Andrea Burden had moved across to the glass, her back to Madelene. Now she turned to face her.

"London is not just an organism that processes animals. There is far more to it than that. Our biologists calculate that this city contains more than thirty million non-human creatures, representing 10,000 distinct species. They give the animal biomass as being 75,000 kilos per square kilo. Do you know what that tells us?"

Madelene shook her head.

"It means that not only are there more animals in London than in any British oak forest, or anywhere else in the British Isles for that matter. It means there is a greater incidence of animal life here than, for example, in Mato Grosso in the dry season. London is one of *the* largest habitats for non-human creatures on earth."

Madelene looked out across the city, down into her now empty glass and out across the city again.

"So what?" she said.

She did not mean to be rude but explicit politeness takes energy and Madelene was running on empty.

"Now let me see you out," said Andrea Burden.

She helped Madelene out of the chair. The carpet beneath her feet had acquired a muddy cast.

"But we humans," said Madelene, "we matter too, don't we?"

"We made a choice. Animals were brought here. It's the victims that concern me."

Andrea Burden put the gin bottle in a brown paper bag and handed it to Madelene.

"Take the bottle for the trip back. It was lovely to see you. Be an angel and call before you come next time."

Madelene steadied herself against the doorpost and scanned the face opposite her. It struck her that the other woman had set her a test. And that she had failed it, without ever having worked out in which field she was being examined.

"You forgot something," she said. "The animals the behavioural scientists work with."

Adam's sister gripped her arm, ready to throw her out. Already her gaze had grown distant.

In Madelene's mind five images converged on one another:

London, the ape, Adam, Priscilla and the coldness of the face before her. They ran together and burst into flames.

"Actually what I came to say was that I had a very strict up-bringing," she said. "I've always had a terrible problem with any kind of wrongdoing. I can't sleep at night. Get throat infections. It's the ape. At our place. What with Adam's position. It was you who brought it. The boss of this splendid establishment. With never a word to the veterinary authorities. I might have to go to the police. That's what I came to say."

Until now Andrea Burden's movements had been fluttery and spasmodic. The first time Madelene met her she had taken this for the mark of a ditherer, but she had since learned to liken it to a prize fighter bobbing and weaving around his opponent. Now she was still. She had no time to regain her balance before Madelene was on her again.

"Or maybe I should go straight to the papers. I haven't been able to eat for days. I kept hoping someone would give me an explanation."

They were back beside the window and there they stayed, on the brink of the urban abyss.

Andrea Burden lowered her head.

"I would like to invite you to London Zoo," she said. "Tomorrow. Before the workmen arrive. Would seven o'clock suit you?"

"I haven't been to the zoo since I was a child," said Madelene.

They walked again to the door. Andrea Burden opened it, the suit was waiting in the outer office.

"About the papers," said Andrea Burden, "and the police?"

Madelene kept her in suspense for a moment before answering.

"We'll have to talk about that tomorrow," she said. "At the Zoo."

8

At first glance there was nothing remarkable about the way Adam Burden ate dinner. On closer inspection it proved to adhere to a set of rules representing the culmination of a four-hundred-year long process of evolution in upper-class table manners. He received the food with a caress, parted it, conducted steaming hot mouthfuls into his discreetly exposed innards, gently coerced corks out of slender bottle necks, dabbed his lips delicately with a napkin which materialized in his hand then vanished without trace into his lap, that no meat juices would smear the gleaming glass held by the stem alone to prevent the throbbing pulse from affecting the temperature of the wine. When all was done and Mrs Clapham had taken the dishes away and laid bare the tablecloth the white linen would offer no clue as to what had gone before.

Madelene had known from the start that she would never be able to match this regular, daily balancing act. When she sat down to a meal she was hungry, usually extremely hungry, to the extent that the food occupied almost all of her thoughts, with whatever was left being focused on spilling as little as possible and – more and more often – on stopping herself from falling off the chair. So there was very little energy to spare for following Adam's animated conversation. Like a well-mannered season-ticket holder she had long since learned to applaud in all the right places while her attention was somewhere else entirely.

But not this evening. This evening, though tired, she was all ears. Listening not to what Adam was saying but for the break in the flow of words that would facilitate her own entrance. Because this evening Madelene had devised a role for herself.

"There was a man here today," she said. "From the veterinary authorities. He was complaining that Clapham had refused to let him in. He wanted to talk to you."

Adam's face lost its air of preoccupation. First it went blank. Then a fine veil of apprehension settled over it.

"And then this woman rang."

Adam stood up and retreated towards the empty grate. It was a wintertime move, and futile – the fire had been out since April.

"Her name was . . . Priscilla something or other. She wanted to know whether there were any – animals here."

By the fireplace Adam froze.

"The birds, I told her. The ones we feed in the grounds. And Clapham's goldfish. But that's all."

Adam leant his head back against the mantelpiece.

"I thought it best not to mention the ape. I mean maybe it hasn't been, what do you call it? Reported? If that's what you're supposed to do with animals? Or what? Could you tell me, please?"

It took some time for Adam to answer her and when he did his voice was hoarse.

"The Washington Convention lists all wild animals under three different headings depending on how great the threat to each species is reckoned to be. Strictly speaking animals that appear on these lists must be reported to the Ministry of Agriculture's CITE office – that being the body in this country which sees to it that the terms of the convention are observed."

"Which," said Madelene, "just doesn't appear to have happened in this case."

"More often than not the Ministry will contact us. So in a way I represent the controlling body."

"That's what scares me," said Madelene. "That's why I almost confided in this Priscilla woman, and said listen, what if these – what were they called again – controlling bodies, break the law themselves? What then?"

What was running through Adam's mind during the long silence that now settled between them was not the implications of what Madelene had said. Nor was it the painfulness of the situation. It was at Madelene as a person that he stared. Behind the woman across from him he was trying to catch a glimpse of the individual he had married but seventeen months earlier.

"Five days," he said. "It'll be here for another five days. Then it's gone."

Anyone who drinks tends to lose their natural, essential tiredness. In recent months Madelene had been having more and more difficulty in getting to sleep. Nonetheless, that night she took two caffeine tablets and drank three cups of black coffee, wanting to be quite sure she would stay awake. Then she sat down to wait.

At ten o'clock a car drove into the courtyard. From the window she watched Adam come out to meet two men, after which they and Clapham in the course of the next two hours carried boxes of various sizes from the car into the garden room. Then the car drove away. At two in the morning Adam emerged and went up to his rooms. Madelene gave him five minutes then followed him.

When she entered the room it was empty, Adam was in the bathroom. The long table that ran the length of one wall was covered in large sheets of paper and on top of the paper stood a jar containing a huge brain suspended in alcohol.

A good many hours had passed since Madelene had put her mind into neutral. Her actions were now guided by decisions taken at another time of day and so she did not stop to think before pulling out the large rubber cork and sniffing the fluid, with the instinctive curiosity that drives alcoholics to comb every new stretch of terrain for any potential reservoir.

The bouquet that rose to meet her nostrils was the repellent, sickly-sweet odour of formalin.

She replaced the cork and straightened up. The feeling that washed over her was not disappointment that the brain had not been preserved in alcohol. It was the fear that this might be the ape's brain. That, having completed their examination, they had then cut open the skull and removed its brain.

The bathroom door opened and Adam came out. His face was grey with fatigue, his eyes red as an albino rabbit's.

He stopped dead. Saw Madelene's hand on the glass, read her thoughts and remembered dinner.

"It's the brain of a chimpanzee," he said. "From the Institute collection."

Remembering her mission, Madelene walked over to her husband and put her arms around him.

"I'm not quite myself," she said. "But I just wanted to touch you before I went to bed."

This close, convincing hug was what she had come to give. With it she wiped the exhaustion from his face. With it she erased the memory of that evening's discord. And with it, as the tips of her fingers ran up over his buttocks, from the clip on his belt, she stole his keys.

She waited in her bedroom for twenty minutes. Then she crept through the darkened rooms, found the keys to the potting shed and garden room on Adam's key ring and let herself in.

A forest of boxes, lamps and instruments had sprung up around and in front of the cage and this she worked her way through, paying it no heed. She knew that these things were intended for use on the ape and that they would never have the chance to fulfil their purpose.

She unlocked the cage and remained in the doorway for a moment looking at the animal. She was never going to see it again and so she tried to imprint its image on her memory, to take a mental farewell photograph.

The ape was in the process of feeding. It ate absorbedly, egoistically, as Madelene herself had always dreamed of eating, with every sense other than those of taste and smell suspended, stripped of all mannerliness and with that same fearlessness which had, from the beginning, seemed like a question aimed at her, a question which, she now realized, had been asking: How do you really want to be? And to this question her heart had answered: I want – in some way – to be like you.

"I've come to let you out," she said.

The ape rose. It placed its fists on the ground and pushed itself into a position which, while erect, still left it on all fours. From there it kept on going, relinquished its hold on the ground, straightened its back, lifted its head and clasped its hands across its chest.

Madelene had been aware that the ape had – to some degree and in a way she did not understand – been learning from the people and goings-on around it. Even so, she was staggered. For a moment they stood there, quite still, she and the ape face to face. Then she turned towards the grille and opened first it and then the conservatory door. They stepped out into the park.

The wind had got up. In a cold, midnight-blue sky it chased the clouds across the face of the man in the moon. The ape bent its head back, seeming to drink in the wind and the moonlight.

Madelene crossed to the wall, set her carafe on the top and clambered up after it. The ape materialized alongside her.

This was as far as Madelene had planned. She would now pick out an escape route for the ape, it would set out for home and she would be left standing in the moonlight, smiling, shedding a tear, looking wonderful and drinking one for the road.

She was, at this point, sitting six feet above the ground. Suddenly, just as she raised her hand, she rose up another two hundred feet. She grew to the height from which, in the House of the Animals, she had surveyed London. She saw the city not with human eyes but with those of a bird. But this was by no means an objective view. It was a vision. And what she perceived was that the freedom she had been so keen to plot out for the ape no longer existed.

What she had seen from that building at Aldgate was a city that stretched to the ends of the earth. And even though she knew that to be impossible, that even this wilderness of inhabited stonework petered out somewhere or other, the principle of it went on for ever. What mattered was not the city itself, since that too was but one small dot on the face of the planet. What mattered was the principle of the city – modern civilization *per se*. Madelene saw that there was no longer any end to that, it had totally enmeshed the earth. There was no longer any *outside* for the ape at her elbow. Any zoo, any game reserve, any safari park whichever was now contained within the bounds of civilization.

Everyone – even someone who has read as little as Madelene had

74

done – takes for their own the dream of *terra incognita*, the unknown, unexplored world. For one awful moment this dream was bathed in the light of reality, then it dissolved. Madelene knew that this was now beyond her reach for ever. From now on there was no quest for the Golden Fleece, or the jewels of Opar, the centre of the Earth, the Promised Land, lost horizons, El Dorado, Atlantis, the Islands of the Hesperides or simply the land of milk and honey.

She turned to face the ape.

"There's no such thing as *outside* now," she said. "If there's any freedom to be found it'll have to be on the inside."

Over the past few days she had been reminded of her childhood longing, not for some image of bliss, but for bliss itself. Not for herself – her own sober common sense was, in spite of everything, too strong for that – but for the ape. She had grown more and more convinced that she could save it by helping it to make the break for freedom.

Now she abandoned this last illusion.

There is nothing pleasant about abandoning the protection afforded by hopes and daydreams and Madelene shrank from it like a hermit crab forced to leave its whelk shell. There was a hopelessness to her situation that would have prompted stronger characters than she to contemplate a speedier form of suicide than that offered by alcohol and Madelene was struck, momentarily, by the thought of jumping to her death.

A split-second and the thought was gone. Not only because it dawned on her that she was not on the thirteenth floor but only six feet above the ground, but to a much greater extent for another reason. Those alter egos who had taken their place beside her in recent days found the thought that they should suddenly be snuffed out quite unacceptable.

It felt as though yet another woman had settled herself beside her on the wall. Turning towards her Madelene saw that this was Responsibility. A figure both as neutral and as undeniably present as the moonlight and the wind and the smell of earth.

Madelene slid down the wall, the woman followed her, then the ape. They walked back the way they had come. Once inside the cage Madelene locked the door behind them.

"It's not like when we were little," she said. "You can't just run away from home. It's too complicated now. We need more time."

She peered through the glass, across the electronic landscape. She saw the anaesthetic apparatus, trolleys loaded with monitoring equipment, a white box on wheels resembling a twin-size coffin, a hydraulic chair connected to a huge machine which looked – with all its electronic purposefulness – like a domestic version of the electric chair.

"They're coming to get you," she said, "and it's going to be worse than it's ever been before."

She put out her hand and the ape took it. The palm of its hand was as big as a shovel but, contrary to what she had expected, it was soft as silk.

"I'm going now," she said. "But I'll be back for you."

This was not some ritual prognosis, like a wedding vow or a New Year resolution. It was an oath of a kind to which Madelene had not been moved in twenty years. It was a fearless declaration of faith with no thought for the future, such as a child will make to an irreplaceable playmate.

9

As a child Madelene had been dragged along, by people who thought they were doing her a good turn, to Copenhagen Zoo. There she had seen ospreys in budgerigar cages, beasts of prey in menagerie looseboxes, hippos in tiled bathrooms and anthropoid apes that flung first their excrement and then themselves against the bars surrounding them, in mute protest. Since then she had never set foot inside any establishment in which animals were held captive. Now here she was, following Andrea Burden through London Zoo, and on through a little door in the twenty-foot-high fence of wood and wire netting which had, for two years, encircled the construction work on the site overlooking Gloucester Gate. In less than two months this site, together with the extension onto Primrose Hill and Albert Terrace, would be linked up to London Zoo for the inauguration of the New London Regent's Park Zoological Gardens.

Madelene had been prepared for the worst. She had brought along a cardboard tube which might have looked – and was meant to look – as though it might hold a student's, or perhaps an architect's, drawings – which, in a sense, it did – but which also contained a Pyrex flask filled by her on getting up that morning and now only two-thirds full. She had stepped through the door with eyes closed. Now, slowly, she opened them.

The light was golden, the shadows long and green, the air as fresh and cool as a fine spray of atomized spring water. Before them spread a grassy plain on the outskirts of which Madelene could make out a large lake with a llama grazing on its bank. In the middle of the lake was an island, on which an antelope stooped to drink. Beyond the lake a forest reared up – one of the trees swayed back and forth, a group of gorillas having taken up residence in it like a flock of immense, lumbering black birds. To the west the forest ran out into a rocky outcrop atop which a pride of waking lions stretched languorously in the sunlight.

The memory Madelene had retained of the zoos of her childhood was of landscaped animal prisons. What she was confronted with here was a tropical scene, at the point where the savannah meets the jungle.

Only a distant skyline, the odd concrete barricade, a glass wall, a tarmac path betrayed the fact that the scene in front of them was man-made.

"At this hour of the day," said Andrea Burden, "I think I know how God must have felt, walking through the Garden on the morning of the sixth day."

Madelene made a vain attempt to recall the chronology of the Creation.

"How did He feel?" she asked.

"There's a tranquillity to the early morning. One can think clearly. He would have been able to draw up His budget for the next day in peace and quiet."

They sat down on a stone balustrade. At their feet the ground plunged away to a ditch thirty feet below.

"But He didn't have the problems we've had with private land ownership. Or free enterprise. Just as there were no such problems in the last century when Sir Stamford Raffles founded London Zoo, for the edification of an exclusive, blue-blooded public and with a mere handful of specimens of the beasts of the field and the birds of the air. Things are different now. The land on which much of London was built, the ground on which we are sitting now, is owned by the Crown. You cannot imagine – no outsider could possibly imagine – what we have had to go through to acquire a lease on this plot of land. Until the present government came into power all negotiations were channelled through the Royal Parks Agency. Now it's an utter shambles. We eventually found ourselves dealing, on one side, with the Corporation of London and its representatives – the City

78

of Westminster, the Borough of Camden, the London Boroughs' Association, the Common Council of London. On another with the Crown Estate Paving Commission, which handles the conveyancing of Crown property. On a third with the Department of National Heritage. And on a fourth with the developers who held the contract for Albert Terrace. Not to mention the agents of those residents who had to be bought out."

She took a deep breath.

"It's all settled now. We won the first round, now comes the semi-final. Once we're open we'll be having to compete with the safari parks, and with every tourist attraction in the city. Both for visitors and for funding. We'll have to hold our own against 600 zoos in the USA and Europe, 800 throughout the rest of the world. We will be required to keep a running record of results achieved within the fields of breeding, research and acquisitions. If we are to keep our place on the European Endangered Species Programme and in the CBSG, which controls the allocation of all the most valuable wild animals in captivity; decides which zoo is to have charge of the studbook for a particular species. We're banking on becoming studbook keepers for ten species within the first two years. And for ten more over the next ten. We've got our sights set on fifteen million visitors a year. We're budgeting £15 million for research. Two years ago we took over St Francis Forest, for use as a breeding centre. It's going to cost us £10 million a year to run that and Whipsnade together."

Below them, in slow motion, a jaguar made its way across the rocks and down to the water and began to drink.

"Maybe you could get the animals to pay for their board and lodging," said Madelene.

"That's the name of the game if you want to create a zoo on this scale. If God were to take another shot at the Creation *that* couldn't be done from scratch either. Or for the benefit of two spectators in their birthday suits. Nowadays He'd have to get out there and raise the money first. And then He'd have to drum up a mass audience. And then . . ."

"Then maybe He'd just drop the whole idea and leave the animals in peace," said Madelene.

She could have kept her mouth shut. Only a week ago she would have said nothing. But behind her, on the stone balustrade, Priscilla had now perched herself. The jaguar alone had noticed and gazed intently at this third party to the conversation.

Andrea Burden stood up and closed in, making those small, slithery, semi-circular movements that Madelene had learned to recognize.

"So she loves freedom, does she?" she said. "She loves the wide open spaces. The true, the paradisiacal world of nature. The one she heard stories about as a child. So she could cope with the storybooks at home, then? And if not, no doubt there were always the cartoons."

She pointed at the jaguar.

"Do you know what lies in store for that in the swamp forests of western Brazil? Do you know what fate awaits those big cats? Those and all other wild animals? They're destined for the kind of suffering that can only be conceived of in statistical terms. Three out of four cubs die in infancy. Of those who survive the first year, one in two will reach sexual maturity, the others will perish. One in eight will go so far as to mate. Seldom more than once. After that they die of hunger. Or thirst. If they're not eaten by other jaguars. Or gored by wart hogs, after which the wound becomes infected and infested with maggots that crawl up through the musculature and attack the brain, after which . . ."

"Stop," said Madelene.

"God knew nothing of this back then on the sixth morning, when He still believed that everything was just perfect. But eventually it must have dawned on Him – like most behavioural scientists He was probably a bit slow on the uptake – that what He had actually created was a factory for the manufacture of suffering. That the whole point of the jaguar is that by pushing itself to breaking point it should be subjected to a certain number of afflictions which will keep it alive just long enough for it to mate."

"Well, at least it has a taste of love before it dies," Madelene said.

Andrea Burden drew her lips back from her teeth in a smile of sorts.

"You bet your life it does," she said. "And let me tell you how. You see, the jaguar goes through its life alone. Then one day it picks up a scent and follows it, driven by an innate biological urge it cannot understand. It follows this scent and all of a sudden it comes face to face with another big cat. It does not see it as a reflection of itself, because it has no concept of self. It sees it as a mortal threat. It wants to run – both animals want to run – but they cannot. They are pinned to the spot by a set of genetic stocks. She turns her back to him, prostrates herself, he jumps on top of her and digs his teeth into her neck. And do you know why? A sign of passion, perhaps? Of love? I'll tell you why. It is for a reason so glaringly obvious that even the zoologists could not miss it. It is because, if he did not hold her down, the female – terrified out of her wits – would turn on him and kill him. Then he couples with her. And just as he pulls out of her, just as he relinquishes his grip, all she-jaguars, all she-cheetahs, all she-tigers, all she-cats the world over make the same instinctive move. And do you know what that is? Do you know how they show their appreciation of this coupling? They stretch back their necks and swivel their heads round. And then they try to see whether they can get away with ripping his carotid arteries with their eyeteeth."

The two women circled around one another. The jaguar and Priscilla followed them with their eyes.

"None of you ever asked a jaguar," said Madelene. "It is quite possible to look as though you're suffering even when you're enjoying yourself."

"Every he-cat's penis is equipped with a number of barbs. As it withdraws these barbs tear into the she-cat's flesh. The pain of this triggers ovulation. And that – through pain – is how Nature guarantees the greatest possible likelihood of fertilization and the continuation of the species."

Madelene looked away.

"Even so," she said, "no-one can know . . . how . . ."

Andrea Burden leant on the balustrade and looked at the jaguar. Her face shone with the utter fulfilment of a mother watching her child.

"It is my firm belief," she said, "that the best zoos can provide animals with almost everything that nature could. Food, light, the right breeding conditions. While also to some extent lessening their suffering."

Priscilla motioned to Madelene.

"And the ape?" she said.

Andrea Burden did not answer her directly.

"Until a few years ago," she said slowly, "the polar bear enclosure was thought to be the most dangerous place in a zoo. Those thick, furry coats and brown eyes made people want to stick their hands in and scratch their backs. If they did, one clout from a paw would tear the visitor's arm off at the elbow. I've been having second thoughts about that, though. The way I see it now, the most dangerous enclosures are – those ones over there."

Madelene followed her gaze. Above the ape jungle, on the other side of Prince Albert Road towered the grey silhouette of the Institute of Animal Behavioural Research.

"The academic aviary."

She pointed to the other side of the park.

"Albany Street. Where the top-level civil servants – the decision-makers – have their private residences. Right next door to the burghers of the financial world. The barnyard of political and financial power. With the most rigid pecking order in the animal kingdom. The most disproportionate relationship between body and brain size. Real peacocks throw themselves into a brief and bloody skirmish, after which they live in sly peace, with the victor as their leader. But out there there's no end to the lunacy of it, the in-fighting. Over there they give to the World Wildlife Fund with the one hand and sell weapons and trees from the rain forests with the other. Over there they had revoked London Zoo's funding and starved the place to the point where the animals were dying off in their cages. Until we embarked upon our . . . campaign. It is the members of these worthy bodies who will decide who is to be the new director, when London's two zoological gardens become united two months from now."

Andrea Burden paused. Somewhere a bird screeched – a harsh, abrupt primeval cry.

"This is going to be one of the most powerful posts in the zoological world. And I've made up my mind that they should appoint your husband to it. The ape will clinch his appointment. It will bring the last of the sceptics into the fold. You see, it's not enough that Adam is smarter than all of the others put together. Not enough that he has written forty papers and three books in five languages. Applications will be sent in from every corner of the globe. The ballot will be secret and thoroughly corrupt. But if he has a three-week start on the others, alone with the ape, no-one else will be able to touch him. Which is why it's being kept at your place. Under conditions which are in every way defensible. And why we've strayed, very slightly, from the terms of the convention. To ensure that much greater respect for it in the future."

"Adam says it's some kind of dwarf chimpanzee," said Madelene. "What do you think?"

Andrea Burden hesitated for a second.

"I'm not a zoologist," she said.

She took Madelene's arm and drew her along beside her. Madelene pulled up short. Someone – herself or Priscilla – reached out a hand and grasped the other woman by the arm.

"Why Adam?"

Andrea Burden tried to extricate herself. But via Madelene's hand Priscilla hung on to her arm with a grip accustomed to manhandling butcher's hooks and half-ton beef carcasses.

"Adam," said Madelene, "likes animals because . . . because they can't do him any harm. Because he's superior to them. But he doesn't trust them. He doesn't trust any living creature. Not even me."

A third woman had joined Madelene and Priscilla, invisible and as yet nameless, but quite distinct from Madelene herself. A person of a certain straightforward integrity. It was she who now spoke.

"Even at those times when we're really close, when you think that now everything is going to be different, he never lets go. He's afraid . . . that I'm going to turn my head round and rip his carotid arteries. And now it's worse than ever. It has something to do with the ape. He's very frightened. Very dangerous."

Andrea Burden lifted a face that was, for an instant, naked.

"Boarding schools," she said. "You're packed off to school some-where between the ages of four and ten. That's quite usual for our class. It's considered to give one the best possible start in life. Sport, art and literature, four foreign languages. Courses on running a gracious establishment and household accounts for us girls. You get everything that's going. Except love. For ten years. After that it's too late. For the rest of your life you're like a soldier at the front. Covering your back. Because no-one else is going to. Like in Churchill's memoirs. The letter from Afghanistan. To his mother. In the break in his account of how they destroyed the irrigation network. About his time at Sandhurst. Where he calls himself a stunted tree. He didn't have the courage to say it straight out. That's why you make the choice not to have children. Because you know what they would have to go through."

The two women enjoyed a split-second of intimacy, as people do when they stop insisting on their own private masks, if only for a moment. Then Andrea Burden shrugged off this weakness.

"You're a foreigner," she said. "You'll never understand. But, no matter what, Adam is a lion. He has style, ambition and the knack for dealing with the ministries, the boards of directors and the university. He has the capability to run the zoo without any internal wrangling. He knows how to cut the outside opposition down to size. He's tamed the environmentalists, the local action groups *and* the Royal Institute of British Architects. We have to respect him for that. You and I both."

"I'm married to him," said Madelene. "And a marriage is not a zoo."

The two women looked one another in the eye. Under different circumstances Madelene would have dropped her gaze. But that was before she had tried looking into the eyes of the ape Erasmus. And so it was Andrea who was forced to look away.

They had reached the door in the fence. They stepped through into London Zoo. The gardens were open, the first visitors of the day had shown up.

"I'm going to stay here for a little while," said Madelene. "See if I can pick up what was running through God's head later on that day."

Andrea Burden stood her ground.

"What you said . . . about going to the papers . . . ?" she said.

Like all she-animals Madelene cherished a powerful desire for everything to end well, for every leave-taking to be uncomplicated and warm and wistful. This one too looked set to go that way, Madelene was prepared for a reconciliation. But at her back were two other women and she was required to answer for all of them.

"It's been postponed," she said. "Indefinitely. But it hasn't been cancelled."

Once alone she made her way through the zoo until she came to a telephone box. She sat herself down on the low wall surrounding the enclosure that housed the anteaters, viscachas and guanacos, pulled out her flask, saluted the animals and took a swig. She looked up at the Institute windows and tried to locate Adam's office.

She knew there was no time to lose. That she was in much the same situation as Eve would have been in the Garden of Eden if, as soon as she herself had been created, she had discovered that God was about to go too far and decided to stop Him. She would have been every bit as bewildered and overtaxed as Madelene was now. Because whatever it was that Andrea and Adam were putting together it was close to completion.

She walked over to the telephone box. Dialled the direct line to his front office.

The secretary announced herself.

"It's me," said Madelene. "Is he there?"

"I'll put you through."

Madelene glanced up at the grey edifice. Her head spun. She had been so sure he would not be there, that today too he would have stayed at home, in the garden room.

"Yes?"

"It's me," said Madelene.

Even without being all that well acquainted with the secretary Madelene knew for a fact that she was listening in. The ethanol and the early hour made her voice rasp like gravel on the seashore. Beneath this surface racket Adam recognized his wife's voice. The voice his secretary heard was that of Priscilla from the Meat Market.

"I had to hear your voice," she said.

Adam growled seductively, flattered. Madelene tried to think. She

85

had to get into the Institute. But without any risk of running into him. She had to make sure that he stayed in his office until she was back outside again.

"If only I could touch you," she said.

"Mm."

She knew Adam's sounds. She knew he now had an erection.

She glanced round about. A group of pensioners went by carrying peanuts for the monkeys.

"I've got this urge to talk dirty to you," she rasped. "Can I call you back in fifteen minutes?"

She could hear his breathing growing heavier. Lust outweighs logic every time. It did not occur to Adam to ask why their conversation had to be cut short just then.

"I'll be glued to the phone," he said.

Madelene hung up.

Heading at a jog for the main entrance, she pinned up her hair, put on her sunglasses and unbelted her coat to let it hang loosely round about her. Parked at the kerb was a truck with a picture of a dog on the door. It was empty. She walked into the Institute foyer to find the driver of this vehicle standing at the reception desk, being treated to a snarling rebuff from the terrier. Madelene took the elevator up and hurried past the door behind which the secretary and Adam sat waiting for her call.

The vet's office was empty. Madelene sat down to wait. She had ten minutes.

He came in after five. With a cup of tea and a muffin.

"Sorry about this," said Madelene.

The doctor sat down.

"Why don't you just move in," he said. "I can have a bed set up for you."

"I don't know who else to ask but you," said Madelene.

In her own voice, under the huskiness, she caught the sound of that new and somewhat honest side of herself, with which she was not yet quite at home.

The doctor waggled his head.

"I like a bit of company over a morning cuppa. And no-one here talks to me any more."

"Why not?"

He pondered this question.

"Maybe because I'm growing senile. Maybe because we're on the threshold of a new age. And I belong to the old one. Or maybe for some other reason. What can I offer you?"

Madelene removed her sunglasses.

"You wouldn't happen to have a Special Brew?"

The doctor reached into a small refrigerator at his back then set a bottle and a glass in front of her.

Madelene poured the beer and drank. She opened the cardboard tube, put her flask on the desk and shook out a small bundle of white papers – sketches of the equipment she had seen outside the ape's cage the day before. Drawn from memory, but not with eyeliner. With black ink, very early that morning while she was still sober.

She handed the vet the first sketch, of the twin-size coffin on wheels and the electric chair.

"Brain scanning," said the doctor. "Equipment for brain-scanning."

"How does it work?"

He shook his head.

"That belongs under the heading of this new age," he said.

Madelene handed him the next sketch.

"A sleep monitor. They have one like this directly below where we are now. In the Institute for Sleep Research. This one is designed for larger animals. You hook the beast up to it and switch on. When it falls asleep, force of gravity will cause some part of the body, an arm, a trunk, the neck to droop. At which point it will receive a shock and wake up. They measure the length of time they can keep the animals awake. It's a method that's been well-used. They've proved that animals can do without sleep. They haven't managed to convince the animals of this, though."

Madelene held out two more drawings.

"Those collapsible boxes are part of an obstacle course. Those, as far as I can see, are draughtboards."

He took yet another sheet from her.

"A stimulation simulator. Straight out of the Institute for neuro-etiology, two floors below us. They've cast some doubt on the extent to which animals can feel pain. And suggested that until animals can tell us in proper English that they *are* in pain there is no reason to suppose that cruelty to animals is being practised."

He looked at Madelene.

"This machine is designed to carry out an extensive test on a fair-sized animal. Have they started doing behavioural research at the slaughterhouses?"

"Testing for what? What type of behaviour?"

"Intelligence tests I would say. Problem solving. But we're looking at some pretty hard-handed methods here. That sleep monitor, for example. It's become extremely difficult to obtain permission from the Animal Procedure Committee for its use. But perhaps this research won't wait?"

Madelene gathered up her papers.

"Can I borrow your phone?" she asked.

The vet flung out a hand.

"It's all yours. Keep it if you want. I'll be retiring next year. And no-one calls now anyway."

Madelene dialled Adam's number. It took the secretary a moment to compose herself sufficiently to put her through.

"Are you alone?" Adam asked.

"Completely."

"Are you wearing anything?"

Madelene eyed the vet.

"No," she said. "Not a thing."

Adam whistled under his breath.

"It's stiff as a poker," he said.

Madelene cast an eye around the room, looking for inspiration. This was a tricky situation. She considered a row of dental charts hanging on the wall behind the vet.

"Can it be felt with the tongue?" she asked softly.

A moan issued from the receiver.

"I'll be . . . coming soon," said Madelene. "So I'm going to have to hang up."

She hung up and picked up her sketches.

"How's that allergy of yours?" the doctor asked.

"Better, thanks."

"I rang the Meat Marketing Board Research Centre. They'd never heard of you."

Madelene took a deep breath.

"They've forgotten all about me. No sooner am I out of the door than people have forgotten me."

"I've gone through the newsletters. For six months back. No theft of any large ape or apelike creature has been reported."

"You're an angel," said Madelene.

"Of course, there are always rumours. Once or twice over the past ten years there's been the odd whisper of an unidentified species of ape, some sort of primate, being offered for sale. We, of course, do not deal on the black market. And such a thing is, of course, impossible. With the Vu Quang ox the last of the big mammals was discovered and documented. It has to have been a cross between some known species of ape."

Madelene stepped into the corridor, pushed off and made an unsteady attempt at a run, wanting to get past Adam's office.

The office door swung open and out came the secretary. It was evident, even to Madelene, that while this woman would usually have the most precise and rational grounds for her actions, on this occasion she was driven solely by an overwhelming desire to get away and to give vent to her indignation. On being confronted with Priscilla in the corridor she flattened herself against the wall.

Madelene flashed her a big smile. A smile of relief at the fact that it was not Adam she was faced with and a smile that said: Just because we've had our occasional differences that doesn't mean we can't all get on. Then she went on her way.

The first button she pushed in the elevator took her to the basement, but on her next attempt she made it to the foyer. Her senses told her she had enough in reserve for tying up one more loose end. She walked over to the reception desk.

"I'm expecting a car," she said. "That man who was here earlier, might he have been my driver?"

The terrier clenched her teeth.

Madelene placed her cardboard tube on the desktop. The woman regarded it coldly.

"These," said Madelene, "are urgent brain-scan results. Anxiously awaited by government ministers and princes. We're talking life or death. If you've let that car drive away without me, tomorrow you'll be so far out of a job you won't even be allowed to shovel the shit from under sea cows."

The woman weighed up the advantages and disadvantages of continued insolence.

"It was the street sweeper," she said at long last. "He wanted the director's car moved. Wanted to know who it belonged to. Wanted to sweep beneath it. Naturally I sent him away with a flea in his ear."

Madelene pulled herself up, swayed and winked.

"That's the way to treat them," she said.

She emerged into the sunshine and into the final, euphoric phase of her drunkenness. Singing a little song to herself, with no clear direction, she set out on her magical mystery tour through a benign and joyful world. Her mind seethed with thoughts of the zoological building site, Andrea Burden, potential and abandoned dreams, strange and unforeseen women friends, Adam's erection, a sketch of a sleep monitor and a drive that could not be explained away in purely chemical terms.

She passed the van with the dog on the door. Up in the cab the street sweeper with the flea in his ear sat staring into space, like the young man in the fairy tale just at the point when his strength and his spirits are at their lowest ebb, the point at which the witch comes to his aid.

Madelene reached up, opened the cab door and climbed up. She made herself comfortable next to Johnny, opened the cardboard tube, took out the flask containing her last centilitre of propellant and removed the cork.

Johnny did not move a muscle.

"Well?" he said.

"I've a street I want swept," said Madelene.

She drank from the flask and held it out to Johnny. He took a sniff and sipped cautiously. His eyes filled first with tears and then with respect.

"That's some booze."

Madelene took off her sunglasses. Only then did she notice a plaster-encased Samson in the bunk behind the driver's seat.

"You're his wife," said Johnny.

Madelene smiled. Halfway through the smile the downturn kicked in.

The effect was instantaneous. All reserves were exhausted, the rocket decelerated, stalled and jettisoned its empty tanks. After which it plummeted earthwards like a stone.

Madelene opened the door through which she had entered and hung out. Passers-by on the pavement saw the look on her face and got out of the way. All except one. Adam's secretary, possibly on her way to lunch, still pale and shaken, stayed where she was. Madelene threw up. The secretary backed away.

Madelene would have fallen out if an arm that had in its time supported gnus and hippos had not wrapped itself around her and hauled her back into the cab. Johnny handed her a large, blue, freshly pressed and folded handkerchief and a thermos.

"Drink," he said. "It's water."

Madelene gulped greedily. In her coat pocket she found her Vitamin B tablets, popped a handful in her mouth and took another gulp.

Johnny started the truck and pulled away from the kerb.

Inside, Madelene was plunging downwards at an ever-increasing rate of knots. Far down the slope self-loathing lay in wait and, farther down, the corpse-filled catacombs referred to by the outside world, with inexcusable understatement, as a hangover. She had no energy left now for being enigmatic. At the same time she saw everything with the hysterical clarity that precedes utter collapse.

"That dog," she said. "It's the one Bower was talking about. You had the ape in the van."

"It ran off," said Johnny. "First time it's ever happened. I didn't know it was there."

"How did you track it down it again?"

Johnny tapped the radio.

"I know the police wave length," he said. "The veterinary police transmit a couple of megahertz down from them."

Madelene had never communicated with workers – skilled or unskilled – on anything other than clearly defined prior conditions. They had furnished her with the material side of her existence and then they had carted off the rubbish. She had engaged them, received them, let them in and out and treated them with an overdone friendliness born of the fact that she feared them without having any idea of what made them tick, and that – deep down – she was completely at their mercy, she herself being incapable of changing a fuse, digging a septic tank or baking a *kransekage*. In a taxi she always sat in the back. Now she was sitting up beside Johnny. On a drive that she herself had instigated. And for which no estimate had been tendered in advance.

When faced with a dilemma all living creatures will resort to the patterns of behaviour they know best.

"You'll be looking for compensation," she said.

Johnny shook his head.

"How much?"

Johnny shook his head again.

Madelene looked at him with fresh eyes, the way one looks at some rare animal – a hornbill or a pygmy tapir. Or a person who is not on the make.

"What do you want then?" she asked.

Through Johnny's limbs and across his face there swept a cavalcade of emotions, none of which found verbal expression. Madelene saw that beside her sat someone who, like her, did not know where he was headed, but who – again like her – was positive that he was on the right track.

"I'd just like to see it again," he said.

They drove for a while in silence. Both of them were conscious of the fact that the ape had been there, in the cab in which they now sat.

"I've promised to help it," said Madelene.

Johnny nodded.

"I see."

"But I don't know how."

"I've driven the lot," said Johnny. "Rutting bull giraffes. Impalas. Which die if they so much as suspect they're no longer in Africa."

He stopped the truck. Only then did Madelene recognize the area. They were only a stone's throw from Mombasa Manor. Gingerly she climbed out.

"I could help you," said Johnny.

Madelene looked him in the eye. For her to trust a strange man from a different social stratum was an impossibility. But she was not alone. In her pain-racked state of clarity she sensed that the hazy women behind her had taken a liking to Johnny.

"I'll park here from now on," he said. "I live in the van."

He passed the cardboard tube down to her.

"Tell it . . . say that me and Samson, we've forgiven it for what it did to him. It didn't have no choice."

Madelene shut the cab door, turned on her heel and started to fight her way homewards, with never a backward glance.

10

She was woken by light, the throb of an engine and a feeling of owing something to someone.

It was two in the morning, but the noise was nothing new to her. Over the past few months a six-lane motorway had been driven through her skull – a road on which traffic was especially heavy at night, at which time it was also lit by searchlights that played and flickered across the inside of her corneae. She had had time to get used to that particular inferno of light and sound. What bothered her this time was that these sensations were being picked up from outside.

She positioned herself by the window. In the courtyard, in the glow of dimmed floodlights, about a dozen men were hard at work securing and sealing off the garden room. During the two hours she stood there, they hung grilles over the windows, replaced the doors and built a small run that extended from the side wing into the yard out of fifteen-foot high wire fencing topped off by three rows of electric cable stretched over insulators. That done, they departed.

Madelene went back to bed but, when sleep eluded her, she got up once more. In the dawn light she saw Adam welcoming three men. Having pulled on lab coats they all went through the door into the garden room. Not long afterwards they were joined by Clapham.

As the day gradually grew lighter Madelene battled the effects of the previous day's alcoholic poisoning with yet more alcohol. At first this looked set to succeed.

Over the next three days Adam and his four assistants only came out to eat, to go to the lavatory or to catch an hour or two's sleep on a sofa or in an armchair. And through those three days Madelene drank steadily and without a break. Initially in order to take the edge off her confusion, later – when this failed – to put herself, if possible, to sleep. And when that too failed she drank to keep the hangover at bay and to save herself from sobering up.

In the course of those three days, the people living in that house acquired something of an animal air. The five men as well as Madelene. The first time they emerged they had bathed and changed their clothes. But by their second sortie, twelve hours later, they had already taken to sitting round the kitchen table in their grey overalls, eating in silence. After that mealtimes were disbanded. The men forgot all about them or sent for a sandwich or trooped into the kitchen in twos and threes, grabbed a slice of meat, flopped into a chair and fell asleep, slept for a couple of hours then went back to work. The first twenty-four hours saw the eradication of all social differences between them. When they hissed at one another or sat slumped over the furniture, it would no longer have been possible for an outsider to work out who was the workman, who the butler and who the future director of the most prestigious establishment the zoological world had ever seen.

They had set to work glowing with scientific optimism. And over those three days, through her own deepening alcoholic haze, Madelene had watched this optimism turn first to expectancy, then dogged determination, then depression and finally panic.

When Adam staggered upstairs to his bedroom at twenty-hour intervals, Madelene went with him and coupled with him and sometimes even dozed off for a few hours. It was here that she awoke, in the night of the third day, during the gap between one nightmare and the next, to the certainty of her system's organic collapse.

The alcohol had drained her fluid reserves. It had drawn off serum from her cells to effect its breakdown, paralysed the auto-regulation function of her kidneys and contaminated the remaining ducts through its production of ammonium compounds. She was acutely aware of her fluttering heart, her overburdened liver, the deathly ineffectuality of her intestine. And above this internal

95

catastrophe hovered the reptiles of her dreams, the great white, venereal amphibians of alcoholic nightmare.

She struggled out of bed and over to the window. In the light of the waning moon she saw the ape. It made its way out into the pen, supervised by Clapham, and completed one slow circuit. It was wrapped in a blanket, its face was in shadow, it was limping and its exhaustion was five times greater than that of all five men put together.

And yet Madelene could see that whatever it was they had been trying to get out of it they had drawn a blank.

The animal made just the one circuit then disappeared into the building and Clapham closed the door behind it.

Madelene looked at the window frame, the park and, beyond that, across the city. From conversations overheard in her childhood home she had retained a vague and repulsive impression of what conditions were like for domestic animals on factory farms. She knew the meaning of such terms as spontaneous fracture, tongue rolling, somatotropin, urine drinking, manger biting, neighbour pecking and monotonization of mating behaviour. Now, in these terms, she spied herself. Swaying from side to side she saw herself and the city reflected in the animal kingdom. She had been inwardly devastated, as though it were emptiness she had ingested, emptiness Adam had discharged into her. She thought of all the protests she had refrained from making, the chances she had wasted. Guilt assailed her. Not a bad conscience, not some petty, unpaid mental account, no tuppenny-ha'penny debt, but a suicide's accumulated arrears. On the slippery slope that she herself had chosen she had slid to the level where lies remorse.

Her thoughts turned to the ape. From her internal, alcoholic nature reserve to the reptiles of her hallucinations, across her family's stock-piled sows, cattle and poultry, a link was established with the incarcerated ape.

And so Madelene came to the realization that she was no longer a tourist travelling through a series of fascinating, alcohol-induced landscapes. She was – and had been for some time – a permanent resident, confined to a chemical prison.

The moonlight, which a moment before had seemed so pallid, now streamed into the room, stark as an X-ray. In this light Madelene saw her own weakness, saw it clearly, saw herself as the ape had seen her, and then she gave up. She gave up hope, she gave up her role as a drunk, gave up the gentle, spiritous tail wind that had blown her through the events of the past few weeks. She gave up her martyrdom to the hard stuff, her alcoholic identity. She gave up drinking.

11

She woke to find that she was not alone. Beside her – in that spot from which Adam had fled during the night – lay the previous day's acknowledgement of her own frailty.

Madelene sized it up. It seemed alarmingly undiminished and yet alien to her.

She got up. Shaking, she took the first steps across the room, turned around and walked back.

She seemed to be heading back towards the bed and the comfort of her carafe. But these she passed by, making for Adam's worktable. There she rolled up a selection of the hundreds of large printed sheets he had carried upstairs from the garden room and slid them into her cardboard tube. From the top drawer of the desk she took two bundles of bank notes. Then she walked across the room and out. And with this action – modest in physical terms though it was – she put a part of her life behind her.

In the hall she cast a fleeting glance at the telephone, but all the phones in the house were connected to a switchboard in Clapham's office. She forged on – out into the garden, through the narrow door in the wall and onto the pavement.

Before she had quite reached it, Johnny had the rear door of the van open.

Madelene had never lived at any address that did not boast at least nine-thousand square feet of living accommodation plus full base-ment space plus grounds. Johnny's mobile home contained a bed, a desk, a television, a minibar, a telephone, kitchen, hi-fi system, rugs, plush wall-covering, lamps and built-in cupboards all in an area measuring eight-feet by ten. In the thirty seconds it took her to clamber in, collapse into a chair and drink the glass of water held out to her by Johnny she formed a number of what were to be lifelong impressions regarding the relationship between social standing and territorial limits.

"I've stopped drinking," she said.

From his childhood and from his own personal experience Johnny knew the power of the rush to be had from alcohol. He looked at Madelene with respect.

She drew the sheets out of the tube and spread them out on the desk.

"Have you any idea what this is?" she asked.

Confronted by a mass of symbols Johnny seized up.

"I had five years at school."

Madelene nodded. Much the same as herself. Once you deducted all the absences.

She reached for the telephone and dialled a number.

Adam's secretary had abandoned all thought of resistance, her voice was subdued, her tone resigned.

"He's out of town. He'll be back the day after tomorrow. Can I give him a message?"

Madelene hung up. Johnny watched her, blank-faced. She made another call. Was transferred twice before getting through, to Andrea Burden.

"Now that we're bosom pals," said Madelene, "and have no secrets from one another, could you please tell me how much longer that thing's going to be staying with us."

"He hasn't told you?"

"He's trying to protect me."

"They'll be winding up tomorrow."

"And where do you suppose it will go from there?"

Her response was all too snappy, all too slick.

"Oh, but the Institute has St Francis Forest. Well out of the way and delightfully secluded."

"That sounds wonderful," said Madelene. "I feel much happier now."

She hung up.

"We've got twenty-four hours," she said. "Before they move it. How do you move animals?"

"It'll be put in an ape box."

"Where do they find those?"

"Bower makes them. Bally always said, when it came to boxes Bower was one of the best."

"Bower?" said Madelene. "And Bally?"

"The one who brought in the ape."

Madelene looked at Johnny. At the cardboard tube. At the graphs. At Samson and his bandages. She looked out of the window. At the morning light. At the man in the grey suit strolling down the street with a perky little cappuccino-coloured, wire-haired fox terrier on a leash, a man she was now observing outside Mombasa Manor for the third time. She became aware of a vibration deep inside her body, apart from and different from the shakes of withdrawal. This sensation grew into a tremor that ran through her from top to toe, as if she had just had her first drink of the morning. But there had been no drink. What she was experiencing was something else again. It was the materialization, out of the blue, of the galaxy of intoxicating possibilities which present themselves to someone who has made up her mind to be creative and left all her options open.

She lifted Samson's leash from a hook, clipped it to his collar, opened the van door and climbed down, with the dog, onto the pavement.

At sight of Madelene the grey man tensed imperceptibly, wheeled about and began to walk away.

Madelene could have let him go. But a nasty migraine had started spreading throughout her body, working downwards from the back of her head. Where there had always been a volatile energy – readily ignited and quick to burn out – to be derived from drink, she now found there was a destructive, brazen power in coming off it. She and Samson caught up with the man and his terrier.

"So how's everything down at veterinary police headquarters?" she asked.

Until this moment she had only ever seen him sitting down, in the white car that time when Clapham had turned him away at the gate and on those occasions when he had been parked outside the grounds. On his feet and close to he proved to be tall, lean and tough, every inch of him born, raised and trained to be nobody's fool.

He took his time, letting the dogs have a sniff at one another before replying.

"Well of course it's quite a big place now. There used to be just four or five of us. Now we have the race meets, all the doping cases to see to. And the petnappings. We have twenty men checking the pet shops alone. With vets and blank search warrants."

Madelene's upbringing and her interest in men had taught her how to distinguish unerringly between those people, like Adam, who had stepped into the station to which they had been born and those, like the man facing her, who had worked their way up.

"How come," she asked, "a man armed with search warrants would suffer to be seen off by our doorman?"

The man had given up following the dogs with his eyes. He now looked only at Madelene.

"Search warrants are fine for pet shops and poky flats with folk who keep protected reptiles in shoe boxes. But among the upper echelons of society they can be chancy bits of paper."

People who had pulled themselves up by their bootstraps fell, Madelene knew, into two sub-categories: those, like her father, who had striven all their lives to distance themselves from their origins and those, like this man, who had found it simplest to adopt a white car, a suit and a moustache but who had remained steadfastly working-class.

"You wanted to ask about the ape?" she said.

The man made no reply.

"We could do a trade," said Madelene. "I tell you where it is. You tell me why you find it so fascinating."

The man said not a word.

"It's in one of the wings," said Madelene. "With a truckload of machinery. They've been studying it. They're looking for something. Something they haven't found yet. It's worn out, but alive. Now keep your part of the deal."

In the space that elapsed before he answered, Madelene was struck by a rare flash of inexplicable, intuitive insight into the character of another human being. All at once she knew that the man opposite her had got as far as he had through being hard-nosed and intelligent and that, in addition to these traits, he also possessed a formidable sense of justice – which explained why he had risen no further.

"We're not so much interested in the animal," he said. "Our prime interest is in the skipper of the boat that brought it here."

"Bally," said Madelene.

The man nodded.

"If there's such a place as an animal Hell, then, when his time comes, Bally will make chief demon down there."

"Deputy chief," said Madelene. "The chief demon, that's my father."

The man extended an arm. Madelene thought he wanted to shake her hand, but it was his card he gave her.

"Smailes," he said. "We fished Mister Bally out of the Thames and remanded him in custody. But we've nothing to go on. We'll have to let him go soon. We had been wondering whether we should obtain a warrant anyway, and just barge our way in and demand an explanation."

"Give me twenty-four hours," said Madelene.

"What do we get in return?"

"The evidence to nail Bally."

Smailes started to lead the terrier away.

"Where had the boat come from?" Madelene asked.

"From Denmark. Like you."

"What a lot you know. Considering you didn't make it past the gate."

"I've been taking the dog for walks in the neighbourhood."

Madelene looked down at Samson.

"I've always been a believer in that myself," she murmured.

Smailes was almost out of earshot when he turned around one last time.

"Twenty-four hours," he called softly. "And not a minute more."

12

The Holland Park Veterinary Clinic invited unconditional surrender. Not only was it the most expensive, most up-to-date private animal hospital in London, it was also known as the "Smiling Clinic" because the people who worked there all wore a smile. The affable doorman smiled, the charming nurse in reception smiled, the helpful porter smiled and the clinic supervisor who lifted Samson up onto a low table smiled warmly and compliantly.

"I'd like to speak to Alexander Bower," Madelene said.

The woman's smile was apologetic.

"You'd have to make an appointment," she said.

Madelene plucked a piece of white card and a ballpoint pen from the desk, scribbled a line on the card, wrapped it in a fifty-pound note from Adam's bankroll and handed it to the porter.

"The operation was touch and go," she said. "Alex begged me to be sure and send for him. So he could see Samson personally."

Three minutes later Alexander Bower walked in, wearing a white coat and a smile.

It was a half-hearted smile. Despite his powerful position the vet's life was a life spent on the edge and the situation he had just walked into was even more of a cliffhanger than most.

On the piece of white card Madelene had written "£1,000 as arranged – Lady Mortensen". Alexander Bower knew *Debrett's Peerage and Baronetage* inside out, he could recall every animal he had ever treated and by far the majority of invoices written in connection with their treatment and he knew that he had never heard of a Lady Mortensen or come across the woman in sunglasses and a duster coat with whom he was now confronted. But he also knew that this dog was the Dobermann he had not dared to put down, for fear of that driver – what was his name again? – the one who had done the carrying for Bally.

What had prompted him to show face was the reference to the thousand pounds. What held him there was partly fear, partly curiosity.

In the prevailing behavioural vacuum he opted for an approach that was forceful but noncommittal. Briskly and solicitously he approached the dog.

"How is he?" he asked.

"Better," said Madelene.

She held out the big sheets from her cardboard tube. In the same move she slid ten one-hundred-pound notes from her bundle on to the desk.

"I brought his X-rays," she said.

Madelene had grown up in a home where the women purchased the men with sex, the adults bribed the children with toys, the children procured concessions by means of tantrums or caresses and the whole clan had bought its way to a position in high society and a place in Danish history. From infancy she had been trained in the virtuoso techniques called for in the art of bribery. Had the vet's face displayed the merest hint of resentment she could have placed a hand over the notes and blotted out this tiny slip-up. But his face evinced no suspicion. On the contrary, his features cleared and became more composed.

"These aren't X-rays," he said. "They're MRI scans. And that's no dog."

"Our chimpanzee," said Madelene. "I must have picked up the wrong ones."

The doctor shook his head.

"See that frontal lobe," he said. "Seat of the higher cognitive functions. That's a human being. Although obviously a very large human."

He ran his finger out to a column of figures to the right of the picture.

"A volume of 2,700 cubic centimetres. Abnormally large."

He flicked through the sheets and stopped at one particular frame. The colours were dazzling – ruby-red, shimmering gold, royal blue.

"Him again. An EEG superimposed on PET. Not many people in Europe can do that. Where did you say these were from?"

"What's PET?" Madelene asked.

"*Positron Emission Tomography*. He's been injected with radioactive water, which causes the brain to increase the cerebral blood flow. Then it's just a matter of monitoring the level of radioactivity."

Treading warily, Madelene fingered the bankroll and furtively planted one more of Adam's notes onto the desk.

"At least let me reimburse you for your time," she said.

The doctor's eyes clouded over. An insidious stream of distractedness, boyhood memories and titillated vanity had taken hold of him and swept him along in its wake.

"PET," he said. "Excellent spatial resolution. Accurate to between three and five millimetres. But poor time resolution. Takes as long as ninety seconds. Which is why you superimpose it onto an encephalogram. That way you can see everything that's going on in the brain, down to the last millisecond. It's fantastic. And when you think that this is a piece of mobile equipment. They've put a helmet on him. That's the latest thing. I didn't think there was anyone but us who could do that."

His finger slid down the column of figures.

"They've sent him round an obstacle course. Is there something wrong with his motor functions? Language tests, eye tests, various practical exercises. Anatomical localization, extremely detailed, thirty cross-sections from all four angles."

"What were they looking for?" Madelene asked.

She threw down yet another note. The doctor's face had a far-away look, like that of someone in a hypnotic trance. Madelene knew she had him anaesthetized. Now it was a matter of keeping his suspicions dormant but his mental faculties intact.

"Ah yes, what are we looking for?" he said. "Can anyone answer that?"

"We?"

"I too have sought."

"Did you find what you were looking for?"

The doctor's eyes were fixed on some distant point, visible only to himself.

"Does one ever?"

"These pictures, did you take them?"

He shook his head.

"I think back on the old days," he said. "Those golden days. Barely ten years ago. When one still dared to hope."

Madelene stroked the arm of his white coat, probing.

"I think of them," he said. "But I don't speak of them. It's better that way. As matters stand."

"Just say it," Madelene urged gently. "The dog won't understand a word of it anyway."

Alexander Bower was aware of a pleasant lack of clarity. His surroundings put him in mind of his own hospital, the scans implied that he was a speaker at a scientific symposium, the listening woman might have suggested a board meeting, the money pointed to an appointment with his lawyer. This situation seemed to reconcile all of the deeply incompatible sides of his character in the most delightful manner.

"Massachusetts," he said. "The question of the nature of intelligence. Pioneering research – nothing to touch it. So far in front that the rest of the field was nowhere to be seen. We believed we were so close. You must understand: we were actually inside the brain itself. As far in as you can go. You don't get any closer. It was so . . . staggeringly intimate. Even if they were only apes. We came so close. To becoming one. With an unknown intelligence. Picture the disappointment. When everything suddenly melts into thin air. Comes to nothing. There you are, left with that awful emptiness. While everyone around you is still living in hope. But *you* know it's all over. *Horror vacui.*"

"Like a love affair," said Madelene.

The vet stared at her.

"Were you there, too?"

"I know how it feels."

"You understand me," the vet said. "Like a marriage. That's exactly how it was. You felt cheated. Because in fact, even though I would never admit it, not to anyone, not even to you. If we had succeeded in getting to the bottom of the mind, the soul, the intellect, in decoding the brain. And if one could have placed a woman on the table. And run her into the spool . . ."

"Spool?"

"MRI produces a huge magnetic field. You lay people on a trolley and push them into a spool. They don't feel a thing. She wouldn't have felt a thing. There's a fan heater inside it. And a mirror. And they can put on headphones. And listen to sweet music. *Rosenkavalier*, or some other wonderful piece. And then you would talk to her over the headphones, and say: 'Alexander, what do you think of when you hear the name Alexander?' And then it would be possible to stand outside and see her thoughts as they occurred, they would show up as computer images, like *pixels*. Penetrating farther into any woman than any man has ever done. To the heart of the female psyche. She would have no chance of lying. And if there were someone else, if she had someone else, or merely thought of anyone else, it would be spotted straight away."

Madelene handed him her handkerchief.

"You're perspiring," she said.

The vet mopped his brow.

"Then one might have managed to save one's marriage," he said.

Madelene surveyed him pityingly.

"I think it would take more than magnetic scanning to do that," she said.

"I know, but it doesn't stop you hoping. It's only human, isn't it? Right to the last we kept on hoping. But in the end it just couldn't be done. Because what is being measured is the oxygen consumption. And there is no formula for the relationship between oxygen consumption and cerebral activity. Nor will there ever be. No objective measurement of intelligence, no way of pinpointing thought. So we reverted to the old methods. Well, we had over eighty million dollars invested in equipment alone. And the sponsors were looking for results. So back we went to the needles."

"Needles?"

"You know, the way it's always been done. You strap them down. The apes, that is. And remove the brainpan. The top half of the cranium. To expose the brain. And then you have these needles. Terrifically precise. *Single Neuron Recording*. You can pick up a single neuron. See how often it pulsates. See just exactly when a given signal passes through it. Then, of course, there are clusters of needles. *Multiple Neuron Recording*. We should never have dropped that system, even though it too has its drawbacks. In order to get at any spot farther in the needle has to be worked through the overlying tissue. And chimpanzees are getting harder to come by . . ."

Madelene said nothing. The doctor detected an unaccountable shift in mood but could not get a fix on it, could not catch what was being thought of him.

"The limited staying power of the big apes also posed a problem. Three weeks was the most you could count on. After that they began to deteriorate and gradually ceased to function."

"Do you still . . . do that?" Madelene asked. "With the needles, I mean . . ."

Somewhere within the stupor into which the vet had sunk a warning light flashed, harsh and prolonged. He stopped dead.

Madelene grabbed the lapel of his white coat and drove him back towards the wall.

"Go on," she said.

"I believe I have answered your questions."

A low trolley caught Alexander Bower behind the knees and he toppled backwards. Madelene knelt over him.

"I have one last question," she said.

The vet stared at her vacantly. As with every awakening from an anaesthetic this one too was nauseating and painful. And yet there was in addition something mysterious and deliciously illicit about this moment.

As deep down and as far back as he could go – as a boy, in the country, on Jersey, Alexander Bower had been a genuine animal lover. He had grown up taking a delight in being close to a cat or a dog, savouring the smell of a stable and deriving from the presence of cattle a peace of mind that required no explanation. He had made up his mind to become a vet and had then gone to university. And there he had learned that animals are machines. Delicate machines, to be sure, with an ingenious biological mechanism, but still – when all was said and done – machines. And faced with this revelation his mind had, for the first time, split in two. Alongside the original Alexander, he developed a scientific *alter ego*. Now, when he stroked a dog's head this onlooker would think: what is happening here, the feelings of warmth and kindness I am experiencing are but illusions, emergent phenomena made up of millions of processes all of which, taken singly, are quite banal and fully explained. By the time he finished his studies his innate reductionist was fully developed and for the next thirty years he had borne the ever greater burden of that test-tube monstrosity, that inner homunculus. He had come home from the USA with the very best references and a severe case of depression. All actions – whether physical or mental – were, he knew, fundamentally chemical in nature and thus quantum electrical and hence causal and hence deterministic and all, therefore, pre-ordained – if not haphaz-ardly random – and so free will was an illusion, which meant that it made no difference what he did since the solution to what would happen in his life would make itself known of its own accord anyway. Which it did. One grey morning he woke up to the realization that since there is, after all, nothing behind the physical universe except a handful of elementary particles and a standard formula for explaining the interplay between the forces of nature, one might as well go all the way, and this he did – that is to say, all the way into a world which is a little – but not much – simpler than that of physics, namely the world of finance, founded upon a few basic monetary units and the four arithmetical operations. And in this environment he had stayed ever since.

Now, sprawled on the floor, he found himself being momentarily dragged out of that world, something which came as a relief. As with all of those who inhabit a purely scientific or purely financial universe, Alexander Bower dreamt of deliverance and right now Madelene's face was speaking to him of another sort of reality.

"The last question," she said, "is what would it cost to be allowed to remove your brainpan and look for compassion. To see if there is any."

For a second the vet thought he was lying in his father's meadow, on Jersey, under the blue sky.

"More," he said. "Do it again."

Madelene released her hold and fished a card out of her duster-coat pocket. The blend of fatalistic resolve, self-loathing and physical discomfort produced by her withdrawal symptoms honed her actions and her choice of words to a razor edge.

"Read this," she said. "And I'll promise to kick you in the stomach afterwards."

It was Inspector Smaile's card. The doctor read it slowly and with difficulty. Then the hunger, the pain and the confusion cleared from his face and it grew sober.

"He's waiting outside."

She took off her sunglasses.

"Mrs Burden," said the doctor.

Until this moment he had been convinced that this situation, like all others in his life, would ultimately prove to be under control. That any minute now two porters would come rushing in and take this mad-woman away and see to it that she paid a substantial sum in recompense for pain and suffering, in return for which the hospital would agree not to press charges and he himself would return to the meeting he had left fifteen minutes earlier. And the only reminder of what had taken place would be the haematoma he had just been dealt by the linoleum floor. Now he saw that he had lost control of the situation.

Madelene pointed to the scans.

"That's the ape, isn't it?"

"It's a human being."

"Is this where it's supposed to have the top of its skull removed? Now that Adam has given up?"

Alexander Bower's face had turned white, only a shade darker than the tiles on the wall.

"The Washington Convention," Madelene said. "It's a prison sentence for you. And a whopping great fine. And you'll be struck off."

The doctor moistened his lips.

"It's a minor operation. A lot has happened in ten years. It won't feel a thing. It will survive and be none the worse for it."

"You examine all Bally's animals, do you?"

The doctor did not answer.

Madelene gathered up the bank notes and slipped them back into her coat pocket.

"I'll need to owe you for Samson," she said.

The dog jumped down from the table.

"You'll call me if you change your mind?" Madelene said.

The doctor looked at her blankly.

"I mean: if on closer reflection you should decide to let me lift off the top of your skull. It would just be a minor operation. You would function quite normally afterwards."

Johnny's truck was parked by the kerb. Madelene and Samson climbed in.

"Do animals think?" asked Madelene.

They were halfway to South Hill Park before Johnny answered.

"Pit ponies," he said. "I used to look after them, as a lad. In Morton. The mine shaft ran out for seven miles under the Atlantic. You got out there by diesel train. But out by the coal face the tunnels were so narrow that only men and horses could get through. The last bit not even the ponies. There you had to crawl along on your stomach. With a lamp and a hydraulic hand-drill. Seven miles out and half a mile under the sea bed. You couldn't get your mind off the props. Holding up the roof. So spindly. But when you started thinking like that, that's when you looked back. At the horse. They catch any sign of shifting long before a man would. Sense if the air supply is starting to give out. Or if there's a leak. And they can give signals. Like people. But more subtle. If the horse was calm, everything was okay."

"Why didn't you leave?"

"Where would I go?"

Madelene gestured vaguely at the light, the trees, the affluence surrounding them.

Johnny gazed out of the windscreen. At the walls around the houses, at the closely-guarded iron gates, at the fence encircling Parliament Hill.

"Would that have been any better?" he said.

For the third time in less than a week Madelene's notions of freedom listed to one side, then they keeled over and started to break up.

"You got used to the heat. To working lying down. To the air. To the fact that there's no room to move. The hard bit was being alone. Because there wasn't a sound to be heard. It's dead quiet. And suddenly you feel that you've been deserted. That you're the last person alive on earth. Half a mile down. That was when you shoved the lamp back the way and looked at the horse. Its muzzle was all black. Like your own face. Its eyes gleamed. Like your own. It was the same as you. But perfectly calm. Not because it was stupid. But because it wasn't thinking unnecessary thoughts. It wasn't thinking about yesterday, or tomorrow. Nor knocking-off time or the Third World War. It was thinking about here and now. And looking at it you began to feel the way it did. And then you grew quite calm. And sometimes . . . almost happy. Like when I drove the animals. Most of the time your thoughts flit about all over the place. Yesterday. Tomorrow. Problems, problems. But transporting Bally's animals, you didn't think about anything but the driving. No loneliness. And behind you in the dark, their eyes gleaming, you could feel them. Fine, powerful, strange. To be protected. You couldn't make the slightest mistake. Or there would be a cave-in. Your mind was one hundred per cent on the job and there, on the road, you were . . . you became . . ."

"Almost happy," said Madelene.

They sat there, saying nothing.

At last Madelene opened the door.

"Tomorrow," she said. "We have to get it out before tomorrow. If it's to have any brain left for not thinking unnecessary thoughts."

She looked up at Johnny and the dog.

"You two will be here this evening?" she said. "Won't you? You're not suddenly going to take off back to Morton?"

"They closed down the pit in '85. That was all there was to Morton, the pit. There's nothing to go back to."

13

That evening Adam ate with Madelene for the first time in five days and, seen from a distance, he seemed loving and attentive.

But Madelene was not seeing him from a distance. She was seeing him at very close range, and closer still, she was also seeing him from the inside, from a mistress's point of view, and what she saw was his absence. Even though he was sitting opposite her, Adam had not put in a personal appearance at the table. His attention had stayed behind in the laboratory with the ape.

This was not a new state of affairs for Madelene. What *was* new was that she found it less than satisfactory. After the first few minutes she was in no condition to eat or talk and she did not utter one word until the point when they climbed the stairs together and stood outside the door to his rooms and he reached out for her and she pushed his hand away.

"No way," she said.

Then Adam Burden re-entered his body.

Before he met Madelene, Adam had had a number of affairs which, in retrospect, he either could not or would not tell apart. It seemed to him that all of those girls – despite being in their twenties and thirties – had had babyish voices and bedrooms full of cuddly toys, that they dreamed of his turning out to be yet another teddy bear, and that – once he had afforded them a glimpse of the mere shadow of his desire – they had been smitten by mystified panic.

Madelene had been different. The very first time he reached out for her, she had taken on an air of languorous, slack-limbed menace. With half-closed eyes she had watched him dancing closer and when at long last she had chosen to respond to him her response had been whole-hearted. Adam had had no antibodies to combat these moments of female lust, so suddenly aroused, only afterwards, to sink without trace. Madelene had invaded his bloodstream like a fleeting bout of blood poisoning. By the end of their first whole day together he was a sick man. When she spurned him for the first time his sickness was rendered incurable.

For an instant, there on the landing, his face glowed with the sort of hate that moves people to commit murder. But it never found an outlet. The emotion flared up for a split-second, then it was doused and his figure hardened into an excruciating encapsulation of the situation thus presented.

It was then that Madelene was struck, for the first time, by the thought that she was too much for her husband. If one is to survive an attack of desire of the kind by which Adam had been struck one must be able to cope with rejection. For every time that Madelene said yes to him there were three more when she turned her back on him, and she now had a suspicion that he could not bear this, and had never been able to bear it. He was a winner, a born winner, who had in Madelene come up against the trouncing of his life and, what is more, a trouncing which was not to be suffered once and once only, but had to be played out again and again like some perpetually recurring annihilation.

For a moment Adam just stood there. Then he turned around, slowly and stiffly, and went into his room.

Once the door had slammed behind him he walked over to the window, opened it and – as was his habit in situations such as this – committed the first of a series of murders.

From the moment he first laid eyes on Madelene Adam had been dazed, shell-shocked by jealousy. He was convinced that not only was she a danger to himself but that she constituted a threat to mankind as a whole, that any man would give his life to get inside her. Consequently he had appointed himself not only her husband but her bodyguard and eunuch and if he could have infiltrated her soul he would have been her thought police too.

Now, standing by the window, he fancied that he had been caught napping and that she had succeeded in taking a lover and smuggled him into her room. Lingeringly, he grilled his imagination over the spectacle of their undressing and the opening moves in their love-making, at which point he himself stepped in armed with his father's double-barrelled Purdey and discharged both barrels, three hundred and fifty pieces of lead shot at a range of four yards. This done, he then wallowed in his own despair at what was left of Madelene.

This first killing mollified him slightly, and so he committed another, and yet another – feeling a little better for each one. In his normal, pragmatic state of mind he would, with some pride, have described himself as totally lacking in imagination but during the half hour he spent by the window like a lone executioner his fantasies acquired an artistic lifelikeness that made it hard to separate them from reality. When he spied Madelene gliding across the lawn, light-footed as an elf maid, he thought at first that he was gazing upon his own, inner stage. Not until she opened the narrow gate in the wall about the grounds and let in a man did Adam observe that this fantasy did not have the same liberating effect as the others.

The moon was on the wane, the sky somewhat overcast. In such a light it was impossible to make out any details. Although, in his present condition, even broad daylight would hardly have been strong enough for that. He could not see Johnny clearly, did not see the collapsible wheelchair he carried. All he saw were the contours of a short, thickset gnome with a hunchback.

In Adam's fantasies of a moment earlier Madelene's lovers had been members of the royal family, or godlike figures; her infidelity had been upwardly mobile, thus acting as an indirect social leg-up for himself. Now, in this fickle light, he saw a male figure dredged from the sewers of London.

He stood there, rooted to the spot, a quarter of an hour elapsing before he was once more capable of thought, half an hour going by before he could come to a decision. He would go straight to Madelene's room, kick the door in and lay this lover low. And then, with a screaming Madelene kneeling at his feet, he would consider his next move.

He was on the point of turning away when the last act of the evening's drama passed in front of his windows.

In the lead came the hunchback. Behind him, closely entwined, came Madelene and a new male character.

Adam had never seen the ape walking on two legs and he had of course never seen it wearing a long coat and a trilby. So he had not the faintest notion of the humanizing effect clothes and an upright gait can have on an animal. Nevertheless, had he been in possession of just some of his senses, his thoughts would have turned to Erasmus. But all his senses had deserted him, he was completely cut off from the realities of everyday life, he was off somewhere where the ape did not exist. Dwelling in the fiendish realms of jealousy. What his eyes beheld was his wife and her two lovers, two creatures radiating an absolute want of finesse and through his mind paraded the appalling range of sexual degradations made possible by this new, third person.

Not wanting to see more he took two steps back into the room. And so he did not see Erasmus, Madelene and Johnny go out of the grounds through the door in the wall, saw nothing at all, in fact, outside of himself. All his attention was driven inwards and there he found that the Adam Burden he thought he knew had been given his marching orders. Over him and through him and out into the night thundered herds of runaway elephants and enchanted swine. He was incapable of moving a muscle and not until day began to break and his inward bellowing died down to be replaced by a kind of lethargy, was he able to drag himself across the floor and lift the telephone receiver.

14

The Danish Society in London is in Knightsbridge, looking over Hyde Park. It was here, at eleven in the morning, that Madelene presented herself, and she was not alone. In front of her she pushed a wheelchair in which sat an elderly lady enveloped in a voluminous travelling rug, her head shielded from the sun by a black hat complete with veil.

Madelene's being here of all places had come about in the following manner: that same morning, early, after a night spent in Johnny's mobile home in a car park in the far-flung suburb of Hemel Hempstead, north-west of London, Madelene had heard herself being reported as missing on the radio.

Not one of the truck's four passengers had slept a wink that night. With not a word being said, not a move made – apart from Johnny getting up twice to make tea – in silence they had watched the night run past, for all the world as though they were a crew and the van a ship steaming across the ocean, sure of making landfall by dawn. At sunrise, as on every other morning, Johnny had tuned his receiver to the police waveband. The minute he heard Madelene's name mentioned he had curled up into a ball in a corner of the bed like a game bird sensing the approach of the beaters.

Madelene on the other hand showed no sign of surprise or alarm. The all-points bulletin was broadcast just as she was shaving the hair off Erasmus' face and she kept at this task while her description was being read out. She was, this morning, brimming with confidence.

She was not putting her trust in any overt form of justice – since she had never been able to determine that such a thing existed – but on something better. Madelene had her hopes pinned on the law of the jungle. Those environments in which Madelene had grown up: her family, her schools, her marriage, had all been controlled by a social order which – far from being one big, bloody free-for-all (any more than the biological jungle law was) – involved a subtle pecking order which kept the individual in his or her structural place with a minimum of outward conflict. Social legislation was an integral part of this structure and the Washington Convention an integral part of this legislation and Madelene's plan was quite simply to get a vet to testify that the ape was covered by this convention. Then she would take this attestation to Inspector Smailes, whereupon the Convention would come into play and the old order be restored.

She had no idea what would happen to her personally thereafter. But she harboured no illusions. She had lived a pigeon-hole existence – biologically speaking, a highly specialized life, a state of being fitted for a life of wedded idleness, life as a decorative appendage. As with all specialists, in the animal world as in the human, this way of life was extremely sensitive to change. Her confidence in the early hours of this morning was for her companions. For herself she held out no hope. Impassively she heard the bulletin out. Then she reached for the telephone.

The veterinary odontologist did not announce himself. He merely grunted into the telephone and from that sound alone Madelene could tell that something was up.

"I have the ape here," she said.

"There's a hunt on for you."

"You're the only one who can do it . . ."

"There are twenty vets in London who could do it. Almost as well."

"At the Meat Market they're always talking about how brave you are."

There was silence at the other end. When the doctor did reply his voice was so faint that Madelene thought for a moment she was speaking to someone else.

"It's my job that's on the line here."

Madelene had been brought up to take no for an answer. Only a few weeks ago she would have bade him a pleasant good day and acknowledged defeat, then gone over and curled up beside Johnny and left the inevitable and disastrous chain of events to run their course. Or rather: a couple of weeks ago this conversation would never have taken place. But the Madelene who was now on the phone no longer had any clear memory of that time a couple of weeks back, and the thought of giving up never crossed her mind.

"You've only got one year to go anyway," she said.

The odontologist's silence was fraught with uncertainty. Madelene could sense that he was teetering on the brink. She moved in and gave him one last nudge.

"And then there's your reputation as a scientist," she said.

"What about it?"

"When word gets out about this conversation. How you refused to help. After seeing that dental chart. I don't know what the Institute will have to say. But at the Meat Market they'll be dining out on it for years to come."

"You don't work at the Meat Market. You're Burden's wife."

Madelene said nothing. She knew she had penetrated, she had won through.

"Mrs Burden," said the doctor, "strictly between ourselves, are you never scared?"

"Always."

"You do realize that your husband has had you reported missing?"

"A misunderstanding. Happens in the best of families. And please call me Madelene."

"Thank you," said the doctor. "My name is Firkin. Where's it to be?"

Hitherto London had always struck Madelene as being as barren and bereft of possibilities as a desert. Now that she had forfeited her usual routine and her rights, now that she no longer had any place in the day-to-day life of the city it seemed to abound in chaotic eventualities. She shut her eyes and tilted her face upwards, opened up her mind to those veins of inspiration that are always there for those who seek and a moment later she caught the scent of water.

"Do you know the Danish Society?" she said, "In Knightsbridge . . ."

15

To Danes abroad the thought of Denmark changing in their absence is not to be borne. On our return we want to find that country not merely as we left it but as it ought to have been. The desire to meet this wish led, in London, to the setting up of the Danish Society – an institution which, on its founding at the beginning of this century by a group of Danish diplomats and businessmen, was already more retroactively sentimental than Denmark had ever been. Since then, true to the law which says that time, in patriotic societies of any description, will always run backwards, things had gone from bad to worse.

Madelene had been there once, dispatched by Adam to enrol them both as members, and she had never been back. On that one visit she had been filled – instantly, the minute she crossed the threshold and before that even, on seeing the building from the outside – with terror, and what had frightened her was her own acquiescent fascination: she loved the lions in the Danish coat of arms on the door. She loved Philipsen the animal painter's red and white cows in the sunset. She loved the elephant on the Order of the Elephant around the neck of absolute monarch Christian the VII's English wife, Caroline Mathilde. She loved the seagulls on the dinner service in the library and the stylized plum-tree branches on the plates in the restaurant. She loved the porcelain polar bears on the mantelpiece, the poster of city traffic being held up to let a mother duck and her ugly ducklings cross the road and the photostats of the lifelong feathered pairing of a stork couple in Ribe. She loved the bearskins on the heads of Life Guards changing the guard before the statue of Frederik V on horseback on the square at Amalienborg Palace, she loved the pictures of black grouse on moors that were no more. Faced with this whole image of Denmark as a social and zoological paradise which she knew had never existed, she had been irretrievably lost.

Had it been possible, had there been even the slightest chance of getting away with it, back then, on that first visit, Madelene would have scrambled up into the case containing Denmark's best-known butterflies and taken her place among the most unassuming of these – the cabbage white for instance and the small tortoiseshell – and mounted herself there with a pin through her chest and lastly – as a prelude to her full and final surrender – at her feet in her best copper-plate she would have inscribed, "*Madelene Burden, née Mortensen. Widespread and quite, quite common*".

She knew, sadly, that such a venture was doomed to failure, because she had already had a go at it, long before. She had tried to be a good daughter, a good pupil and a breathtaking young girl, but all of these attempts had miscarried. She seemed to have been born not to flutter elegantly hither and thither but to cause trouble. Her first conscious memory was of the leaden yet crisp sound of shattering faïence overlaid by the word "clumsy" uttered coolly and dispassionately in an adult voice which might have been her mother's, or perhaps the Queen's, or God's.

But she had never given up hope altogether. Even though she had bowed her head and tiptoed away from her family and into marriage and out of Denmark, deep down she had always felt that maybe one day, in spite of everything, a reconciliation would be reached and now, as she pushed the wheelchair towards the front steps of the Society and the front door opened and two men came hurrying out to greet her, her past seemed suddenly to stretch out a hand and give her another chance.

The two men who had come down to meet her were the Society's commissionaire and its manager. The latter grasped her hand, shook it then looked at the lady in the wheelchair with an expression that did not so much ask as expect to be put in the picture.

"My grandmother," said Madelene. "Mrs Mortensen."

The manager essayed a peek under the brim of the hat, but could make out nothing behind the veil other than the outline of a large, dark face.

"We are honoured," he said.

The two men took hold of the wheelchair, one on each side and heaved.

Nothing happened.

Smiling still, not batting an eyelid, the manager took a look round the back of the chair to see whether it might have got caught between the paving stones, or was perhaps electrically operated and hence weighed down both by a motor and batteries. This, however, was not the case. It was a flimsy, collapsible model. The two men heaved once more. And succeeded in lifting the chair a few inches off the ground. Then they eased it down again.

It was hard to comment on such a state of affairs and so Madelene kept her mouth shut. But she was seized by a number of urges, strong among them the temptation to do what she usually did, what she had done so often before, to run away. Nonetheless she stayed put. She could not leave the wheelchair. Added to which, several times during the past week or two she had found herself in painful situations and she was starting to discover that if one bided one's time, something usually turned up.

This something turned up at that very moment in the shape of a third person: Sir Toby, Madelene's late father-in-law's brother, joined the group.

On the surface Madelene gave nothing away, dutifully she put out her hand and had it kissed. But inside her an alarm bell rang, as yet faint and far-off, at the sight of Her Majesty's Government's consultant on veterinary matters.

The three men grabbed hold of the wheelchair and lugged it up the steps, through the doors and into the lift – the door of which closed, whereupon it began to ascend.

The men were desperately gasping for breath. Madelene had the feeling that an explanation was in order.

"Comfort eating," she whispered. "Ever since grandad died. She weighs over 25 stone."

The three men regarded the figure beneath the hat, the veil and the travelling rug with sympathy and fascination. The manager alone still felt a faint twinge of unease. Each and every trade tends to develop a form of recall unique to its own field and after forty years of running the Danish Society this man had perfected a memory worthy of the most chauvinistic butler. In this he had filed away data cards on every Dane with whom he had ever come into contact in the United Kingdom. Right now his need to enter the old lady onto this file outweighed his oxygen debt and so he inclined himself towards Madelene.

"Her feet," he gasped.

Madelene looked down. The ape's feet had crept out from beneath the rug. Admittedly they were encased in a pair of Johnny's woollen socks, but in the tiny lift, sitting on the wheelchair footrest, they still seemed unduly large.

"Fluid," she said. "Fluid retention in her feet."

The manager's features exuded palpable sorrow.

"And her head?" he whispered.

In order to get Mrs Clapham's hat over Erasmus' head it had been necessary for Madelene to take the scissors to it. This headgear had now slipped and through the crown peeped the ape's skull – brown, smooth-shaven and enormous.

"Fluid," said Madelene. "In her head too."

The lift came to a halt, the door opened and Madelene pushed the chair out. And there, walking towards her from the far end of the corridor, was Susan.

It did not seem at all odd to Madelene that she should bump into her friend right here. She knew that she had stepped into some sort of alembic. Not an open-necked Pyrex flask like the one in which she had mixed her drink, but a sealed laboratory alembic, a retort containing a goodly proportion of her essential elements. She was also aware that she had now lit the burner under this flask and to this mixture, from the outside, she had added the ape and it was her dream that finally, at long last, if not gold then at least some sort of equilibrium would now manifest itself.

Susan was an intrinsic part of this alloy and Madelene greeted her with a warm smile. But deep inside her the peal of the alarm grew in intensity.

124

Susan had, so she thought, taken in the situation at a glance, but even though she saw things more clearly than the three men in the elevator, nevertheless – as always when people come up against the incomprehensible – first and foremost she was seeing herself.

"Madelene . . . !" she said.

"It's not what you think," said Madelene.

Susan licked her lips. Then her face took on a worried look.

"We're having a meeting," she said. "The Royal Society for the Protection of Animals. We always have our lunch-time meetings here. Because of the cakes. Adam will be here any minute."

Madelene braced herself against the wheelchair. Susan took her by the arm.

"Let me help you two," she said. "I keep a little flat. For just this sort of thing."

Madelene shook her head. At Susan's back a door opened, Dr Firkin stuck out his head. Madelene drove the wheelchair forwards.

Susan gave her arm a squeeze.

"Well, if nothing else I can keep him out on the patio," she said. "Enjoy yourselves!"

Dr Firkin was terrified. Not only was he clad in a broad-shouldered wool jacket, over this he also wore a bulky overcoat and a felt hat on his head, and when he divested himself of the hat and coat it was plain to see that he was frozen, despite the summer heat. His eyes were trained on the floor and he kept them downcast as Madelene trundled the wheelchair into the room. Only once she had brought it to a standstill and removed the travelling rug, the hat, the veil, the gloves and the socks did he lift his head to look at the figure in the chair. Slowly, never taking his eyes off the ape's face, he walked over to it, gently stroked the hair on its arm, measured the length of its forearm with his outstretched palm, turned its hand back and forth several times, circled it, surveying its ears from all angles, ran his fingers over the smooth-shaven cranium, studied its epidermis at some length, delicately parted its lips to disclose its teeth. Finally he knelt down and took one of its feet in his hands, lifted it and gazed long and hard at the sole of the foot. And throughout all of this he kept up a soft, soothing stream of baby talk. When he was done, he stood up and trudged back across to his outdoor things.

"Is he drugged?" he asked.

Madelene shook her head.

"I'm sorry," he said. "But there's nothing I can do."

He shrank from looking Madelene straight in the face.

"It doesn't belong to any known species. So it must be a cross-breed. There were a lot of those produced in the '20s and '30s. But it's rare now. And strictly forbidden. There are 150 species of ape, 180 if we count the prosimians. I can't say which species have been crossed here. I would recommend you to take it over to The Veterinary School of London. They'll prepare a detailed description of it there. And send tissue samples to the genetics laboratory at the Institute for Population Biology."

Neither Madelene nor the ape stirred. Hesitantly the doctor raised his face and looked at Madelene. When he spoke his voice was very hoarse.

"Nothing fits," he said. "The body bears a faint resemblance to that of the dwarf chimpanzee, but it's too tall and too heavy and the facial skin is too pale. The cranium is as big as a gorilla's, but gorillas have a sagittal suture running across their skulls, serving as a linchpin for the masticatory muscles, and this chap's skull is quite smooth. This coat here is a summer pelt with vestiges of a winter one, but we know of no primates from a temperate climate. The hands and feet have the retentive grip found in humans, but the prehensile muscula-ture is formed like that of a gibbon. Had there been no more to it than that I would go along with it, I would sign on the dotted line and report Burden, I would say to myself, well, even if we *are* going to Hell in a basket at least we're doing it in style. But that's *not* all."

He got into his coat.

"Apes can be trained to do the most amazing things. If they are hand-reared. And it goes without saying they end up in a mess. Demonstrate abnormal behaviour, become incapable of mating. But they can be tamed. Were we to assume that this fellow here has been brought up among humans, then that might explain his docility. And if we were less fussy about the scientific details we could perhaps put his appearance down to his being some sort of crossbreed. But what we cannot explain away is the look in his eyes. Even the most psychologically twisted performing chimp cannot withstand eye contact. It's the ultimate challenge of the animal kingdom. What sets us apart from the animals is not language or intelligence. What sets us apart is the fact that we can look each other straight in the eye."

He donned his hat.

"This thing is too big for me. It was your husband who started it. And his sister."

Madelene said nothing.

"My pension," said the doctor. "Have you any idea what it's like to be a seventy-year-old living in Britain without a pension?"

"The veterinary police?" said Madelene.

"They're supposed to hand over wild animals to London Zoo. Which means Burden. A report has to be filled out, and this the Home Office will countersign once it has been ratified by the Animal Procedure Committee. Which again means your husband. And his sister."

He bent his head.

"I'm sorry about this," he said. "That's why I've always got on best with animals. I was always almost as afraid as they were."

"I must remember to tell Erasmus that," said Madelene. "It'll give him something to console himself with when they're pulling him limb from limb."

The doctor turned on his heel, opened the door and was gone.

Madelene stood by the window. Her eye fell on Adam down in the street, standing next to a white car. Out of the car climbed Inspector Smailes and three other men. Out of four other white cars climbed nigh-on a score more, in no great hurry, dressed in pale, lightweight summer clothes. Parked farther down the street was a closed van with the initials RSPCA painted on its side. A collection van from the Royal Society for the Prevention of Cruelty to Animals. It was a tranquil scene, bathed in sunlight. And yet it represented, beyond a shadow of a doubt, the final phase of a hunt.

The men fanned out around the building. Madelene turned back into the room. The ape and the wheelchair were gone. She walked out of the room into the corridor. Some distance away, by a window, stood the ape, looking out. In the walled garden backing onto Hyde Park the committee of the Royal Society for the Protection of Animals were foregathered around a table loaded with Danish cakes and pastries, a sight which stopped Madelene in her tracks.

This table called to mind a birth. It smelled of milk, it ran with strawberry-marbled whipped cream, buttercream and confectioner's custard, so perfectly formed that no-one could have told from looking at it that within the past eight hours it had been both killed off and brought back to life.

The original idea behind this table had been that over this spread Adam would advise the committee of an extraordinary zoological subject which had come into his possession, going on to ask them for their support in keeping this hidden both from the public at large and the Animal Procedure Committee for a few weeks longer.

The table reservation had been suspended at four in the morning when Adam called his sister to tell her that his wife had run off along with the ape. It had been reinstated that very morning when he had rung to assure himself that Smailes had located the truck and that it was in the process of being surrounded.

Twenty minutes later he had called again to report that the van had been taken by storm and the driver arrested. But that Madelene and the ape were nowhere to be found.

Adam had lost two pounds in weight for every one of the past ten days, a fact borne out by the sound of his voice. Not only had he lost his wife and his ape, not only did he now have to watch the most crucial offensive of his career brought to a grinding halt or called off completely, but beneath all this there lay a more profound exhaustion: for three almost sleepless days and nights he had, for the first time in his life, been confronted with a zoological phenomenon that was not open to investigation.

This situation had led to the following conversation between himself and Andrea.

"The papers," said Adam. "She'll go to the papers. And the police. That driver is the one who worked for Bally. We're sunk. I've been considering suicide."

"The newspapers," said Andrea Burden, "know nothing about apes. But everything about the law of libel. Before printing so much as a line they will check with the experts. With the Institute, that is. And that, oh little brother mine, means you. You will examine the ape and conclude that it is a chimpanzee. Of a rare but not unknown species."

"They'll confront me with Madelene."

"And you will reveal – reluctantly, but constrained by circumstances – that your wife is an alcoholic. You won't be spared the front pages. But the headlines will read: 'Zoo director's drunken wife steals rare chimpanzee'."

"This will ruin my prospects."

"It will give them a boost. You will not only have the support of the scientists and politicians. You will be buoyed up by the sympathy of the man in the street."

Andrea Burden paused.

"What it will do to your marriage," she then said airily, "is another matter."

Adam shut his eyes, and came to a decision. Not a personal one, not a subjective nor an emotional decision. What he did was to set up an imaginary chemical balance. In the one pan he placed Madelene, her drinking, her mystery, the now exhilarating, now depressing attraction she held for him. In the other pan he placed his future. His infinite potential, both professional and sexual.

It was not he who wrote off Madelene. It was the law of gravity.

"And this evening," he said, "you and Bower will appear on *Newsnight* and back me up."

And so it was that this cornucopia of cake had been given remission and now here it was, reminding Madelene that she had eaten nothing in sixteen hours and more.

The ape had not had anything to eat either and it was now on the move, making its way down the stairway, tripping lightly as a ballerina with the wheelchair under its arm. Madelene thought at first that it had got wind of what was afoot and was making one last, desperate bid for freedom. But at the foot of the stairs it stopped, swathed itself in the travelling rug, slapped the hat down over its head, seated itself in the wheelchair, drew the veil down into place and bowled through the doorway, heading straight for the party around the table.

The meeting had not formally been called to order and so the circle opened up accommodatingly and with no surprise to admit the elderly lady in the wheelchair. Then silence fell, to be broken eventually by Sir Toby. He was related to this new arrival, he had ridden with her in the lift, his back still ached from carrying her.

"Mrs Mortensen," he said, "Mrs Burden's grandmother."

Everyone bowed politely towards the veiled face. The committee members were twelve in number and these Sir Toby now proceeded to introduce one at a time.

He was halfway round the table when the old woman made a move. An arm shot out from the rug, an inordinately long arm in a dressing-gown sleeve – like a crane at the end of which hung a grab in a workman's glove. With care and exactitude this hand worked its way under an entire chocolate-coated Othello layer cake, lifted it and guided it underneath the veil.

Knowing, as he did, of the old woman's deep sorrow and terrible problem, Sir Toby completed his introductions, his expression deadpan. The dowager's other hand darted out, hovered in mid-air for a moment then snatched up three jugs of cream in rapid succession.

Madelene stepped away from the stairway and out. She crossed the patio, treading slowly and with dignity. She did not acknowledge the committee, did no more than nod at Susan, who registered the clarity and hopelessness in her friend's face. Madelene took hold of the wheelchair, turned it round and pushed it the few paces to the bottom of the garden, down by the high wall adjoining Hyde Park. All she wanted was one last moment away from other people and in physical proximity to Erasmus.

She placed her hands on the ape's shoulders. Then she closed her eyes and measured the full extent of her defeat.

She had believed that the law of the land would protect the ape and she had been wrong. She had expected social convention to allow her at least a breathing space and here, too, she had been wrong. She had pinned her hopes on her own triumphant feeling of being on the right track and this feeling had proved to be an illusion. Now she took stock of the universe and could discern no trace – not even out on the farthest reaches of her experience – of supreme justice. She was being driven, unresisting, towards conceding that the world is a machine in which men and animals are merely components or, at a pinch, minuscule self-contained machines. In other words, lifeless – or worse still, a lifelessness that is lifelike in action, the tiny *perpetuum mobile* of death.

The door to the garden swung open and Adam, Inspector Smailes, the two vets from the RSPCA and a bunch of easy-does-it white men issued onto the patio. They split up into two groups, to skirt round either side of the table.

Madelene lowered her head.

"I'm sorry I couldn't do better," she murmured.

Some yards in front of the wheelchair the men halted for a moment. One of the vets cocked his rifle, the other unfurled a net. Madelene looked back, the wall behind them was yellow, the sun and shadows dancing across its face had a merciless look about them, as though this were the wall before the firing squad, and more than that, a metaphysical wall, a definitive blockade against any hope of a meaning to life.

Then the ape got to its feet. It pulled off the hat, pulled off the rug, the dressing-gown and let them drop. In the sunlight it faced up to the men: tall, short-legged, grotesque, with arms that hung down to the ground and a whipped-cream clown grin on its clean-shaven face.

The men instinctively took a step backwards. The ape wrapped its arm around Madelene's waist.

"Let's go," it said.

It leapt like a cat, with no visible preparation, did an about-face in mid-air and ran, carrying Madelene, up the vertical face of the wall.

It perched for a second on the top of the wall. Then it took off, and to the people on the patio it seemed to spring straight up into the blue sky with Madelene and disappear.

$$\boxed{1}$$

London is a troubled town. Its Stock Exchange and banks form the financial heart of the world; its mass media constitute the eyes and ears of the English-speaking world; its libraries, museums and archives stand anxious guard over the most comprehensive historical memory in Europe; it is the seat of government, it houses both the Lords and the Royal Family and, hence, the world's largest repository of aristocratic genetic material. And through the University of London and that institution's neural links with Oxford and Cambridge it is responsible for the inhabited world's greatest accumulation of civilized intelligence, for the biggest brain on earth. With the result that this city is a hypochondriac, it frets to the point of distraction over its health and boasts therefore one of our planet's most extensive and most paranoid immune systems. It was this monstrous yet timorous piece of surveillance equipment which was activated minutes after the ape's and Madelene's vanishing act.

When Erasmus leapt from the wall Andrea Burden turned on her heel and disappeared. She was gone only for a minute or two – a time frame so short that those who stayed behind in the garden did not even notice its passing, but at the same time a flash of eternity insofar as, staring at the top of the wall, they felt that they were gazing up into infinity. But for Andrea Burden it was just enough time to walk to the nearest telephone and dial a number which bypassed the duty officers and put her straight through to someone in authority.

The man at the other end took down the details.

"Should we try to take it alive?" he asked.

It took Andrea Burden less then a second to weigh up a number of complex considerations.

"There's no reason to take any risks," she said. "The experts consider it to be dangerous."

This done, she returned to the patio, from which Inspector Smailes and his white men had already slipped away, whispered something to Adam, asked the committee to be seated and proceeded to present the first public – more or less – and not untruthful – at least not in all particulars – report on Erasmus the ape.

Within five minutes of her call, Hyde Park had been cordoned off. Five minutes later the first helicopter from the Scotland Yard heliport on Thornhill Road flew over the park. Five minutes after that the first dog patrols went in. And five minutes after that sentry posts were set up at fifty-yard intervals round the entire perimeter of the park.

None of those who knew of or were involved in the search were in any doubt that the runaways would be tracked down within the hour. It is possible, under certain circumstances, for a person to evade detection in London. But not an anthropoid ape. Which happens to be holding a woman captive. And which has already been hemmed in.

Madelene and the ape observed the manner in which they were cut off from the outside world from the top of a lime tree situated next to Speke's Monument between the Round Pond and the Long Water in Kensington Gardens. They were not readily visible, the ape having twined branches and leaves into a little cupola that arched over them and screened them on all sides. But obviously it never occurred to Madelene to cherish any kind of hope. The police were everywhere, the nearest dog patrol was less than thirty yards from the base of the tree in which they sat. Wherever she looked she saw men with walkie-talkies, with television cameras, field glasses and rifles with telescopic sights. She knew nothing of Andrea Burden's telephone call. But she could hazard a guess at what the world around them was gearing up for – as far as the ape was concerned at any rate. Not capture but execution.

Even so, her main feeling was not one of fear. More than anything else, she was filled – in this state of absolute hopelessness – with that curiosity which goes on growing in all living things, like hair and nails after death. She viewed the people and things around her with fresh clarity, freed from any interest in where they had come from and unconcerned as to where they might be going – distinctly, like after the first drink – acutely, like being in the midst of a diabolical but miraculously painless hangover.

She looked at the ape. It was following the course of the hunt, absorbed but unmoving, apart from the odd time when it stopped up a gap in an effort to perfect the leafy cupola. Madelene saw how much it resembled a little boy.

All at once she felt at home. She recognized the green universe that surrounded her – here were the hide-outs of her childhood, in the trees of her childhood, with her childhood playmates. Although actually it was more than that, since in her childhood there had in fact been no trees. Her nursemaids had discouraged her from climbing aloft for fear that she would fall, in which case they would be given the sack; her mother had begged her not to because of a vertigo so severe that it also embraced everyone else around her; and her father had forbidden it on the basis of a vague aversion to the thought that his daughter might climb out of sight and into the heavens while in the company of some boy. So the hide-out that now arched over her head was not something of which she had ever had experience. It was like a dream that was only now coming true. She and the ape were bandits and down below them on the ground there were not only soldiers but a consolidation of all the gangs of boys from strange streets and unknown neighbourhoods whom Madelene had never fought against, and she followed them with eyes that were agog with excitement and yet totally serene.

She knew, of course, as did the ape, that beneath them they had – not real live children but something better, Death itself – and without giving any thought to it they both smiled the same smile. Contrary to what adults believe the joy of children at play comes not from having no knowledge of Death – every living creature has that. It comes from their divining what the grown-ups have lost sight of; that even though Death makes a fierce opponent, it is not invincible. The ape and Madelene laughed, soundlessly and convulsively, holding one another up, because they knew that tomorrow, too, they would be alive.

At sunset the guard on the outer wall of the park was doubled and at nightfall stands rigged with searchlights were erected at hundred-yard intervals, lighting up the park like a football stadium. At the gates, men from the London Fire Brigade armed with ladders and accompanied by the anti-terrorist corps prepared to institute a systematic search of the treetops at daybreak.

Even by London standards this was an impressive display of force. And all prompted – as only a very few, including Andrea Burden, knew – by the fact that an action was being mounted against an unequivocal enemy.

Having once exceeded a certain, critical size every organism develops a number of self-destructive traits and in London's gigantic mycelium of police, military and intelligence units departmental rivalry, hole-in-the-corner intrigue and bureaucratic jealousy had long since borne fruit in the form of well-advanced, tumorous growths. And what a tumour craves, of course, is neither an internal purge nor its own liquidation. What it wants is a good, external foe. Erasmus the ape was not just good, he was wonderful, seemingly heaven-sent – like the Falklands War only on a smaller scale, a dragon, an economy-size King Kong tailor-made for taking the public's mind off such insoluble problems as the general deterioration and impoverishment of the city, race riots and widespread organized crime. Besides, it was completely apolitical. And to top it all, it had kidnapped a princess. Hyde Park had been floodlit to create an arena into which St George of the System might ride.

An hour after nightfall the ape rose, wrapped an arm around Madelene, parted the screen of leaves at a shadowed spot and leapt, nigh-on horizontally, into what seemed to Madelene to be a pitch-black void.

Their glide lasted long enough for her to note the hissing drag of the cool night air, the warmth of the ape's body, its stillness in the air after take-off and its gradual preparation for landing. It lighted upon a branch eight yards farther on with the muffled weight of a tawny owl swooping down into the undergrowth, and then it began to run.

Heading away from the wall of the Danish Society towards the centre of the park, it had propelled itself forward by means of its long arms, in great pendulous swings. Now it had forsaken this sweeping movement, instead forging ahead by means of both feet and its one free hand, and where the trees were too far apart it jumped.

Not once did it get caught in the light. They made the park railings as if through a tunnel of shadow. A good few feet above one of the lookout posts the ape paused. The moment it was waiting for came half a minute later: those few seconds of inattention among the men beneath them which resulted not from negligence or fecklessness or any other reason unique to these men, but because it is in the nature of the human consciousness to switch on and off, on and off. In that second when it was disconnected, while the men were swapping places and exchanging a brief word or two, the ape sprang.

Its spring carried them into a light so bright that they might have been leaping from the wings onto a stage and Madelene shut her eyes. She waited for the shot, or the cry that would give them away, but it never came. The only sound was of the traffic beneath them and the wind whistling in the telegraph wires along which the ape was travelling. Madelene opened her eyes. She saw that the creature was running. Straight ahead – parallel with the street but high above it – it ran, along cables, across scaffolding and buttresses. Its physical and sensory faculties could pick out a path, invisible to human eyes, cutting across the city at third-floor level.

Madelene saw the vehicles below them, she saw people on the pavements, people in cars – saw them quite clearly. She saw the backs of the men patrolling the park. She saw the fire engines with their extending ladders and their crews waiting for the dawn and – directly beneath her, on a low roof – she saw two of the police snipers, saw their faces, their eyes, their night glasses. But they did not see her and they did not see the ape, even though she and it were fully visible, bathed in the light.

The ape was climbing higher now, up drainpipes, over balconies and fire escapes, then up another storey to a heart-stoppingly haphazard network of flag poles, cornices and balustrades. Then further up still, to the lowest unbroken run of rooftops in London.

They passed by windows behind which families huddled round the television. They ran across verandas on which people were watering plants. They came past men and women in lifts and stairwells, people on balconies who looked straight at and past them.

No-one noticed them. This progress of theirs was not just a journey through space, it also constituted a passage through the civilized consciousness, and for the first time ever Madelene had the feeling that this watchfulness was not something omnipresent but that it was, in fact, concentrated. She saw how people on the street only took in what was happening at street level. She saw how those who were searching for her had forgotten themselves and everything else in the outside world other than the spot where they believed their quarry to be. She saw how people sitting in front of a television become oblivious to everything except the tiny patch of flickering unreality before their eyes; how, when engaged in any sort of activity, people paid no heed to anything other than the job in hand.

With Madelene in his arm the ape ran straight across a glass roof beneath which children played; they passed a dinner party on a roof terrace just an arm's length away; they nipped round and past a young couple who looked straight through them and up at the stars, and no-one noticed them. And having come within spitting distance of them Madelene understood why. It was because these people did not expect to see them. Faced by the mass of stimuli and information generated by London its inhabitants had closed their minds, quite categorically, to the possibility of anything truly miraculous.

Until this moment, Madelene had always pictured the British capital as the city liked to think of itself, as a nerve centre of sleepless, hyperactive vitality. Now she discerned a truer picture. Looking into these faces, devoid of all suspicion, she saw that the city had its head in the clouds; that – despite its seven million people, its telephones, its never-ending supply of energy, its feverish activity, its streams of nutrients and effluent – its mind was quite simply elsewhere; that it hung suspended in a permanent and only spasmodically interrupted absence.

Through this gigantic urban daydream the ape moved like a circus performer high above a stunned audience. Where a human being, pulling up short, would be caught off balance just for an instant, the ape could stiffen – even when running, even halfway through a turn – and hold itself still as a statue. If a figure suddenly appeared in a doorway, if a face behind a window was turned in their direction, it would freeze into inertness and always, in such situations, some escape route would present itself – a ledge behind which to duck, or a drainpipe to drop onto, as though the animal itself were creating the world through which it moved. Eyes blank with concentration, it executed a sequence of movements in which the city provided it with a backdrop, while at the same time it was capable, quite suddenly, of becoming one with a grey wall, a ventilation shaft or the shadow of a chimneypot.

But no illusion is ever perfect, and the ape's were no exception. There were times when a section of drainpipe came away from the wall in his hand and plummeted clattering into the abyss. Times when a sudden, unexpected breeze wafted its burnt-rubber odour across a dinner table; when a woman in a kitchen suddenly pulled back a curtain and peered out at their vulnerable double silhouette – exposed, backlit, swinging from three washing lines suspended eighty feet above a back yard.

But no-one paid them any heed, no-one sensed their presence, no-one saw them or smelled them or heard them. Until that moment Madelene had never known any form of unconsciousness other than sleep. Now she realized that even when they are awake people may be asleep. Oblivious to space they slept, their sense of smell slept, their hearing, their vision and their sense of touch. And their imagination slept – their ability to conjure up images, which might have held a channel open to the unknown – that too slept.

In that hour a hush fell over the city. It closed its eyes, its lights went out, its streets emptied, it abandoned the last semblance of vigilance. Its televisions shut down, its traffic came to a standstill. Even around Hyde Park, far behind Erasmus and Madelene, the men on watch withdrew into themselves. During that hour there was something rather moving about London, as if it had cast aside all pretence to disclose its true nature: it was not, after all, some superior life form, since no living organism ever grinds to such a complete halt. Neither was it a forest, nor urban jungle, since no jungle sinks into such a torpor at night. What it in fact now proved to be was a machine. A sorry machine – worn out, dilapidated, to some extent faulty, full of blind spots and flat points, and criss-crossed by the forgotten tracks along which the woman and the ape were now travelling.

2

On a flat roof high above the city the ape set Madelene down then dropped over the rim like a falcon diving. It seemed to pitch headlong from ledge to ledge, disappearing from view to return seconds later carrying a crate full of bananas and oranges. It put the crate down and began to eat as quickly and methodically as does a migrating bird breaking its journey to rest, aware as it does so that the longest stretch still lies ahead.

It dawned on Madelene that the ape still did not know her name. She placed her hand on her chest.

"Madelene," she said.

"Madelene," repeated the ape.

Its voice was dark, darker than any human being's, but its pronunciation was distinct, accentless, perfect.

The feeling of all rules being waived went to Madelene's head like an injection of alcohol and she took a step backwards. Even before this action was effected the ape had anticipated it, risen and stretched out an arm, but Madelene was not about to fall. She was on the point of lifting off. Only an hour earlier she had been awaiting her execution and before that she had been a suicidal alcoholic trapped in a breakneck downward spiral. Now she had ascended out of this pit, less than an hour it had taken her to rise up and she was still climbing.

"I don't know when you . . . that is, animals . . . I mean apes, grow up," she said. "But I've often wondered when humans do. And now I know."

In all the time she had known the ape, she had heard it say a total of three words, but it never occurred to her that it would not be able to understand her. What she now had to say was, she felt, of universal importance, comprehensible to all living creatures.

"I've often thought to myself: now I'm no longer a child. I thought it when I married Adam. And at our high school graduation parties. And with my first boyfriends. But I see now that this was wrong."

"Wrong," repeated the ape, its mouth full of banana.

"Grown-up," she said, "is something you become only once you are free."

"Free," said the ape, and peeled an orange.

The eyes above the steadily working jaws rested on her and Madelene experienced the uplift that comes from talking and being listened to, felt it like a warm, soaring thermal, and she spread her wings and took to the air.

"Something else has happened, too," she said. "I think I know who I am now. I'm a sort of princess."

This was a lightning promotion, one which took even Madelene by surprise and for one brief moment she threatened to metamorphose from a bird into a balloon. Then she felt the ape's hand take her arm in a grip that gently but firmly anchored her to the roof.

"It's got nothing to do with being royal," she said. "It has something to do with being chosen for something important."

The ape moved a few paces away from her and straddled a low parapet.

"Bowel movement," it said in explanation.

It defecated with the horse-dropping weight of the vegetarian, like an earthquake in a compost heap. Then it was by her side once more, put its arm around her, took a few rapidly accelerating strides and leapt into the night.

Two full days had passed since Madelene last had had a drink and even though her liver had had nothing like enough time to clean out the alcohol residue in her body nevertheless in one sense she was more sober now than she had been for two years. In another sense, however, she was more heavily under the influence than ever before.

She let her head fall back against the ape's shoulder. Like one of those birds that flies at night, a wild duck or a nightingale, she looked up at the stars to get her bearings and what met her eyes was more than just tiny, gleaming pinpoints, what she saw shining in the heavens were the images of femininity by which she had steered up till now, those sophisticated, rapidly burned-out personalities: Billie Holiday, Marlene Dietrich's Lola in *The Blue Angel*, Judy Garland, Janis Joplin, Julie Christie – the supernovas of female alcoholism. But now these fixed points paled, now their place was taken by a fierce self-confidence.

Under such conditions London acquired a certain beauty. Madelene viewed the skyscrapers she passed as sleeping cathedrals of solidified lava. She felt in no way irritated by the city's slumbering inhabitants, felt only kindness and pity because these people could not see her, Madelene, demi-goddess, in the moonlight, riding on an ape, heading towards something tremendous. It was as though the Lord God Almighty had made Himself known, like a kind of talent scout whose eye, on this night, had at long last fallen on her, Princess Madelene, and He and she had come to an arrangement, a sort of contract, the first clause of which stated that Madelene was never again to be unhappy.

Reality struck without any warning. She had been aware that they were no longer as high up and that they were now moving through gardens and parks but in the dark, seen from above, looking down on it from treetops and tiled roofs she had not recognized the landscape. Until the ape slid carefully down a dormer and deposited her on the balcony outside her room at Mombasa Manor.

At first she was incapable of movement. The ape had already straightened up, it was ready to take off, in a moment it was going to disappear over the edge of the balcony and leave her here, the way men had always left women, except that this was a hundred times worse because the animal was only an ape, or more horrid still, a talking ape – in other words not even a proper animal.

Madelene blushed, but not out of embarrassment. Out of hate. It had taken her a whole life filled with a long succession of privations plus a fortnight of upheaval plus these past hours of dramatic flight to come to a point where she could feel that fleeting, magnanimous sense of empathy for the people of London of a moment before. Now it took her one second to turn into a demon in female form.

She pulled herself up to her full height, she walked over to the ape, she smiled. The paralysis had lifted, she seemed herself again. But she was no longer herself. Every trace of humanity had gone from her. Although the ape did not know it, opposite him now stood the figure of pure, smiling, feminine ruthlessness.

She laid her hands on its shoulders.

"Wait a minute," she said. "There's a dear."

The ape's eyes searched her face.

"Dear," it said.

Madelene turned round and walked into the house. She walked through her rooms looking neither to right nor to left, touched by no memories of the time she had spent in them. She walked out into the corridor, walked down the stairs and through the public rooms of the house as she had never walked through them before, at speed, paying them no heed, feeling no fear, feeling in fact nothing at all. She climbed more stairs, walked along the corridor and into her husband's room, for the first time ever without knocking first.

Adam Burden was lying on the left side of the bed, on his back, with the telephone on the bedside table right next to his head in order that he could, any minute now, take the call to say that the ape Erasmus had been put down and his wife taken into custody. When Madelene crossed the threshold he was in the middle of a bad dream.

Twelve hours earlier he had taken his leave – silently, in his head – of Madelene. He had excised her from his mind and it was with the feeling that he would soon recover from this operation – or, no, that he was in fact already well again – that he had turned in for the night. Nonetheless her image had come to him in his sleep, pursued him, caught up with him and fallen upon him like the phantom pain of an amputated limb. He had dreamt that she stood before him and that he had stretched out a hand to her, but could not reach her.

It was a nightmare of the kind in which, even while it is happening, one begs to be wakened and when the bedroom door opened the first thing he felt was gratitude. Then, in the moonlight, he recognized Madelene, let out a roar of terror, sat up in bed alive to the fact that his nightmare had been elevated to a higher and more pitiless level of reality and pressed himself back against the wall.

Madelene put out a hand and switched on the light.

"It's out on the balcony," she said. "You have to do something."

Adam saw her lips move, but he did not hear her words. Standing there in front of him, determined and desperate, she radiated a corona that penetrated his sleepiness and firm decisions that insinuated themselves under his quilt and down into his pyjama trousers, causing his entire being to stretch out to her – this woman whom, in the same breath, he also hated – to hold onto her.

Madelene stepped one pace backwards.

"You'd better bring a gun," she said.

Adam swung his legs out of bed, grabbed a rifle from the back of the wardrobe and followed Madelene, befuddled, clad in a dressing-gown, pyjamas and flip-flops and with an erection that refused to subside.

The ape had not moved. It was standing in the position and on the spot in which Madelene had left it and they could see it silhouetted through the French window when they entered Madelene's room. Adam had left his sandals outside the door, they moved in absolute silence with the whole house on their side, not a door hinge or a floor board uttering a sound. But still the ape detected their presence. It drew itself upright and tried to peer through the darkness before it. Madelene pushed Adam forward; they stepped out onto the balcony.

Adam Burden was not a doubter, he was the inexorable man of action. Even so, under other circumstances the situation with which he was here faced might well have cracked and broken him, involving as it did all the conflicting forces and considerations in his life. It involved his career, his marriage, his home, his past and his future, not to mention a number of incalculable legal and political considerations. But he was not aware of these conflicts. For him, the instant he saw Madelene standing at the foot of his bed, the situation had become very, very simple; it revolved around one thing: how he could possibly hold on to her. Right at this minute he could not have cared less about the ape, the outside world, in a way he could not even have cared less about himself. There was one person who mattered and that was Madelene.

When they stepped out of the darkness the ape glanced briefly at Adam and at the rifle. After that its eyes never left Madelene.

" Why?" it said.

Adam stared at its mouth, at the point from which the words had issued. For a second or so the lover in him gave way to the scientist. Then he shook his head.

"This is some kind of hoax," he said.

Madelene was not listening to her husband.

"I don't want to be left here," she said.

A deep furrow appeared in the creature's broad, smooth-shaven brow. It searched – frantically, fruitlessly – through the useless, technical glossary it had gleaned from its keepers in a vain attempt to say something so convoluted that precious few would ever be able to articulate it.

It gave up, pointed round about, in a gesture that embraced the whole house. Then it nodded at Adam and looked quizzically at Madelene.

"He let me down," she said.

Adam moistened his lips.

"It was a mistake," he said. "Everything's going to be all right."

The ape looked out across the park, and beyond, towards Hampstead Heath, which Madelene knew would form its escape route.

"Shoot it in the legs," she said.

Adam lowered the rifle and took aim. The ape ignored him. In its face, a face that Madelene was very gradually getting to know, she saw something new, something quite inconceivable in an animal, nestling like a shadow in the corner of its eye. It was not fear, it was not animal ignorance as to the impending danger of the situation. It was sadness, or possibly despair.

She walked into the line of fire.

"Wait just a moment," she said.

Adam looked from her to the ape and back again.

She walked over to Erasmus.

"I've just had a thought," she said.

"Move," said Adam.

Madelene did not hear him.

"You know," she said, "what I've been chosen for."

The ape regarded Madelene intently. Both it and she had forgotten everything else around them. And so they did not see Adam raise the rifle. He was no longer aiming at the ape's thigh. He was aiming at its head.

"To go with you," said Madelene. "That's what I was meant to do. Observe your behaviour. Like a zoological experiment."

She said it very softly but there was something in her voice, something heard only occasionally, very rarely, in a woman's voice when there is a thing which is vitally important to her and she reaches for it – never forcing it: a kind of music, the music of the spheres, an ultrasonic signal directed straight at a man's central nervous system. And so, too, it struck both the ape's and Adam's. For a split-second they both stood there, vibrating like a pair of tuning forks.

The next instant a surge of murderous jealousy shot through Adam and out of his index finger, and he squeezed the trigger.

Too late. The white-hot projectile sped out into the world, never to find its target. It flew whistling across the southern side of Hampstead Heath then, over the Vale of Heath, it began to waver and rotate and lose height, before falling impotent to earth. For by the time Adam pulled the trigger the ape had already, a moment before, wrapped an arm round Madelene, lifted her off her feet and leapt off the balcony.

3

Seven days they were under way.

The first night brought them to the outskirts of Greater London and after that they travelled during daytime. To begin with through parks and housing estates, later along ditches and hedgerows and later still along the banks of rivers and through orchards and woods. No human set eyes on them and even the wild animals they passed, even the pheasants, foxes, badgers and deer had no time to register them before they were off again, leaving no trace of themselves other than the scent, baffling to animals, of anthropoid ape with a dash of perfume.

The only living creatures in a position to observe them long enough to see which way they went were the birds of prey that overtook them, dropped out of the skies, drew closer and hovered for a moment in the air. Madelene waved when she saw them, as two motorcyclists or two nuns passing one another will signal to say that while everyone else may be tied down they alone are free.

If she could have flown and taken wing with the birds and followed them she would have seen that every single bird was part of a pattern, one among millions of birds traversing at one and the same time throughout Europe the same line of latitude and all with the same purpose in mind: to mate, build nests and have young, and set against this greater design each and every unique and free-as-air bird was fettered and anonymous. But Madelene could not fly and at this point her thoughts barely left the ground, far too taken up was she with being able for the first time in her life to do, brilliantly, exactly as she pleased. She never watched the birds for long and she never guessed that the reason they only ever hung over her and the ape for a very little while was not because they gave up any idea of them as potential prey or gave up trying to understand them. Not at all. It was because the birds had seen that this at once shaggy and smooth-skinned, multi-headed creature was neither hunter nor hunted. It was making its way towards a definite geographical and psychic location. It was migrating, just as they were.

It might have looked as though it was the ape who chose their route and it may even have seemed that way to the creature itself. But in fact – as is so often the case – it was Madelene, the woman, who with the minimum of almost passive but nonetheless unremitting, intuitive obstinacy dictated their course.

That first night, in the still dusky light of dawn, while she kicked her heels the ape had broken into a department store, neat as you like, and helped itself to two air beds, two sleeping mats, two extra-long goose-down quilts, two sets of bed linen and a large expedition ruck-sack in which most comfortably to carry it all. The first time it made up beds for them on the mats, in a tall oak on the edge of suburban St Alban's botanic gardens, Madelene – noticing that it had had the nerve in the gloom of the department store to grope its way to bedclothes of especially soft, long-fibred Egyptian cotton – realized that besides being a large anthropoid ape it was also an arrant free-loader and from that moment on she steered them in one particular direction.

At a crossroads, having divined the wording on a road sign from some distance off, she made an imperceptible decision. When they left the shadow of a forest and had to choose which way to go next, she came with an all but invisible suggestion based on a tenuous under-standing of the four points of the compass. She compared – virtually without being aware of it – the names of the villages they passed with a cartographical snippet in her head.

Erasmus ate, she discovered, 20 to 30 pounds of fresh fruit in a day, supplemented if possible by nuts and raisins, better still by honey, best of all by five pints of double cream. And to crown it all these provisions should be easily obtainable, within easy reach – in a cold store, for instance, or a parked lorry. And the ape did not care for cold water.

Like Madelene it had a profound and possibly neurological, genetic need for a hot bath every day.

Having once grasped this fact Madelene understood also that they would have to keep to the outskirts of villages and other built-up areas. On that first night of their journey, she had felt that they had the whole of England at their feet. Now she took yet another step towards grasping the nature of freedom. She realized that they would have to walk a line, a tightrope, between – on the one hand – the destructiveness of technological civilization and – on the other – Mother Nature's exasperating lack of creature comforts. That right from the start there had been only one course for them to take: to a place where one could stay under cover and have one's food laid on, a place which could accommodate both their congenital yearning for freedom and their congenital laziness. She had spent eighteen months awash with zoological information. She knew that in the whole of Britain there was only one such place.

When, on the sixth day, they reached the fringes of the town of Chatteris, she made the crucial choice. Had they turned east, as any *homo ferus* or any honest-to-goodness wild animal would have done, they would have ended up in the most out-of-the-way, the most desolate, the most isolated spot in England, in the impenetrable marshlands of Bedford Level. Instead Madelene led them northwards. Towards St Francis Forest, London Zoo's private wildlife reserve, the largest zoological breeding and research centre in Europe.

Throughout their journey Madelene had given Erasmus lessons in both English and Danish and the ape had learned fast – not as a child learns, since children learn under great pressure from the need to express themselves – but playfully, effortlessly. On the seventh day they travelled in silence, with no language lessons, no behavioural studying, no waving to birds. Late in the afternoon they crossed a high wall, exactly like so many others and yet significantly different and on the edge of a wood, overlooking a grassy plain, they halted. Madelene's inner compass was now spinning wildly and erratically. They had arrived.

A grey boulder meandered across the plain, coming their way.

"That thing there," the ape asked, "climb trees?"

Madelene shook her head.

"Eat people?"

Madelene had been brought up in the suburbs of a large city and for a moment there was some doubt in her mind. Then she shook her head once more.

"That's an elephant," she said.

When darkness fell they lit a fire in the fork of a tree and watched it flare up before dying down into glowing embers as fires are wont to do when the wood is dry and piled on top of half a dozen firelighters. After that they propped themselves up against one another on the two air beds which were spread on a flat, solid and comfortable foundation of spruce branches. The twilight hour, the teaching hour was upon them.

Like their journey, their language lessons had followed – without their being altogether aware of it – a quite specific route. From the personal pronouns they had sallied forth into the surrounding world's forest of nouns, moving on from there into ever more abstract linguistic territory. But just at this moment Madelene woke up to the fact that there was something they lacked, something important which they had come to quite naturally in a roundabout way. What they lacked was the body, the human anatomy.

She ran the tips of her fingers along the sole of one of Erasmus' feet.

"Foot," she said.

The animal jumped and they both laughed. A little and near soundless laugh, much like people giggling before the altar – the last brief burst of self-consciousness before the moment of truth.

Madelene slid her hand up to the ape's knee.

"Skin," she said.

Erasmus made no reply. She placed her outstretched palm on its chest and ran it downwards. The creature's body as such remained motionless. But directly below its navel its member rose to meet her. Madelene wrapped her fingers around it. It was white and at first sight almost unreal. It had the smoothness of ice, or of a cool breeze against a cheek, but at the same time, beneath this elusive softness, there was a rigidity as substantial as fired granite.

Madelene looked up. She placed her other hand on the ape's face and felt the same thing there. The skin was pale, quite fine, transparent. Beneath and across it she could feel the microscopic, fast alternating surges of feeling, the thready, capillary trees of blood. And underlying this fragility was something else – its pulse, the solid urgency of its arousal.

She nodded in the direction of its penis.

"Cock," she said.

The ape stretched out an arm, laid the back of one hand on her leg then eased it under her dress. Madelene felt the warmth of its hand in her crotch, but it did not touch her. It looked at her inquisitively.

"Pussy," she said hoarsely, enlightening him.

Without taking her eyes off the ape's she lifted up her dress until her breasts broke free. Slowly the ape leaned forward, bent his head as if in some ritual salute and took a nipple between his teeth.

It straightened up and they looked into one another's eyes as no living creatures are ever given to looking at one another. Then it took hold of her knickers – very gently with hands that had no difficulty differentiating, even in the pitch dark, between satin-weave cotton and plain mercerized – and pulled them off. Madelene slid backwards, still in slow motion and the ape came after her.

They kissed one another only fleetingly. The potential lip-smacking, familial quality of a kiss would in this case have been but a digression. Madelene was very soft, very warm and very ready to clench him between her thighs. But just at this point Erasmus stopped and for a second Madelene thought there was some misunderstanding.

"Come on," she said.

Nothing happened, impatiently she pushed herself up onto her elbows and looked at the ape.

The combination of the flickering light from the embers and the dense shadows made it hard to read the ape's expression accurately. Nonetheless as far as Madelene was concerned there could be no doubt. What she saw in its eyes was not simply lust, not merely the beast in him, not only naïvety. There was something else there, too, the subtle sadism of the wide boy. The animal had not left off on account of some misapprehension. It was holding her at bay.

She tried to get out of it, of course she tried to get out of it. She waited for disgust to flood through her from top to toe. But it never came. Something else came instead – more desire, a need, pressing, beyond all question of pride and submission.

"Please," she said.

Erasmus entered her with a kind of sensitive ruthlessness, along the golden mean between pain and sensual delight and as he did so she bit his ear lobe, gently but deeply, until on the tip of her tongue she felt the first metallic hint of blood and her nostrils were filled with a scent, a savannah of scent, a continent of scent, of animal, man, stars, glowing embers, air beds and burning rubber.

4

St Francis Forest was established by the first Duke of Bedford in the seventeenth century in an attempt to re-create the Garden of Eden. The duke was a devout man, he named his park after the patron saint of animals and planned it out in strict accordance with the few, vague directions afforded in Genesis and the detailed description given in the *Divine Comedy* – in the twenty-eighth canto of the *Purgatorio* – of the garden outside which Virgil leaves Dante and in which he meets Beatrice. As with all the great gardens in European history it was based upon the proposition that nothing, and especially not nature, is good enough as it stands. What the duke and his successors had in mind was not a mild adjustment of the landscape, what they had wanted to construct was a machine, a horticultural machine designed to seize the awareness of the visitor and turn his thoughts to God. It had been their wish to create a *drug* of a garden, a landscaped hallucinogen.

This was, of course, a preposterous idea, not to say blasphemous, since any god whose work is deemed to leave that much room for improvement can obviously not be omnipotent, at best he may be a great – though not infallible – landscape gardener and, as one might expect, this scheme came to grief. In an endeavour to stick as closely as possible to the letter of the Bible, in which we are told so elevating is the effect of Paradise that the lion and the lamb graze there side by side, the duke introduced a number of wild animals to the park. Just when it seemed that his enterprise was to be crowned by success, at the point where he had been hand-feeding fourteen Judaean lions with roast potatoes for thirty-one days and was about to declare these wild beasts to be tamed and converted to vegetarianism, they betrayed the trust shown in them and ate him. Over the next three centuries the park underwent numerous changes of ownership and extensive restructuring – under the supervision in the nineteenth century of a follower of the renowned landscape gardener Capability Brown – and at the time of its purchase by the Royal Zoological Society in the early 1970s it epitomized quite perfectly – with its rolling luxuriance, its lakes and streams, its groves, its exotic flowers and trees, its rockeries and perfumed Persian rose gardens – what people look for in a paradise.

It had, by that time, a reputation so bad that for two hundred years its owners had found it impossible to recruit workers locally. It had been hit by so many floods, droughts, lightning bolts, forest fires, outbreaks of Dutch elm disease, fire blight, attacks of red admiral caterpillars and heart-rot fungus and the park's owners similarly plagued by such an endless succession of human natural catastrophes that the very earth seemed to be against it. It was as though the land itself were an enormous creature, a buried whale which, when folk scratched its back, shook itself to throw them off. Just as there are children who are extremely difficult to rear, and areas of the human psyche which are very hard to control, so intractable was St Francis Forest that some inexplicable form of geographical and biological anarchy appeared to reign there. The last owner managed, shortly after the Second World War, to see the park completed and for a few, fleeting moments he thought that he had got the better of the place. Neither his wife running off with the gardener nor his daughter running off with the gardener's son could induce him to give up. Not until the whippet his wife had left behind then had a litter of mongrel pups by the gardener's mongrel dog did he perceive that what he had been experiencing was not a lasting victory, but merely the momentary check of the pendulum at the outermost point of its swing and that ahead of him lay the downswing. The following day he put the park up for sale.

St Francis Forest met with success for the first time as a game reserve. It became the first breeding ground outside of Africa of the mountain gorilla, the first breeding ground outside of the Russian taiga of the Siberian tiger, the first hatching ground outside of Australia of the penduline owl. During the '70s and '80s it boasted the most impressive results ever of any zoo or wildlife park in the breeding of certain endangered species. These results were reported to the general public, which formed the impression that the wild animals in St Francis Forest had found an Eden – a place even better than their place of origin – that they lived a life of mild-mannered zoological ease. This, too, was the reason given publicly by Adam Burden, on his appointment as head of the Institute of Behavioural Research – under whose auspices St Francis Forest fell – for the park remaining a restricted area. The reason no outsiders were allowed access, Adam explained – no representatives of animal protection agencies, no research scientists who had not first been approved and sworn in and, under no circumstances, journalists or representatives of the public at large – was so as not to disturb the park's distinctive air of high zoological spirits.

In actual fact this was not merely an embellished rewrite of the truth, it was a downright, if necessary, lie. St Francis Forest was one of the first research centres to have been arranged according to the modern-day acceptance of the fact that the more animals are left to themselves the better they will thrive. The place was run with the minimum of interference and consequently a balance of sorts came into play, not a divine harmony however but the unfolding of the animal kingdom's own unsentimental brutality.

Adam knew that what the public wanted to see in a zoo were lovable tiger cubs, cuddly old bears, garrulous seals, communicative baboons, child-loving elephants and an all-pervading sense of positive control. What they would have encountered in St Francis Forest was the animal kingdom's volatile ruthlessness towards the small, the old, the sick and the misfitting. They would have seen spotted wood-peckers stealing fledgling tits from the nest, anteaters sucking the entrails out of baby mara, lions serving up cheetah kittens to their cubs, zebras safeguarding their territory by slaughtering waterbuck calves, squirrels demolishing goshawk nests and eating the goshawk's young, pike clearing a river bank of ducklings. They would have seen what was at this point known only to the zoologists: that what really vitalized the animals and caused them to thrive and grow and breed was the opposite of indolence and protection. It was the fact that their days were fully taken up with the struggle simply to stay alive.

What Madelene and Erasmus had fetched up in was the first garden in Europe ever truly to come to resemble its ideal. Not some nice cosy paradise, but the game reserve that Adam and Eve must have beheld, with its mixture of the fascinating, the thought-provoking, the appalling and the utterly catastrophic ways in which the animal world can develop when left to its own devices.

All this they saw. And they also divined something else, something which none of the biologists, gardeners nor any of the park's four centuries of workers and owners had cottoned on to. They discerned the essence of the place, its topographical soul.

Madelene was the first to see it, that first morning. She woke up, Erasmus was gone. She sat up and her eye fell on him. He was squatting by the river bank, drinking as he always drank, by sticking his whole hand into the stream then licking off the water soaked up by the mat of hair on its back. Sitting there, in the sun, his hairless buttocks looked like two halves of a honeydew melon, only twice as large. At that moment Madelene realized where they had landed. That it was to the pornographic Garden of Eden they had come.

5

They stayed in St Francis Forest for seven weeks and during that time the place posed for them three questions, the first of which was put that very first morning just after Madelene had woken up. She was making her way across the meadow at the time, towards the ape, she was naked, she was strolling along and she had the feeling that she was shining. Her face shone, her breasts, her genitals, the palms of her hands. In a moment Erasmus would turn around and be dazzled.

The ape had his back to her. When they were five paces apart it turned.

"Morningsleepwell?" it said.

Madelene froze in her tracks. The ape's face looked open, rested and full of pride at having remembered the correct form of greeting. But of the gratitude she had expected, to which she was entitled, there was no sign. Yesterday was gone, the night was gone, leaving not the slightest trace.

At that moment Madelene grew afraid.

Madelene lived by love, she always had done. Or, rather, she lived by dependence. The few times in her life when she had taken a risk, the few independent steps she had taken in her thirty years – up until three weeks ago – she had ventured only because she knew that beneath her there hung a safety net. A net formed by the conviction that the men who loved her would go into a decline and die were she to leave them. This certainty constituted the essential amino acids of her character. What was not in evidence in the ape, as it stood there facing her, was fear. There ought to have been a touch, just the faintest hint, of meekness and dread. But there was none, the animal was utterly fearless.

It was then that the garden posed her the first question, as distinctly as if it had been voiced by a narrator, and the question was this: Who has made the decisions in the love affairs in your life? And even as she heard it uttered, before it was finished, she knew that she did not see herself as staying there long enough to hear the answer.

For the next three days she kept her distance from Erasmus. Together they patched up their nest in the trees, they tracked down one of the park's feeding sites, where fruit was put out each day, and they found out at what times the site was not under surveillance. And throughout all of this Madelene treated the animal with quiet friendliness, on the face of it she was a happy and contented girl of summer.

But in her heart winter had set in. Her eyes took in the ape with a new scrutiny. She used it to get her bearings in the garden, to discover the location of the closest point of the outer wall, to calculate the risk of going on foot, she used it to gather provisions. She was preparing for her break-out and her attempt at escape from Paradise.

The third day was warmer than the previous two. On the grassy plain running down to the river bloomed three immense rhododendron bushes and in the shade of these Madelene and the ape lay resting. The bushes floated like green and violet mountains on a sea of grass. Madelene had barely slept at all over the past three bitterly cold nights. Now she had dozed off.

She was woken by the ape licking her, here and there, working from her knees up the length of her thighs, its tongue possessing the same superficial softness and underlying insistence as its penis. It took Madelene some time to come to, sleep had disarmed her and by the time she was fully conscious it was too late. Desire bore down upon her slowly, like a ship it came sailing across the plain and when it drew close enough and she saw that she herself was on board and that there was no chance of getting off she was struck by a sudden clarity. In a flash of erotic *satori* she saw that even this final vestige of her freedom of movement had been an illusion. She had been led, to this place and the tongue now sliding over her belly. And not only she, the ape too had been led there for, even if there was something importunate about its mouth at this moment, there also was an entreaty, it was begging her to surrender. Mutely Erasmus pleaded, because he too was a victim.

The last thing Madelene heard before she yielded was the answer to the garden's first question. She it was who answered it, and the answer was: whoever made the decision it was neither him nor me.

What happened to Erasmus and Madelene was what happens to all of those who pass through Paradise, either of their own free will or ostensibly by chance: love took possession of them and did with them as it pleased. But unlike so many others they did not fight it. They had no time to prepare themselves, no time to build up hopes or develop prejudices and when it hit them they had nowhere to run to and no-one from whom to seek help. They simply gave up, they abandoned themselves to the basic uncertainty of this unpredictable state of affairs.

At no point, while they were in the garden, did Erasmus make Madelene any promises whatsoever. To begin with she persuaded herself – half in anger, half in panic – that the animal was retarded or at any rate that its language skills were at too low a level for it to understand all the cunning little ways in which human lovers are forever reassuring one another that they and their love are alive and well and that they are still bound together by a warm umbilical cord. But after a day or two it dawned on her that this was not because Erasmus could not. It was just that it never occurred to him. And what was more *she* did not want it either. She felt the fantasies with which she had comforted herself dying out, she noted how she had rejected her own promises before they could be put into words. For the first time in her life she walked along a tightrope without looking down. For the first time she began to lose interest in the future.

They were heading into a variant of eternity. One night, while Madelene was sitting astride Erasmus, she realized that they were not alone. She was not only with him but with two men, one of whom she had inside her while the other caressed her, and with eyes closed she sensed who that other was, it was Death. She dropped her head back, looked up at the heavens, abandoned all resistance and saw that, when time ceases to exist, the present moment that arises is not without its dark side, not even in Paradise.

6

Their life in the garden revolved around three distinct occupations – hunting for food, sleeping and attending to their love and their language lessons. Imperceptibly the barrier between them was dissolved. They experienced a didactic breakthrough when Madelene reached the section dealing with the bawdy element in language. She had him inside her at the time and she said: "Lie still and tell me what I'm doing to you, what am I doing now? And now? Describe that!" Or she would shift Erasmus' hands and say: "No, look me in the eye, don't do a thing, just tell me what you feel like doing," and then Erasmus would speak without thinking first, then language broke through to him, and at that moment in the shade of the rhododendron bushes they were joined by the ghosts of Denmark's world-famous language teachers: Diderichsen, Hjelmslev, of the glossematists and of the entire Copenhagen School of Linguistics.

They frequently forgot to eat, with the result that they experienced real hunger, experienced being weak from starvation – experiences indistinguishable from the intimacy they shared. When they had gone for a night, for several days, for a week without laying hands on one another Madelene was filled with yearning, and then it struck her that not since she was a child had she been truly hungry. Whenever the animal inside her had growled she had tossed a meal down to it – one pound of chocolates, a caress, a cocktail, a glass of pure alcohol – not out of hunger, but as a means of repression, to quell the fear and the disagreeable noises.

Now she was becoming acquainted with want. She was treated to the experience of watching Erasmus moving across the meadow, sometimes on two legs, sometimes on four and had the feeling that it was not only she who wanted him, it was the grass that stretched out after him, the air that longed to stroke him, the water that wished to straddle him.

Little by little they lost interest in consummation, in bringing their lovemaking to a conclusion. They wanted to be wide awake and on one such night of famished, crystal-clear wakefulness Madelene caught Erasmus unawares. She had dozed off, she opened her eyes, the ape was sitting looking at her. Thinking itself unobserved. Gone was its alertness, gone its brute strength, its indifference. It was engrossed in the sight of her, the look on its face was one of profound happiness. It caught on to the fact that it was being watched, but it did not alter its expression, it could not, what it was feeling held it transfixed.

"Lovely," it said.

And a moment later it formulated – quietly, wonderingly, despairingly, chiefly for its own benefit, as it placed its hand on its chest – the empirical law which says that there is no light without darkness.

"Hurts," it said. "In heart."

That same night, later, Madelene awoke and perceived how the world is ordered.

The ape was sleeping a little way off from her, its body stretched along a branch and its arms dangling in mid-air. She got up and through a gap in the treetops she saw the sky and the stars, saw too that what the grand scheme of things amounted to was a perpetual act of unconsummated, uninterrupted coitus between heaven and earth. Then she lay down again and went back to sleep.

Early in the morning after that same night the garden posed them the second question. This presented itself as a sharp pain which made Madelene sit up with a start.

"It's not enough," she said.

The ape never passed through any sort of waking-up phase, moving instead – this time, too – straight from deep sleep into total readiness. It sat up and looked at her.

What Madelene was trying to say was something she could only feel because now, for the first time since her childhood, she was living her life without an anaesthetic. What she wanted to say was that she had seen, half in a dream, how right at the heart of the ultimate in sensual intoxication and ecstasy lies a spot stricken by famine. What she was endeavouring to explain was that even while she was experiencing the most intense erotic hunger and the most lavish sexual feast of her life, it had suddenly struck her that one can never eat one's fill.

The ape grasped her meaning immediately.

"Never enough," it said.

Then it was that the garden posed them the second question. Madelene was the one who put it into words, and it was the question concerning the course of love.

"So what's going to happen to us?" she said. "Where is all this leading?"

It was Erasmus who provided the answer, later that same day.

They were sitting with their backs against a tree gazing out across the river where it divided into two around a long, narrow islet.

"What's the word," asked the ape, "for when there's water all the way round?"

"Island," said Madelene. "An island."

"Erasmus comes from an island," said the ape.

Something chill breathed on Madelene. It was time, a reminder that something else did exist apart from the two of them, that the universe went on revolving beyond the garden wall.

"How big is it?"

"From the top of the tallest trees you can see the water on the one side and on the other side and behind. But not ahead."

"Is there fruit?"

The ape nodded.

"On the trees?"

The ape considered this.

"It's easier in the shops," it said.

"Are there people living there? Like me?"

The ape took her hand.

"Lots," it said. "But none like you."

It was the first compliment Erasmus had ever paid and under other circumstances it might have been hard to swallow. But at this time and in this place Madelene shut her eyes and relished its honeyed sweetness. When she opened them again the ape's face was nose-to-nose with her own. It rested the palm of its hand on her abdomen.

"Couldn't there be a child?"

Madelene had always regarded children with indifference. Whenever she had seen them on the street or in playgrounds they had seemed so helpless to her and she had thought with pity of how they were now covering the same bleak distance that she herself had once, miraculously, completed. Once they left her field of vision she forgot all about them.

Not so with Adam Burden. To him children were not irrelevant and he had eyed them, not with pity, but with positive distaste.

Madelene had read in books that you can expect to become one with the person you love. But she had never become one with Adam. She had become two. She had split into two people – the one viewed the world as Madelene had always done, the other learned to view it from Adam's point of view and this other Madelene had looked at children through his eyes.

She had seen how children evoked the animal in people. She had perceived – still with Adam's eyes – that children are themselves animals. Cubs is what they are, ungainly, attention grabbing, bumptious, raw creatures of instinct.

And they turned their parents into animals. These parents were, she observed, exhausted, they were in a state of animal exhaustion. They could not have cared less about themselves or their appearance, they were colourless, as though the children had sucked out all of their human energy surplus. They had become sexless, the women especially, they seemed milked dry, drained, desiccated.

Adam wanted to travel. He wanted to get on in the world. He wanted to make love. He wanted to look good. He wanted to be attractive and he was, he radiated energy. There were moments when Madelene pictured him not as a lion but as one of the little electrical substations from her childhood in Vedbæk – tall, straight, bursting with volts and amps and with a sign on the back bearing a death's head and the words "High Voltage".

She had been the very same, she knew that; it was what Adam had expected, and naturally she had accommodated him.

To be the focus of an electrical charge such as his and to light up and glow, that had been her life.

Children had constituted a threat to all of this. Children had had nothing to offer her and Adam, they would have appeared on the scene complete with a greed that would have run down their batteries and deprived them of everything they had. This they had both accepted. Together they had cut the switch to the question of children.

Now, when Erasmus placed his hand on her belly, a dazzling white light was shed on this darkness. And in this light Madelene could see that the ape's question was also an answer, a possible answer to where the mutual magnetism of two people may lead when it is strong enough.

The third and final question was the one put by every person who suddenly finds happiness, the one that asks: how long will it last?

For a long time this question seemed to answer itself by fading away and then vanishing altogether. There was nothing in Madelene's and Erasmus' life to suggest that it would not last for ever, that this idyll of theirs was not solid as a rock.

In the mornings when they woke, the garden was covered in a dew which caught and refracted the light like a mother-of-pearl veneer. Every leaf on a tree curled like an open pearl oyster around its own drop, the tree trunks were moist and slippery and when they walked hand in hand down to the river through the grass they seemed to be walking through cool, shallow waters on which lilies of the valley floated like water lilies and from which the flowering meadowsweet reared up like upstanding liquid columns. Down by the river they met the other animals in the garden, and at this time of day in this under-water world all natural enmities were suspended. Sable antelope drank alongside elephants, alongside a cheetah, alongside a capybara, alongside the reddish-grey and white sarus crane, alongside a group of red lemurs. Even the monkeys held their peace and at times such as these the garden showed that side of itself which so many had dreamt of but so few had seen: in Old Testament harmony.

While Erasmus and Madelene washed, daylight broke. Not gradually but all of a sudden, and in a cloud of mist it swept the waters aside. Then came the heat, the sounds, the smells, and then the garden's heartbeat jumped from its tick-over pulse to its maximum rate of turnover.

Around noon a short hiatus occurred, not out of lethargy, but because so great was the intensity of the place that every living thing in it had need of a break. Madelene and Erasmus rested then, too, in their tree, on their air beds, and often when they awoke they would just sit there, sit quite still, surveying the burgeoning life around them: the fiery rays of the red lemurs, flashing like miniature comets through the treetops. Birds of paradise like some divine joke, three feather boas knotted together and tossed up into the air. The stillness of the cheetah, its infinite patience, its impossible, slingshot acceleration. The indefatigable industry of the she-gorillas. The dominant males' endless forbearance with the young ones. The wariness of the field mouse, a wariness so unconfined that it prompted Madelene to think that here at last was a creature which was undeniably more afraid than she had ever been. They witnessed the extremes of the adder, from deathly inertia to movements too swift for either Madelene's or the ape's eyes. One day a golden eagle flew over their heads – first high above, rectangular, like a flying door, then quite close to – and this time Madelene did not wave, this time she simply thought: we are just like it.

They ate early in the evening. When darkness began to fall, the ape lit a fire in the fork of a tree, a tiny fire, for all the world as if it had grabbed a fistful of flame from the sun now fading from view. Not setting – for in recent nights even the sun had seemed too elated to go down – but withdrawing behind the midnight-blue membrane of the skies on which throughout the long, light night it would recline, permeating it with a lustre that would trickle down to the dark earth as a reddish-grey glimmer of light.

In this life there was no time – at least only of a sporadic and soon forgotten sort – and hence no question of duration, and so Madelene and Erasmus lost all interest in the problem of how long. They lost interest in time.

The truth, when it presented itself, sneaked up on them all-unnoticed like a beast of prey one noontime, in the shade, in the middle of a lesson.

They had abandoned any idea of a systematic approach to their language lessons. Madelene had stopped trying to call to mind the oddments of grammar she had once learned and they were now journeying through language on instinct. She would gauge where the ape had not yet been and lead it there. On this particular day she had conducted it to the Danish conditional conjunctions.

"If I could," said the ape, "I would fly."

"If I could," said Madelene, "I would fly with you."

"If we could," said the ape, "we would stay here for ever."

At this Madelene felt the earth give way and sensed that it was too late to turn back.

"If we wanted to," she said, "couldn't we?"

The ape shook its head.

"There are all the others, you see," it said.

They fell silent. They listened in disbelief to the echo of what they had said.

They were not three feet apart apart. A space now populated by living creatures, by apes like Erasmus. In a vision, a shared mirage, they saw a congregation of apes, a body of apes, a nation. Madelene could tell that Erasmus was every bit as staggered as she herself was. That the reason he had not spoken about the future was that, like her, he had forgotten it. But somewhere there were hundreds of apes like him, maybe even thousands. Their existence must be threatened. And he, with the knowledge he possessed, must owe them something. His situation differed from her own. Her departure from civilization had been a quite definitive one. She had put everything behind her. There was not one soul on earth with whom she had shared anything she feared to lose.

Once she had thought this far the space before her grew very crowded. Between herself and Erasmus, mingling with the imaginary apes, there appeared a new group, a group of people. In the forefront, Adam and Madelene's parents and Susan and her children, and behind them other acquaintances, relations, forgotten school friends, and behind them again the faceless silhouettes of people who had once meant something to her. All of them were looking at her, like children who have asked a grown-up a question and not yet been given an answer.

"Yes," said Madelene. "The others. We'd almost forgotten them."

What they both hit upon, together, at that moment, was a natural law which always takes the form of a reminder, a law that has prevailed in every hermit and stylite regardless of religion or historical era and revealed itself to each and every pair of lovers. It is the reminder that there is no such thing, nor can there ever be any such thing, as a private Paradise.

Madelene shut her eyes and took a deep breath.

"What do you call yourselves?" she asked. "I mean you don't say 'apes', do you?"

The ape thought this over, trying vainly to reconcile two incompatible languages before coming up with an acceptable compromise.

"'People'," it said. "We call ourselves 'people'."

"And us? What do you call us?"

"'Animals'," said the ape, "is what we call you."

Madelene opened her eyes.

"Do you miss them?" she asked. "Your people."

The ape did not answer her straight.

"Princesses," it said, "what was it they were again?"

For seven weeks Madelene had been living in one flowing here and now. It was with some reluctance that her memory began once more to function.

"'Chosen'," she said. "That there's something you have to do."

The ape nodded.

"There's something I have to do," it said. "That's why I came."

Around them the garden hummed, warm and drowsy. Everything was as before. But nothing would ever be the same again.

"The animals," said the ape, "here in the garden, they don't know what to make of us. That's why they're afraid of us. Why they run away. In order to stay invisible they run away. It's a good way of doing it. Something we all have to learn. But there's another way too: if you have the measure of what is coming you don't need to run. You can hold your ground, hold it even when it's just about on you and still be invisible. Because you know where to stand. That's how we live – we people."

"Are none of you ever seen?"

"It might be that we're sensed. It might be that your people sense us. As something missing. Or as something that ought not to have been there. But you don't see us. And even if you do, you still don't see us."

Madelene threw the last shred of caution to the wind.

"Was it a good life?" she asked. "Were you happy? Are the others happy?"

The ape nodded.

"And yet you are here," she said. "But maybe that was a mistake."

The ape drew itself up, with unquestionable arrogance it drew itself up and in a flash Madelene recalled the stiff-legged strutting of the male gorillas.

"Erasmus," it said, "*allowed* himself to be caught."

"And what about me," said Madelene, "I suppose I was just meant to lend you a hand?"

It was a quiet remark, and those are the most difficult of all to answer, especially in a language other than one's mother tongue. But Erasmus had learned a great deal and to his lessons he had brought some of his physical agility.

"When we go down to the river to drink," he said, "sometimes, quite often, the sun appears. Even though that wasn't what we were after. Now and again, when you go looking for something small, you come up with something big."

Madelene shut her eyes. Like a ripe peach, she savoured her lover's rapidly developing eloquence.

"Even if one is content," the ape went on, "even if it was, even if it still is a good life for us, even if we are quite, quite content, there would still be, there are, always . . . the others, your people."

They looked at one another and knew that they had arrived at the answer to the garden's final question. They said not another word. They had reached the outer limits of language and what now occurred, the last stage of their journey, its farthest point, was wordless. They sat on a promontory, a linguistic *ultima Thule* and what they spied far off in the distance were the contours of an answer to their question: why can't two people or a band of apes shut themselves off in Paradise?

They perceived that this question is part and parcel of a bigger, a much bigger one: why hasn't everything gone on being the same as it was in the beginning, why is the paradisiacal condition not a *steady state*?

The answer one arrives at depends on the point from which one asks the question and Madelene and Erasmus asked it from a position 80 feet above the ground in the Garden of Eden, sitting hand in hand on two air beds, and the answer they reached in the same breath was that when the world starts to move it does so thanks to love. They saw – they thought they saw – that either above or below them there sat a god, perhaps the Almighty, holding something or someone by the hand, perhaps an ape, and who was happy and for that very reason could by no stretch of the imagination be sufficient unto Himself.

1

If, on that July evening, one had come gliding in over London and dropped down towards the city, close enough to make out the facial features of isolated individuals, one would at that distance have gained the impression that the city had forgotten Erasmus and Madelene. That it had picked up the threads of its life again as if nothing had ever happened.

In South Hill Park, at Mombasa Manor, Adam Burden stands before his bedroom mirror rehearsing something or other, something reminiscent of a conjuring trick, something which evidently calls for practice and a clear idea of the positioning of one's audience and of what they may and may not be permitted to see. Working away at this, he seems quite his old self again, with all the assurance of a seasoned trouper.

Elsewhere, in Mayfair, Andrea Burden is in the act of trying on a hat, again in front of a mirror, looking as though she has not a care in the world, radiating serenity and vitality.

At the other end of town, at Millwall Dock, at the very back of a pub situated at the very end of a narrow side street, Johnny peers into the bottom of his beer glass. It is not so much at his own dispiriting reflection that he is staring, but rather it is as though he were looking out across that Sea of Futility which has for so many years been lapping at his feet and on which he has now finally abandoned hope of ever making land.

Some way from there, on the outskirts of the Isle of Dogs, the man who until not so long ago had gone by the name of Bally, is gazing down into the Thames just at the point where it flows past the boat which not so long ago was known as *The Ark* but which has now taken a new name, and the look on his face is, as it has been for many years, equable and inscrutable.

On the opposite bank of the Thames, at veterinary police HQ at St Thomas' Hospital, Inspector Smailes gets up from his chair and walks over to the window. What he is contemplating is not to be found beyond the glass, what he is staring at with something akin to jaded force of habit, is his own face in the windowpane.

In another office, much bigger, in the Holland Park Veterinary Clinic, sits Alexander Bower, jittery as ever, clutching a telephone receiver. He has dialled the number, but this call goes – as is so often the case with telephone calls – unanswered. There is no-one at the place he has rung to take the call, no-one apart from Firkin the veterinary odontologist who is wandering up and down through suite upon suite of offices and laboratories paying no heed to the instrument's peal. He has stayed on at the Institute long after the end of his working day but even that, under normal circumstances, would give no cause for wonder.

At this distance, at such close range, it is as though Madelene and Erasmus had never existed.

But if one pulls back, just a little farther back, a new picture comes into focus.

Adam Burden has been appointed the new director of the New London Regent's Park Zoological Garden. He was elected to great acclaim, not a single voice raised against him. His reputation as a scientist and his *curriculum vitae* are impeccable, he has the support of Andrea Burden and all the animal protection societies, he has the backing of the investors, he has the Department of National Heritage's seal of approval and comes recommended by the Royal Zoological Society. Furthermore, due to that dreadful incident with his wife he has the most cordial sympathies of the public and of the media. At the end of July – a week from now – he would be officially installed in his new post.

It is his induction he is now rehearsing. This will be held in the assembly hall of the new zoo, in the presence of representatives of

Her Majesty's Government, the patron of the Royal Zoological Society Her Royal Highness Princess Anne and other members of the Royal Family.

The subject of his speech will be Erasmus.

This will be one of the most momentous zoological speeches of the twentieth century. The totally unforeseen disclosure of the discovery of a new and hitherto unknown mammal, an apparently highly intelligent anthropoid ape. His speech would be supplemented by slides, drawings, the brain-scan results, a complete anatomical description of Erasmus, a physio-chemical analysis of his feed, excreta and metabolism, an outline of his behavioural pattern and a genetic record compiled by the DNA laboratory at the Institute for Population Biology. It is Alexander Bower who is supposed to furnish this last record, but as yet it has not been forthcoming, hence Bower's call and his impatience. The DNA laboratory is attached to the Institute of Animal Behavioural Research – where Firkin works. Which is how Firkin caught wind of the inquiry. Which is why he is roaming the laboratories after hours.

Firkin is thinking about the ape and about Madelene. Since their disappearance he has not been able to stop thinking about them. Nor has Inspector Smailes, and it is the unpleasant feeling induced by the memory of them, the feeling of something unresolved, that moves the inspector to gravitate towards his own reflection.

Once the scientific proof has been set forth, it is Adam's and Andrea's wish that one particular testimony dealing with the circumstances of the ape's capture should be presented and it is the man formerly known as Bally who is to present it, and it is for doing this that his boat and his liberty have been restored to him. There is, however, another testimony – having to do with Bally's true identity and how the ape actually arrived in London – which must absolutely not be given, and one person who must therefore on no account show his face and that person is Johnny, and as an incentive to stay well out of it he has received a number of threats and a sum of money which he is now in the process of drinking away. Johnny has been on the bottle for seven weeks, ever since Madelene and Erasmus disappeared, and where other people will take as many as twenty years to drink themselves to death Johnny has displayed such a singular talent for alcoholism that in his case it looks as though the process is going to be speeded up considerably.

This speech is not only scientifically unique, not only the most crucial of Adam's career. It is also of critical importance to Andrea Burden. It is going to supply the zoo with its first official accreditation. It would be made clear that it was this new zoo and its scientific resources which had made the discovery and detailing of the new ape possible.

The speech will conclude with the announcement that the New London Regent's Park Zoo is to include a large – a vast – enclosure for apes like Erasmus, an ape island. And, last of all, Adam was going to name the new ape, not – as is the custom – after whoever discovered the animal, or after certain characteristics of the animal, or after the place where it had been found. Instead it was to be named after that place where it would be on display for evermore, home of the zoological pioneers who had unearthed it from its hiding place, site of the scientific bodies which had been the first to classify it. Erasmus was to be known as *Pongo hominoides londiniensis*.

So, at such a remove there can be no doubt that for these people everything over the past seven weeks has revolved around Erasmus and Madelene.

Or rather: around what they would like to remember them for. And around what they have dared to remember. Because there are some things, particularly concerning the moment when the ape sprang aloft with Madelene and disappeared, which they are trying to forget, things which – were they to rise to the surface – would ruin the impression of sensational credibility which Adam's speech is meant to create.

The woman and the ape have gone. Now it is a matter of getting the best possible mileage out of the trail they have left behind them.

But Madelene and Erasmus have not gone. They are closer than anyone imagines, crouched on the edge of a wood atop a ridge overlooking Edgware, in north-west London. And from this point the city presents a third view of itself. From here its concrete silhouette arches into a dome not unlike the skull of a malevolent gnome creeping out from under the stone beneath which it has lain for two thousand years, to find a butterfly and rip off its wings.

They are hunkered down on a branch, the ape is naked and Madelene wears nothing but a bit of cloth around the top half of her body and another bit of cloth around her bottom half. Outwardly they look like two displaced apes – for Madelene, too, could pass for an ape. Erasmus rarely carries her now, she can manage on her own, even 70 or 80 feet above the ground. And the way she sits there on the branch, curling her toes around it, one might think she was growing fingers on her feet. Erasmus' face is clean-shaven – Madelene insists upon this, she wants to be able to lay eyes and hands on him directly – but on the top of his head grows a layer of fine, white down. So, too, with Madelene's head. Her hair has been bleached white by the sun and cropped to make it easier to get at the head lice. And while she surveys the city she catches a louse and crushes it between her thumbnails.

There is a new coolness in the air and Madelene shudders. They look so frail sitting there on that branch she and Erasmus, so helpless. They seem, on this night in July, like the feeblest, most improbable hit squad ever to strike London Town.

2

There was one other person who had been thinking about Madelene and Erasmus, who had possibly thought about them more than anyone else, and that someone else was Susan. Today was the first day in seven weeks that they had not been in her thoughts. She had forced herself out of the depression that had fallen on her at their disappearance by coaxing her husband and children into leaving the flat for an hour and a half. And during this time her lover paid her a call.

Susan had a penchant for compact sexual encounters. They were apt for London life. There was something provocatively unnerving about knowing that even as such a scenario called for particular care in its planning, implementation and mopping up – all the while in a state of utter abandonment – the whole thing had to be over, leaving no traces in its wake, inside ninety minutes.

Here she was getting undressed. Here she was stepping into the shower. Here she turned on the hot water.

"Are you coming?" she called.

In the living room Donny LaBrillo peeled off his jacket, unbuttoned his white shirt, slipped it off his shoulders and contemplated his mirror image in a piece of Japanese lacquerwork.

Donny was one of a new generation of boxers – handsomer, slimmer and smarter than Henry Cooper in his heyday ever dared to dream of being. After seventeen wins in as many sensational professional light-heavyweight bouts under the British Boxing Board of Control he looked like an angel straight from Heaven, and one who had never donned a boxing glove.

He liked this set-up. Very elegant. The woman had class. The fancy apartment and the park-like grounds in which it lay. He liked the thought of being in strange pastures. LaBrillo the Stud among another man's flowers.

He looked around him. He liked the exotic antiques. The lacquer-work. The blue porcelain elephants in the window bay. The life-size doll on the sofa. The elongated masks on the wall.

His eyes slid back to the sofa. That was no doll sitting there at all. It was a man. Flat-skulled and with a blanket round his shoulders, like a punchy at a toga party.

"What the hell?" said Donny.

Erasmus eased himself to his feet. This man was the first human being other than Madelene with whom he was to communicate. It was imperative that he be correct in every detail of grammar and etiquette.

"How do you do?" he said, slowly and distinctly. "Now let me show you out."

LaBrillo stared at the ape.

"I have an appointment here," he said.

"I am delighted to hear it," said Erasmus.

He ushered the boxer solicitously through the hall and opened the door.

"Thank you so much for calling."

LaBrillo made a little side step and dropped his right shoulder ever so slightly. Then he belted Erasmus in the midriff, just under the breastbone and level with the solar plexus, at a point where the layer of muscle is very thin.

It was not like hitting a concrete wall, because there was a certain superficial elasticity to the torso beneath the blanket. It was like ramming your fist into the wall of a padded cell.

LaBrillo straightened up and stared at the ape. He had earned a few KOs with that punch. Being hit like that would give any ordinary untrained man in the street a heart attack.

The ape's expression remained deadpan. Gently it nudged LaBrillo through the doorway.

"Very best wishes for the future," it said. "Come back soon."

Then it shut the door.

LaBrillo grabbed hold of the banister, looking for some sort of mainstay in his life. He stood there, outside the closed door, for some time. Then he turned around and slowly, barechested, he started down the stairs, walking away from his first defeat as a professional.

Erasmus and Madelene sat down opposite one another in the living room. The ape picked up the boxer's jacket and put it on. The sleeves were too short. It pulled a pair of sunglasses out of an inside pocket and placed them on its nose. Madelene reached for the ape's hand, it stretched out an arm that extended with ease from the sofa back across the coffee table. Madelene put its hand over her crotch and before her eyes the ape's face gradually changed colour, from pale yellow to chocolate. It was blushing.

"Donny," called Susan from the bathroom. "Grunt like a pig."

The bathroom door opened. Susan gaped at them.

"Donny's gone," said Madelene. "He wanted his Mummy."

It was more than fifteen years since Susan had begun experimenting with the quicksilver of hastily improvised sex and she had developed the reflexes of an explosives expert. Losing none of her outward composure, she wrapped herself in a large bath towel, hugged Madelene, shook Erasmus by the hand and sat down on the sofa.

But inwardly she was terrified.

It was their poverty which scared her. The experience of being confronted, for the very first time, by two people with not a thing to their name – not even clothes for their backs – and no social backup. "We've been . . . out of town," said Madelene. "We know nothing."

Every unforeseen catastrophe separates people into two groups. Those who panic and those who operate at maximum efficiency and save the fear and trembling for later. Susan launched into a meticulous and unexpurgated account of what she knew – of Adam, of Andrea Burden and of the New London Regent's Park Zoological Garden.

As she spoke she became aware of a warmth which prompted her to glance towards the radiator and the grate, but both were out of action. The radiation emanated from somewhere on the other side of the coffee table and after a while she succeeded in locating it. It was the heat of people in love. It glowed in the space between Madelene and the ape as if they had brought along an invisible, portable sauna from which they were constantly letting out heat. Susan snuggled up to this warmth and slowly, as the heat spread, while she was talking, she began to suspect that perhaps these two indigents were not totally lost after all.

For a while after she finished, there was silence. Then she asked her first question.

"Couldn't we just try to get you two away from here?" she said. "Out of the country?"

Madelene shook her head.

"There are the others," she said, "Other apes, like Erasmus. If the outside world gets to hear of their existence they'll be hunted down as never before. Trophy hunters. Reporters and photographers. The international zoological underworld. Hordes of scientists. Just the fact of knowing – Adam's way of knowing – destroys anything of which we have any knowledge. Or changes it."

She stood up.

"Johnny," she said. "The man who drove us. We have to find Johnny."

Susan looked keenly at her friend. The cloven-hoofed obstinacy upon which she had remarked not so long ago had now been joined by a new trait: the panoramic perspective of a bird of prey. She checked her watch.

"You'll need clothes," she said. "And money."

"Would it," inquired the ape, "be too much to ask to have a hot shower? And if I might borrow a scraper?"

Susan let them out through the back door.

Erasmus was kitted out in a pair of flip-flops, the baggy trousers from a karate suit, a tee-shirt ripped at the sleeves – this, however, being topped by LaBrillo's jacket – sunglasses and a felt hat with slits cut in its brim and crown.

The overall effect, while not exactly harmonious, was in no way alarming. The ape paused for a moment on the landing, resting on its knuckles, then it straightened up, rectified its posture and tipped the sunglasses forward. Erasmus had entered the world of man.

Madelene and Susan stood facing one another. Madelene had borrowed some sandals, a long skirt, a blouse and a cardigan. She was her old self again and yet at the same time someone whom Susan had never seen before: a woman with a share in a sauna.

Susan followed Erasmus with her eyes. His careful tread, the mindfulness around hip level.

"We've never taken any of one another's belongings," she said. "But maybe sometime I could borrow him . . ."

It sounded like a joke and Madelene smiled at it, too, and leant forwards to kiss her friend on the cheek.

But it was not just a joke and this Madelene knew and her kiss was not merely a show of affection. As she leant forwards – cautiously, consciously – she rubbed her temple against Susan's and ten head lice, ten bloodthirsty, ineradicable *anoplura* which Madelene and Erasmus had caught from the red lemurs, and twenty-five of the lice's sticky, robust eggs passed from Madelene's cropped scrubland to Susan's rampant temperate rain forest.

"That," said Madelene, "we will have to talk about."

3

Hampton Park racecourse has accomplished the feat of lying on the same spot and maintaining the same appearance for twenty-five years while everything it has enclosed for all that time has been going downhill. The horses are going downhill, the jockeys are going downhill, and so are the spectators. On this particular afternoon no-one was going downhill faster than Johnny.

The two thousand pounds and the threats he had received from Andrea Burden upon his incomprehensible release from custody had produced much the same effect as if she had put a pair of gilded lead shoes on him and tossed him into deep water. Now, seven weeks on, he was settling on the sea bed.

At his side stood Samson. Johnny looked down at the dog with bleary but fond eyes. Its coat was thick and glossy, its nails clipped short, its eyes clear, its nose cool. It stood as only a Dobermann can stand, as though perpetually posing for a photograph for next year's Kennel Club calendar. When – and it would be soon – Johnny was no more, the van was to be sold and all the money raised from its sale would go to Samson, and he would have a good life. At this moment the dog radiated the carefree contentment and the pluck that Johnny had never himself possessed.

But now a sudden change occurred. The gleaming hair on Samson's back lifted and stood on end, giving him instantly the look of a wire-bristled brush. Then his ears were pressed back flat against his head and his teeth bared. Then he rolled over onto his back, gave a little whine and stuck all four legs in the air.

Johnny bent down. Samson was not sick, he was not having a fit;

he had not thrown himself to the ground in pain. He had prostrated himself in an act of unconditional submission.

Johnny looked round about. The only living creature anywhere near them was a man standing a few yards away, leaning on the rail looking across at the horses.

"So what d'you think?" said Johnny.

Slowly the man turned around.

"I beg your pardon?" he said.

At the sound of his voice Samson turned to stone.

"Who's going to win?" Johnny asked.

"The horse with the red coat," said the man.

Johnny tried to focus on the face before him. Hampton Park is a popular spot for daytripping loonies from London. The face he confronted was broad and innocent-looking. The face of a loony. Sometimes nutters brought good luck. Johnny waved a bookie over and put his last hundred pounds on the horse with the red blanket.

It was a week or so since Johnny had sold his field glasses because he had had to give up trying to hold them steady. Now he followed the field with the naked eye. His and the stranger's horse came in a full length ahead of the favourite.

Johnny collected his winnings. Then he fixed his eyes on the man.

"How could you tell?" he asked.

The man removed his sunglasses.

"I could . . . smell the hormones," he said.

There was something disquietingly familiar about his face. Johnny turned his back and started to walk away.

The man was right on his tail. Johnny speeded up. The man was still there. Johnny stopped dead, spun round and thrust half his wad of notes at him.

The man shook his head.

The hair on the back of Johnny's neck rose. He had not thought of the Devil since he was little. Now seven weeks of alcoholic poisoning had toned down the present and revived his boyhood. The Devil had come to get him.

He shoved the whole bankroll into the man's jacket pocket. The man stepped right up to him and Johnny inhaled the scorched reek of the flames of Hell. An arm went round him and he was swept off his feet. Johnny closed his eyes.

"Take me," he said. "But spare the dog."

The night, two months earlier, when he had put up Erasmus and Madelene in his mobile home had been the most wonderful night of Johnny's life. Out of the mire that for so many years had passed for his life he had suddenly pulled a sparkling existential highlight.

He had known that what had been granted him that night was too intense to last. Meekly he had taken the moment off the hook and thrown it back without any hope of a repeat performance. Now the same situation was being re-enacted, more forcibly than before. In the van, sitting at the table beneath which Samson lay quaking, close beside him, were Madelene and the ape.

"We were thinking of asking whether we could stay here for a while," said Madelene.

Faint with joy Johnny stretched out a hand towards the sink in which dreg-sticky glasses had been dumped to make space for his guests. Madelene placed her hand over his.

"We were also wondering whether you would do the driving for us," she said. "So you're going to have to stop drinking."

She looked over at Erasmus.

"We have to talk to Bower," she said. "If he recognizes us he'll call the police. How can we get him away from the hospital?"

"Perhaps," said Erasmus, "I could."

Madelene lifted Johnny's telephone on to the table, dialled a number and handed the receiver to Erasmus. Only when a woman's voice said: "Holland Park Clinic", and Erasmus took the receiver away from his ear and looked round the back of the phone to see where the voice was coming from did Madelene remember that this was the first telephone conversation of the ape's life.

She curled her fingers round the receiver and pressed it gently but firmly to its ear.

"I would be most obliged to you if I might please speak to Dr Alexander Bower," said Erasmus.

"Who may I say is calling?"

"If you would be so kind as to say that it concerns a large ape that has gone missing."

It took the vet five seconds to extricate himself from whatever he was doing.

"Do you remember," said Erasmus, "the man in whose garden you picked up the big ape. It's back. The ape. The same one."

Several seconds passed before the vet was capable of answering.

"What is its general condition?"

Erasmus glanced down at himself.

"Good," he said. "What do you think we should do?"

"Stay where you are," said the doctor. "I'm on my way."

The line went dead and instinctively the ape pulled the receiver away to see where the doctor had gone. Madelene took it out of his hand and handed him the hat and the sunglasses. She stroked Johnny's cheek.

"Let's go," she said.

Madelene and Erasmus climbed from the gloom of the van into the bright Dulwich sunlight. They then walked sixty yards down the road to the house in the garden of which, two months earlier, Andrea Burden had first set eyes on Erasmus and rang the bell. A maid opened the door.

"My uncle has been taken unwell," said Madelene, "could we possibly come in and sit down?"

There were black and white marble tiles in the hall, and white lacquered furniture. The maid brought two chairs.

"I'm very thirsty," said the ape.

It searched its increasing, but as yet incomplete, vocabulary.

"A bucket," it said. "Could you please let me have a bucket of water?"

Three months earlier the man who came walking towards them would have scared Madelene out of her wits. Now – from her new viewpoint on society and the people in it – she nonchalantly classified him as a layer cake: a base of irritation at being disturbed, a layer of fear of burglars in disguise, a layer of insecurity at the prospect of physical closeness, all topped off by a frosting of urbane politeness.

"We're terribly sorry for bothering you," she said. "An ambulance has been called. It will be here any minute."

The man relaxed and walked over to the ape.

"How are you feeling?" he asked.

"Very well thanks," said Erasmus. "How are you feeling?"

At this most inappropriate of moments Madelene learned something new about the man she loved. That he was incapable – physically and mentally incapable – of lying.

The man blinked.

"I'm glad to hear you're feeling better," he said.

"I'm glad that you're glad," said Erasmus.

The man started to rock back and forth on the balls of his feet. The maid brought a bucket. Erasmus raised it to his lips and drank down a gallon and a half of water.

The man stopped rocking. Now he stood stock-still looking at the ape.

The doorbell rang. No-one moved. The door opened and Alexander Bower walked in. Wearing his white coat and carrying a small leather bag.

Dazzled by the sunlight in the street, all he could make out in the hall were the man of the house and the maid.

"Where is it?" he asked.

The man motioned towards Erasmus. The doctor moved a little closer then stopped short.

"We're so pleased to see you again," said Madelene from the shadows.

She and Erasmus positioned themselves one on either side of the doctor and escorted him to the door. The owner of the house took a couple of hesitant steps after them, caught up in an overwhelming moment of déjà vu.

In the doorway the ape doffed its felt hat and bowed to the maid. The man stared at the white down covering its cranium.

"Many thanks for providing shelter and refreshment," it said. "To you and to your husband."

4

The ambulance was parked 25 yards away. They got into the back. Up front, on the other side of the Plexiglass partition, sat two porters. It was Madelene who slid back the partition, but it was Priscilla who gave the order.

"Drive round the corner and pull in to the kerb."

The doctor's eyes had not left Erasmus.

"It's true then," he said. "It does talk."

The ambulanceman drove around the corner and stopped. The doctor was still staring at Erasmus.

"You're going to be rolling in it," he told Madelene. "I hope it's got a good agent. And a good accountant."

Hysteria drew a snigger from him.

"Its first tax return is going to be a farce. There's no regulation governing the income of apes."

Madelene poked a bank note through the partition.

"You've got the rest of the day off," she said. "Take a taxi home. And buy your wives some flowers on the way."

The two men got out. Madelene drew the ambulance's grey curtains. She opened the leather briefcase the doctor had brought with him. Nestling in blue velvet lay an air gun, a hypodermic syringe and two glass ampoules.

"'Pentabarb'," said Madelene. "Sodium pentabarbital. Adam says it homes straight in on the central nervous system. Two seconds and you're dead."

In the ambulance all was silent.

"I could cry for help," the doctor said.

Madelene did not answer.

"I suppose it's those results you're interested in. They're from the DNA laboratory. At the Institute for Population Biology. The best in the business. They're the ones who backcrossed Przewalski's horse. DNA sequencing. That's what it's called. They set pseudogenes side by side. Then they can see the number of phenotypically neutral differences. These differences go to make up a molecular clock from which they can tell the length of time between two species. How long ago they broke away from one another. It's by dint of this method that they've been able to show exactly how close we come to chimpanzees. Six million years. Give or take a million."

He paused, a market trader's tactical pause.

"What do I get for telling you all this?"

It was the ape that answered.

"The best we can do for you," it said quietly, "is to allow you to go on living."

Thoughtfully Madelene noted this fresh expression of her lover's characteristic candour. The ape had not made a threat, since a threat is all part of a game and the ape possessed none of the strategist's craft. It had stated a lethal fact.

The vet had gone rather white around the gills. He looked at Madelene, at the ape, and reassessed his position. Then he threw in his hand.

"The first time I saw it – I'm sorry, I mean you – I thought to myself, it's some new species of chimpanzee, that's what we all thought, Burden and his sister, too. A sensational new type of chimpanzee. From a temperate zone. That's what we took as our starting point. That's what we told the molecular taxonomists. Of course we didn't show them any pictures. All they were given were the cell samples. They sequenced 30,000 genes. It must have cost Miss Burden a fortune. But we had got it wrong. It – I'm sorry – you were not close to the chimpanzee. It came close, horrifyingly close to – was impossible to tell apart from – ourselves. It – I beg your pardon, you – are, at least in genetic terms, not so much an ape, more a human being."

Madelene glanced round about. She saw the grey light on the built-in cots, the oxygen cylinders, the instrument drawers, the bags and the tubes for blood transfusions. She looked at what the doctor had said and she looked at the doctor himself, at the triumph with which he was regarding them. She opened her mouth to say something nasty, but the ape stopped her.

"We are very grateful to you," it said steadily. "And we would make so bold as to ask you to do us one more small favour – to drive us to Mr Bally."

"I don't have my driving licence on me," said the doctor. "I haven't been behind the wheel in ten years. And I've never heard of anyone by that name."

Gently Madelene and Priscilla lifted the ampoule free of the blue velvet.

"Oh, but you have to," she said. "Otherwise I'll need to ask you to guzzle this."

5

The man who had some months previously been calling himself Bally was, at this particular moment, doing quite nicely, thank you. After having been fished out of the Thames by the London Port Authority, after having been identified and then put in solitary for three weeks, he had received a visit from Andrea Burden, had been released and had *The Ark* – with a market value of half a million pounds – plus another quarter of a million pounds' worth of veterinary equipment, returned to him. In three days' time, once he had given his testimony – under immunity promised to him – he would set sail from London, on course for an objective which, for the first time in a good many years, was not primarily money-oriented and which filled him with a hopefulness he had not known he possessed: Bally had made up his mind to catch another ape like the one that had given him the slip. Not so as to sell it, but to sit once more across from it in the cramped confines of the cockpit, once more to encounter something like Erasmus.

In recent months he had returned again and again in his thoughts to his last few minutes with the ape and it was on this memory that he was reflecting, leaning on the boom that had swept him overboard, when an ambulance from the Holland Park Clinic drove out onto the wharf and drew to a halt.

A woman in a blue lab coat got out and walked over to the boat.

Making no other move to speak of, Bally slipped his hand down through the hatch and released the two catches around a shotgun the barrel of which had been sawn off just beyond the forend of the stock. Not that there was anything menacing about the woman as such, but Bally had not been expecting her and it was just this insouciantly cautious approach to the unexpected that had made him a prince in the hazardous, international principality of those who made their living by breaking the Washington Convention.

"Mr Bally," said the woman, "Dr Bower is in the van there."

Bally nodded politely. Then he stepped onto the quayside and followed her, the shotgun hanging down at his side like a gleaming rolled umbrella.

A man, also wearing a blue overall, opened the back door of the ambulance. Looking past him at the driver's seat Bally recognized Alexander Bower. He ducked his head to climb inside.

"Excuse me," said Erasmus, pointing at his weapon. "Would it be too much to ask for you to leave that outside?"

Bally looked at Erasmus. He sensed the danger, but could not figure out whence it came.

With an obliging smile he bent down and propped the gun up against the pressurized cylinders in the ambulance. Then he kicked Erasmus.

There are not many people who can boast of having kicked the legs from under a half-ton rhino calf on the rampage, but Bally could. He caught the outer edge of the ape's right kneecap, the leg gave way and Erasmus dropped to his knees, never uttering a sound.

Then Bally aimed a kick at the ape's head.

His first kick had been first-rate, but it had been delivered with the left leg and the left side was Bally's weak one. The second was made with the right, it was all one could have asked for and it wrenched the vehicle's bumper free of its bodywork. But it did not make contact with Erasmus because Erasmus had suddenly – and, to Bally, quite unaccountably – dodged half a yard to one side.

Keeping his eyes pinned on the ape Bally lifted his gun from where he had left it. But he had no chance to use it. He had no chance even to cock it. Just as he was about to draw himself up Erasmus hit him.

It was a wild blow with the flat of the hand and had it been dealt by a human being it would have amounted to a casual clip round the ear. But it was not dealt by a human being. It struck Bally with all the force of a pneumatic hammer, produced a crack like a pistol shot, lifted him off his feet and hurled him up against the ambulance door.

At this point he momentarily lost consciousness and, left unsupported, he would have collapsed. But the ape supported him. Its left hand shot out, grabbed Bally by the jaw and held him upright.

But it also cut off his air supply and it was the feeling of being suffocated that brought Bally round. He opened his eyes, and looked up the length of the arm at the ape's face bearing down on him. When Erasmus was about as close as he could get, a bare inch or so from Bally's jugular, he drew his lips back and opened his mouth. Bally felt the ape's breath, the heat of its throat, saw its glittering, conical three-inch long canines.

"Erasmus!" said Madelene.

Erasmus released his grip. Bally crumpled to a heap on the ground.

Alexander Bower had flattened himself against the dashboard.

"I'm holding you responsible," he said. "You're going to reimburse me. For any and all damage to vehicle and/or equipment."

The ape deposited Bally on a cot. Madelene lifted the receiver of the ambulance telephone.

6

Half an hour later there came a knock on the ambulance's rear door. Erasmus opened up and Johnny climbed in, dragging a trembling Samson with him. He glanced at Bally, then sat down.

A quarter of an hour went by, and not a word said. Then came another knock. Erasmus let in Dr Firkin, the veterinary odontologist. Five minutes later, yet another knock.

"There is a limit," said Dr Bower, "to the number of passengers this vehicle is permitted to carry. If it comes to a fine . . ."

Erasmus opened the door. Outside stood Susan.

"I had to bring the children along," she said.

Confinement within a small space heightens and accentuates all human relationships. The ambulance now contained ten individuals – six adults, two children, one dog and one ape. They were there because they had been forced to be or because Madelene had summoned them, none of them knowing why. Now they looked at her, feeling giddy, like passengers on a ship that is too small, steering an uncertain course onto the high seas.

"The day after tomorrow," said Madelene, "Adam becomes director of London's new zoo. At the ceremony he's going to make a speech, revealing everything he knows about Erasmus. I've been married to Adam. I know that if you try to learn too much too fast, in his way, you wipe out whatever it was you wanted to learn about. I have been wondering whether those of us who are gathered here might not be able to persuade him not to say anything after all."

She had spoken softly, but they listened, they heard every word. The children had forgotten the dog, the dog had forgotten the ape,

Bally had forgotten his bruises, Johnny had forgotten his withdrawal symptoms.

"I thought we could give him a call. Now. And then we could each say something to him, just a few words. So he knows that we have joined forces, that our knowledge has been pooled, and that if he proceeds he is going to founder, his life will go under."

She lifted the receiver.

Adam Burden's secretary had had two months in which to forget, to recover, but as soon as she recognized that low, husky and penetrating voice on the telephone, she realized that while she might well be on the mend she was anything but cured.

"He's out of town," she said. "No-one knows where he is. He has gone away with his sister. They're getting ready for the ceremony two days from now. I don't see what I can do . . ."

Madelene stood where she was, unmoving, with the receiver pressed to her ear. She did not try to argue, she knew the woman was speaking the truth.

"What about the day after tomorrow, before the ceremony?"

"He's going straight there. They'll be checking everyone at the door. And only 200 personally addressed invitations have been sent out. But I could fix up something after that . . ."

The secretary's voice had grown tearful.

"After that," said Madelene, "it will be too late."

She put down the receiver.

They were all watching her. She could sense the instability of them. And all at once it occurred to her that she must have been mad to pin her hopes on such a crew. What were they after all but children, dogs, quacks, smugglers and addicts? Losers, the lot of them and she – the one who had assembled all this human flotsam and jetsam – was the biggest loser of them all. She sat down.

The ape placed a hand on her thigh. A dry, warm and perfectly steady hand. She relaxed, they all relaxed. The ape's steadiness coiled itself around them, like the onset of a fair wind, their wait had proved suddenly fertile.

It was Susan who at last broke the silence.

"My God!" she said. "Of course! Frank and I are invited. I have two invitations. And we can rustle up a couple more."

Madelene stared at her friend.

"You go in my place," said Susan. "And Johnny will go. And the man who's all battered and bruised. And when Adam sees you . . . I know him, I know all about men, Adam's a canny one, if you gave him an apple he wouldn't bite into it until he'd had it laboratory tested . . . When he sees you . . ."

Everyone looked at Madelene. All his life Adam Burden had been a mystery to everyone around him. Madelene had been married to this mystery. Now they wanted her to solve it.

She gazed into space.

"I don't think," she said, "that Adam has ever truly had any interest in animals. They were more . . . a sort of underpinning for him. When he sees me and Johnny and Bally there in the audience, he'll realize that now it's purely a matter of staying afloat."

They all sat there quietly, listening, rapt, like the crew of a vessel heading out of the doldrums. The ambulance was starting to pitch and roll. The wind had risen.

Madelene walked her friend and the two children to their car.

"So what was Adam actually making for?" asked Susan. "By way of the animals, I mean."

"Sometimes I think it was me."

"And now?"

Madelene stared straight ahead with that expression of dearly-paid-for lucidity accorded only to those who have staked their existence on another human being, lost everything and discovered that there is life to be found even on the other side of the great crash.

"That's a question he would always have been too busy to ask himself."

Susan helped the children into their car.

"What if their father asks where they've been?" Madelene asked.

Susan straightened up and scratched her head. Over the past twenty-four hours her scalp had begun to itch.

"D'you know what?" she said, "That's a question their father would always be too busy to ask."

Erasmus escorted Bally back to the boat, assisted him into the cockpit and climbed in after him.

"When is Mr Burden making his speech?" asked the ape

"Day after tomorrow. Friday."

"How many times do we have to sleep before it's Friday?"

"Two, said Bally."

"Do you happen to know where he will make this speech?"

Bally avoided looking the ape in the eye. He knew it did not waste time on irony. He stuck a hand through the hatch, took a telephone directory from the shelf under the ladder, wrote the telephone number and address of London Zoo on a slip of paper and pushed it across to the ape.

It did not touch it.

"In that book, can you also see where people live?"

Bally nodded.

"Could I trouble you to look for someone for me?"

Slowly, deliberately, it pronounced the first name for Bally.

Not until there were twelve addresses and telephone numbers on the sheet of paper did the ape pick it up without looking at it, fold it and tuck it carefully away in a pocket. Then it stood up. In its hand it was still holding the sawn-off shotgun. It raised it to eye level.

"Where I come from," it said, "we usually give one another presents. When we . . . understand one another."

It wrapped both hands round the gun. The muscles around its wrists flexed. With a series of muffled cracks, of bolts snapping, varnished wood splintering and clips being torn apart it bent the two cylindrical barrel stumps round to meet the neck of the butt. This done, it set the mangled weapon down on the seat.

"I would most earnestly request you not to tell anyone about our being here," it said. "And to take care that nothing befalls Mrs Burden on Friday. After we have slept two times."

*   *   *

The ape found the ambulance empty save for Alexander Bower.

"I'll be missed soon," said the vet. "They'll be looking for me."

The ape sat down.

"No-one will miss you," it said. "You have no friends."

The doctor's unfailingly *en garde* expression gave way to a stunned stare. The ape's clairvoyant frankness affected him more deeply than any threat.

"It's true," he said. "Not a single one. Isn't that awful?"

"But you might be able to make one."

"It's too late for that."

Out of its pocket the ape drew the paper given to it by Bally. He pointed to the bottommost line.

"This place here," it said. "Pick me up there, in this van, before sunrise, after we have slept two times. And you'll have taken the first step towards having a friend for once in your life."

"That would be breaking the law. There's a hunt on for you two."

The ape's eyes gleamed, with a cocky, streetwise glint that would have elicited a nod of recognition from Madelene.

"But then," it said, "With you people nothing's for free."

At this point an amazing thing happened. Across Alexander Bower's face there travelled a spasm which might possibly have formed the beginnings of – albeit inhibited and strained, yet nonetheless, in a sense, sincere – a smile.

"I can see," he said, "that you really are beginning to get the hang of things around here."

7

The full moon had always gone to Madelene's head. Formerly it had made her long to wander, to drink a litre of pure alcohol, to have three lovers in one night. Now it made her transparently happy.

She lay on the double bed in Johnny's mobile home and every 15 minutes the moonlight shook her gently so she could reassure herself that Erasmus was lying beside her.

The tenth time she woke up, he was gone.

On the other side of the panel through to the cab she could hear the deep breathing of Johnny and Samson. Even the dog had not heard him leave.

Over the minutes that followed she suffered a relapse, a *de facto* physical slide back into an insecurity she had forgotten. In rapid succession she was presented with those sides of herself which she had in recent months started to believe she had put behind her: The searing jealousy, the stupefying anger, the bitter vindictiveness, the porous self-pity, the bleeding vanity. Every one of the multitude of masks assumed by her self-loathing presented itself – as if for a party, a jet-black midnight feast, they presented themselves.

Once they were all assembled Madelene made them a speech, a speech which was very short but conclusive.

"He weighs 300 pounds," she said. "The way I see it, if he loves me, he can live with you lot too."

She had made her speech soundlessly and with eyes closed. Now she opened them. The van was empty. The guests had vanished. Through the glass roof fell a blue cone of moonlight.

The light was cut off by Erasmus' shadow.

There was no sound to be heard, all Madelene was aware of was a faint rippling of the mattress and duvet. And there he was.

She did not open her eyes. She did not say a word. All she did was to put out a hand and run her fingers through the thick coat. Deep inside her, for the first time in her life, she came to terms with the fact that even the one you love you cannot ever fully understand.

8

The 200 people who had gathered on that Friday afternoon in late July to take part in the inauguration of the New London Regent's Park Zoological Garden and to hail its new director, were fewer by far than the assembly hall was capable of holding, but they had been selected with great care. Not one of them had been invited as an individual, in their own right. They had been invited for the fact of their representing hundreds or thousands of others, or because they controlled substantial amounts of capital, or a substantial measure of political and administrative power, or real estate, or knowledge, or because they tended to crystallize public opinion. And each and every one of them symbolized some significant aspect of society's stance vis-à-vis dumb animals.

In attendance were representatives of Her Majesty's Government, of the Corporation of London, of the twelve largest animal protection organisations, of the British Society of Zoological Gardens, of the European Society of Zoological Gardens, of the Safari Parks' Association, of the natural science faculties of Britain's universities, investors, sponsors, representatives of the veterinary police, of the Royal Institute of British Architects, of the British Association of Zoological museums, of the Association of Practising Veterinary Surgeons and of the World Wildlife Fund. The Royal Family was represented by HRH Princess Anne, patron of the Royal Zoological Society.

Twenty-two specially invited journalists and three selected television stations were to convey the afternoon's events to the nation, and not the nation only but to every corner of the globe, since it was not only the British who rejoiced that afternoon but the world at large.

They were rejoicing because this inauguration was a touching demonstration of unity. A demonstration of how a group of well-to-do citizens and property owners, a national administration and the people of a city – in the midst of what was otherwise, in many respects, a heartless civilization – had seen reason and seen fit to endow the world and themselves and the wild beasts with a place of refuge. From an international point of view it was an occasion as uplifting as any sporting event, though with none of the nationalistic aggressiveness of sport. And so on this day the world rejoiced, from Tristan da Cunha to Spitsbergen it was a day that had been as eagerly awaited as the start of carnival in Rio, and with a touch of the emotion aroused by the fiftieth anniversary of VE Day or the fall of the Berlin Wall.

All this London knew, knew that on this day it had the rostrum to itself – hence the deliberate downplaying of the festivities. Like a coquettish little mannequin well aware that she is in a class by herself, the city paraded itself before the eyes of the world wearing a quiet smile and a ravishing yet understated outfit, for the benefit of endangered species.

The mood of irresistible optimism in the air had penetrated even into those places where people live by expecting the worst; penetrated to the core of the Metropolitan Police Special Branch, which had the job of guarding the assembly hall. With the result that – by showing the invitations and other proofs of identity procured for them by Susan – Madelene, Johnny and Bally experienced no difficulty passing through the first two checkpoints in the security cordons set up by the police round Primrose Hill, Albert Terrace and Regent's Park.

For the first time in their lives Johnny and Bally were in morning coats. They looked and felt like two Antarctic penguins banished to the tropics and the weather this afternoon was indeed tropical. The sun blazed in a cloudless sky and alongside the two men Madelene, in the dress she had borrowed from Susan, resembled an Amazonian parakeet, bright-hued and glossy-plumed.

The entrance to the hall itself was manned by two security guards and a woman who greeted every guest personally, ostensibly to bid them welcome, but in fact to verify the identity of each one.

This woman was Adam's secretary.

She recognized Priscilla and stood stock-still.

"He says he doesn't know you," she said. "I've just asked him. He's never heard of you."

"That's what they all say when they've been having a bit of a fling," said Madelene. "What does yours say?"

The secretary backed away, one step at a time.

"I live alone," she said. "I have done for some years."

Then she halted and summoned up all her courage.

"You can't threaten to go to his wife now," she said.

The two guards were closing in. Madelene leaned forward.

"Look at me," she said.

The secretary looked at her. Madelene took off her sunglasses. The secretary felt a wave of heat wash over her, different from the meteorological heat of the day – a warm front carrying with it a smell of burning, as from a sauna.

"There is no Priscilla," said Madelene. "There never has been. There's only me. Madelene Burden. I *have* to get in. It's all to do with love. Can't you tell by looking at me?"

The guards were upon them. Bally and Johnny stood rooted to the marble floor.

The secretary pulled back her shoulders.

"We're so pleased to see you," she said. "Please go on in."

The guards moved off, the secretary stepped aside, two glass doors opened. The way was clear.

Meanwhile, at the kerb in Albany Street overlooking Gloucester Gate sat an ambulance from the Holland Park Veterinary Clinic. At the wheel sat Alexander Bower, wearing a blue lab coat over his dress suit. In the back of the van, on the cot, knelt Erasmus, still attired in tee-shirt, jacket, karate trousers and sunglasses.

"There's a road block," said the doctor. "We'll need to produce some form of identification. And you don't have any."

His voice was thick, his hands shook. He had not been this scared since he sat his finals.

"Could you please switch on the light on the roof," said the ape. "The one that flashes and says mee-maw."

The doctor switched on the flashing light and the siren.

"If you would be so good as to drive very fast."

Light flashing, siren blaring, the ambulance pulled out into the road, heading straight for the entrance to the New London Regent's Park Zoological Garden.

A policeman stepped out into the middle of the road and signalled to them to stop.

"I'll lose everything," said the doctor.

Erasmus removed his sunglasses. His voice was almost passive in its calmness.

"You're carrying a sick ape," he said.

Bower rolled down the window.

"This is an emergency," he said. "An ape. It's dying."

The policeman stuck his head through the window and peered into the back. Bower closed his eyes. When nothing happened he opened them again and looked in the mirror.

Erasmus was laid out on the bed, covered by a white sheet and with an oxygen mask over his shaven face.

The policeman stepped back.

"We'll give you a motorcycle escort," he said. "I hope you make it."

Accompanied by the police motorbike the ambulance negotiated the second road block, inside the Outer Circle.

"You're learning," said Bower. "That honesty gets you nowhere."

He waved the motorbike away and carried on slowly past the assembly hall. The doors were closed. Outside stood Adam's secretary, the two security men and a number of uniformed police officers.

"Inside there are 200 of the most influential people in Britain," said Bower. "You'll never get in."

He drove round the corner and stopped. When he opened the rear door, Erasmus stepped down onto the pavement clad in a blue coat, green surgical apron and surgical cap. In his hand he held a foam extinguisher, into his pockets he had shoved an assortment of shining instruments.

"I've dressed up as a doctor," he said.

Alexander Bower relieved the ape of the fire extinguisher, took off the apron and removed the instruments.

"The key to impersonating a scientist," he said, "lies in striking a balance between making use of all the means at one's disposal and not appearing conscious of that fact."

He removed the surgical cap from the ape's head.

"Now," he said, "you look like a senior consultant. More than most senior consultants do."

Erasmus took Bower's hand in his own.

"I would like to say thanks for now," said the ape. "In case there shouldn't be another time. You have taken the first steps towards making a friend."

The ape was walking away when Bower stayed it.

"The DNA analysis," he said. "There was something else."

The doctor clenched the surgical cap between his fingers.

"I didn't want to tell Burden's wife – sorry: ex-wife. I know what she would think. Here's science passing another turd. And taking it for a sacred pearl. But I will tell you. You see, it's very difficult to tell the difference between the brains of the larger apes and our own. The chimpanzee brain looks exactly like ours. But, all things being equal, what one can say is that the more convoluted it is, the bigger the neocortex, the more intelligent the animal. Your brain, I noticed the minute Mrs Burden – forgive me – your friend, showed me the scans, is the most convoluted ever seen. With the largest frontal lobe. The greatest volume. Now I know we've had no chance to talk about your life. Probably never will have. All the same, I want to tell you that you . . . that is to say your ancestors, your race, after breaking away from us a million years ago on the shores of Lake Turkana, travelled northwards. And after that you outstripped us. We had it all wrong. Burden, his sister and I. We thought we would learn something about one of those hominids which came before man. But you are not what went before. You are, rather, what comes afterwards."

9

That afternoon, even Adam Burden was not representing himself, appearing instead as an image of the historic compacts arrived at between the general public, the Royal Family, the zoological world and the investors, who between them had made this new zoo possible. He personified the myth that exceptional people enjoy exceptional success. And – his wife having been kidnapped and presumably murdered by a crazed ape – he bore the stigmata of the self-sacrificing man of science, bore them meekly, as Livingstone his malaria in Lualaba, as Darwin his failing health following his circum-navigation of the globe.

Circumstances can make a person greater in size than they actually are and Adam had grown, this Madelene noted the instant he strode out and across the rostrum. He was no longer simply a strikingly handsome man. Responsibility had rendered him charismatic.

On reaching the lectern, looking out across the footlights at the upturned faces and the black newspaper and television camera lenses behind which sat millions of spectators, he swelled even further. At that moment he caught sight of Madelene.

He turned pale, as though suddenly drained of blood, and would have keeled over had not a hand gripped his arm and held him upright. At his side stood Andrea Burden. She put out her free hand and cut the switch on the public address panel. She and Adam were still in full view. But now they were out of hearing range.

"It's Madelene," said Adam. "And Bally. And the driver."

"They're ants," said Andrea Burden. "Industrious. But still nothing but ants."

"The press?"

Under such extreme conditions, Andrea Burden's commanding nature blossomed like a lotus flower. She took her time, took plenty of time. As a coach will fuss like a mother with a new-born babe over a heavyweight champ already knocked nearly senseless, thereby cajoling him into going out and winning that final round, she stroked Adam's muscular back and whispered softly, slowly, clearly into his ear.

"This is England," she whispered. "They'll never get to speak to the press. And if they do, Toby will see to it that the papers don't print it. Toby could stop word of the end of the world from being printed. If it were seen as a threat to national security."

Adam shut his eyes for a moment. Then he relinquished his misgivings and his self-will and sank, so it seemed, at long last into arms he could trust.

He switched on the PA system.

"Your Royal Highness," he said, "my lords, ladies and gentlemen, honoured guests. Nature is bountiful."

The spectators in the auditorium had seen him stagger and had held their breath. At his first words they breathed out. On hearing the sound of his own voice Adam drew himself up to his full height, sparkling with zoological star quality. His rehearsals in front of the mirror stood him in good stead – the prepared text, his whole choreography of gestures, opened up before him like a motorway. He raised his eyes and stepped on the accelerator.

"It gives me great pleasure to declare the New London Regent's Park Zoological Garden – the world's largest, most modern, urban zoological garden – open."

The walls and the roof of the assembly hall were made of glass, encased by a network of stainless steel venetian blinds. The blinds had been closed, now they gradually opened. Behind Adam, beyond the end wall of the hall, the zoo – its enclosures, its jungles, its savannah, its lakes and its cliffs – stood revealed.

"A pact," said Adam. "An understanding, between technological civilization and the natural world. Proof that peaceful coexistence between animals and humans is possible. A technological miracle.

And yet even this pales when set alongside what I now have the pleasure of presenting to you."

A slide was projected, 24 feet by 12, onto a screen to Adam's left. A picture of Erasmus, photographed in the Mombasa Manor conservatory, with the plants forming a backdrop and in a light reminiscent of dawn over the rain forest.

"It is my moving duty today to bring you news of the most important zoological discovery of this century, perhaps the most important ever. A hitherto unknown mammal. More closely related to us than the chimpanzee. A highly intelligent anthropoid ape."

Adam had designed his speech as an emotive guided tour. After building up the suspense with his opening remarks and reaching an interim climax with the slide depicting Erasmus, he intended to explain, in a few restrained phrases, that the reason for his showing them a picture and not the animal itself was that this was the ape which had abducted his wife. He would then have moved on to a résumé of the scientific documentation.

He did not get beyond his opening remarks. As he opened his mouth and spread his arms wide he became aware of a surge of tension in the hall, a surge that went over his head, directed as it was at something behind him. He turned around.

Behind the assembly hall lay a building which could have been taken for a large greenhouse, but which was in fact that section visible from the hall of the magnificent enclosure intended to house *Pongo hominoides londiniensis*. On the roof of this building stood a figure in a blue coat. Just as Adam turned, the figure took one pace backwards, executed a brief run-up and leapt into the air.

It was a stupendous leap. With the deep preparatory bound of a trampolinist, the soar of a human cannonball and a suicidal trajectory, aiming straight for the glass wall of the assembly hall.

It landed as lightly as a fly on a cube of sugar. The man – for now it could be seen that it was a man – hung for a second from the steel slats. Then he scrambled upwards like a sprinter on a flat track, up onto the roof where a row of windows stood open. To enhance the organic lightness of the building the structural framework of the ceiling had been left exposed – a hexagonal system of slender steel piping, not unlike the rudiments of a honeycomb. Along these the blue man swung until he came to one of the cables holding up the light fittings. Down this cable he slid, to the lamp and from there he dropped. To land beside the lectern.

There were fifteen police officers in the hall, all of them armed, and any one of them could easily have shot the new arrival. But none of them did. In these surroundings it was impossible to perceive him as a threat. Adam, the man at the lectern, exuded self-confidence, the invited guests exuded self-confidence, as did the journalists, the policemen. The entire building, the entire zoo, smacked of a torrid yet perfectly safe flirtation with nature and its savagery, a flirtation one can get away with because everything is under control.

Adam pulled back a pace or two. The blue man mounted the lectern. He straightened his back, stood for a moment quite still, surveying the gathering. Then he grasped his coat, dragged it off and stepped out of his white trousers. There he stood, Erasmus the ape – naked, hairy, short in the leg, colossal – for all the world to see.

Up to this point the audience had been stunned and confused. Now the penny dropped. This scene that they were witnessing had been staged. It was all part of Adam's speech. An illustration of the amazing animal training techniques they had heard of and observed at both London and Glasgow Zoos. An actual "live" presentation of the momentous ape. Not only tracked down and captured by British scientists, but also – already – tamed, broken-in and trained.

There was a burst of applause, wild applause. The policemen clapped, and the journalists, there was no end to it. It subsided only when the ape picked up a microphone.

"We have come," it said, "to say goodbye."

The members of the audience did not merely stiffen. They lapsed into lifelessness. Their sense of well-being and their view of the world were founded on the conviction that the horrors of this world can be identified, pinned down and kept within bounds. But the beast in front of them spoke a perfect dusky English and out of the blue, with this language, it came too close for comfort – in the same way as unemployment, as the threat of war, as AIDS, as pollution.

"Where we come from," Erasmus went on, "we say that if a . . . person is on his knees you offer him your hand. If he rejects it you offer him both hands. And even if he rejects them both you still have to help him up. But if, even so, he turns his back on you then you have to let go of him. I hope I won't hurt anyone's feelings when I say that you are on your knees, you are all on your knees. So we decided to try. But it didn't work out. We were wrong . . ."

By now the audience were shivering, in spite of the afternoon heat they were shivering. In their morning coats and capes, beneath their jewels and medals, cameras and handguns, they shivered.

"We have tried, tried in many different countries at once and mine was the final attempt."

Erasmus swivelled round, slowly he swivelled right round on himself, like a male model at a fashion show. Quite distinctly the members of the audience could make out the operation scars, the bite marks, the still-raw burns and the numerous shaven patches to which Adam's electrodes had been affixed.

"I tried to fit in," said the ape. "We've all tried. But things haven't been working out too well. We're all agreed that the time is not yet ripe. We can do no more. Not this time round. It's too . . . difficult. So now we're going home."

There was some movement on the floor of the hall. Up onto the rostrum strode a dean from the University of London. Renowned and forever barred from becoming rector by reason of his criticism of the scientific world's contempt for the notion of global responsibility. He positioned himself alongside the lectern and for a second or so he stood there like that, perfectly still, a tall, grey-bearded man. Then he tucked the fingers of one hand in at his morning coat lapel, gripped his shirt front, yanked it up and ripped it off. Beneath it his chest was hairy. Not a human hairiness, though, but off-white in colour, wavy and long as a full-bottomed wig. He pulled off his coat, undid his trousers and climbed out of them. Stark naked he stood there now, next to the lectern, wearing nothing but a pair of enormous patent leather shoes. An ape, a creature just like Erasmus, only larger, older, with silver-tipped hair.

A woman walked up to take her place beside him; a big woman, a distinguished celebrity, vice-president of the Royal Zoological Society, a public figure, spokeswoman for the animal-rights lobby, an intellectual, an advocate of the total abolition of animal testing, the one person who had done most to persuade fifty-two nations to take part in the Great Ape Project, which had accorded the anthropoid apes of the world the same legal, economic, moral and social status as mentally sub-normal humans. As with the dean she, too, stood for a moment quite still.

Out of the auditorium came a scream, heart-rending, imploring. It came from her husband. Like one possessed, he struggled to push his way through the audience in order to prevent what was about to happen. But it got him nowhere, people stood as if frozen to the spot, like icicles they stood there, blocking his path.

The woman drew her dress over her head and tossed it aside. Her face was clean-shaven but for the rest she was long haired, naked, clad only in a pair of knickers so vast they might have been sewn out of a lugsail.

Two civil servants in the Ministry of Agriculture made their way to the front of the hall. Although strangers to the 200 guests, within the Ministry and in government circles they were notorious, singled out and long since ostracized and politically defused for their unremitting, unrelenting, unobtrusive underscoring of the fact that there is no way the question of the survival of wild animals can be dissociated from that of the insatiable, grasping materialism of the world's wealthiest nations. These two were followed by a policeman, two zoo keepers and a television producer, people who until this moment had been quite unknown to the 200 guests in the hall but whom their workaday contacts had long both feared and felt themselves attracted to for their unfathomable, radical integrity – acting as it did as a permanent, non-aggressive reminder that there was something – something or other – very wrong with life today. People fell back before them and the little procession marched up onto the stage, where they divested themselves of their lounge suits and morning coats, their uniforms, their handguns and press card, laying them aside. They were all apes.

Later, at the hearings, not one member of the audience would be able to recall how many apes there had been on the rostrum by the end. But they all believed that they had filled the stage, that there must have been somewhere between one and two hundred of them.

In fact there were twelve. They stood very still and yet they raised a storm that swept through the brains of the guests, a storm of bewildering images of lions, prehistoric monsters, snakes, dragons, rabid dogs, crocodiles and demented mandrills. Their entire childhood chamber of horrors.

Erasmus picked up the microphone.

"When we are gone," he said, "you will forget us. Until we come again. Till then there is only one thing I would ask you to remember. And that is how hard it is to tell, in each one of us, where the part that you call human ends and the part you call animal begins."

He jumped down from the lectern and for an instant all twelve apes stood there, side by side. Then slowly they backed away, making for the rostrum steps, and after that they were gone.

For a minute the hall was held spellbound, stunned into immobility by terror and the vague recollection of the ape's words. Then people started to come to, their first signs of life irrational, devoid of thought and hence totally genuine. They were stricken by grief. They recognized that they had been forsaken, something precious had forsaken them, some great force had withdrawn its protection. They took to milling aimlessly around, like a bunch of toddlers looking for their mummies and daddies, they bumped into one another and only gradually, over a matter of minutes, did their distress give way to rage, to a child's urge to avenge itself on the adults who have abandoned it. They started yelling, they screamed, like animals they screamed, weapons were drawn, they would give chase, they broke down the doors to the dressing-rooms backstage, they raced shrieking along the corridors and through the cloakrooms, they tore up and down the stairways, but the apes were nowhere to be found.

Then, amid all this rancorous desperation, the old backbone-of-steel reflex came into play. One man spoke from the rostrum, an evacuation was organized.

They filed out of the hall, apathetic, like cattle. They bore the marks of what had passed, they were shocked, sick with worry for the future, unsure whether the world to which they were returning would still be there.

10

Even before the last guest had left the assembly hall every corner of the British Isles, from Jersey to the Hebrides, had been thrown into a fever of activity which lasted for about two hours. Thereafter the nation seized up and ground to a halt.

The first, frantic stirrings occurred when – on hearing the first vague live transmissions and the first alarming rumours – everyone, all and sundry, in the country and in the cities, dropped everything and rushed home. They panicked, they stampeded, they trampled one another underfoot, stole other people's cars, commandeered buses and forced the drivers to run taxi services. They all wanted to get home, as quickly as possible, whatever the cost, to see whether their husbands, their wives, their children were still there or whether they were actually apes and even now slipping away.

Once inside, they locked the doors, drew the curtains, slammed the shutters to, pulled down the blinds and switched on the television.

There was nothing on the box but a laconic announcement that all programmes had been temporarily interrupted.

Even the BBC, whose proud boast it was that come hell or high water it would always manage to broadcast and which would have made it a point of honour, in the event of a third world war, for the last person left alive on Earth to be a newscaster sending a balanced and well-formulated report on Armageddon into the void – even the BBC had closed down. When the *Newsnight* team turned up for work, in response to an urgent summons, they had looked at one another and seen that any of them – or all the others – could be apes; that so great was the risk that any move might prove to be a false one, in which case it was better to do nothing and so, muttering inaudibly, they had turned their backs on one another and gone home.

At 8 p.m. the announcement regarding the break in transmission also vanished, when the screen was blacked out, when the power stations which feed London shut down due to staff shortages. One by one they shut down: Dungeness A and B, the French interconnecter, Barking in Essex, the coal-fired stations at Kingsnorth and Tilbury. And deprived of its oxygen supply the city fell into a coma.

With the going down of the sun London was plunged into darkness. The last of the traffic petered out, all shops were closed, the streets deserted and black – pitch-black they were, as they had not been since the wartime blackout. Every visible human activity ceased, even crime came to a standstill, paralysed by a fear greater than greed. For even in the world of cutthroats, ticket touts, muggers, pushers, con men and organized prostitution one needs to know that one's mate, one's bodyguard, one's pimp, one's bookie and, yes, even one's executioner or victim is a human being and not an animal.

Seven million Londoners in four million homes suffered a psychotic identity crisis. They had no access to information regarding the fate of the remainder of Britain, of Europe, of the rest of the world. They grew suspicious of their own government, their own society. They could not be certain of the identity of their bosses, or their friends. They eyed one another fearfully, tried to remember how their children and their spouses looked naked, wondered when exactly they had first met their wives, frantically they wondered whether she might be an ape, or the daughter of an ape. They gazed into the light of the paraffin lamps or candles they had lit and contemplated the most solid and glorious thing they knew – the Crown. They hardly dared entertain such an appalling possibility, but on the other hand they could not help themselves. Running over a long span of years, accessions and outrageous questions concerning the order of succession they realized they had no guarantee that they did not have an ape for a queen.

11

A light swept the night, a solitary car drove through London, at a snail's pace, past the barricaded shop windows, through the extinguished traffic lights, round cars abandoned in the middle of the road.

Between Johnny and Bally, in the front seat, sat Madelene. White-faced, tense, she guided them through a city she barely recognized, through districts she had never seen while sober and which she had never before been responsible for finding a way across.

But find a way she did, with the blind certainty of a homing pigeon. By the time she gave the signal to stop, in the heart of Mayfair, Bally and Johnny had long since lost their bearings. They had been snivelling for some time, trapped betwixt fear of the unaccustomed darkness and desolation outside and fear of the desperation in the woman sitting between them.

Madelene took them by the hand like children and ushered them across the road, through a gate, up a stairway and through suite after suite of darkened rooms that seemed to lead inwards then close up behind them like a lobster creel.

At length they came to a door. Madelene turned the handle and it gave onto another door behind which the sun had not set but burned white-hot in a stainless steel basin positioned alongside an electric shredder and a heap of paraffin cans.

Dazzled, they halted just inside the door.

"Come in and have a cup of tea," said Andrea Burden.

She was standing beside the fire, her arms full of papers contained within yellow files. She dropped all she held in her embrace into the steel basin, the files landing like bricks and flaring up like petrol. The heat of the blaze could be felt all the way over by the door.

"As a child," said Andrea Burden, "I was very fond of jigsaw puzzles. 'Sunrise over the Savannah of the Serengeti'. Seven thousand pieces. The other children never so much as made a start but once you got your teeth into it there was no stopping. Eventually, when there were only a couple of dozen pieces left, always of the sky – well, there were three thousand pieces of blue sky, all virtually identical – it became like an obsession. Mother told me that during the war, during the Blitz, people were killed because they just had to see that last piece of the sky. They ignored the air-raid sirens. Ever since the first time I laid eyes on you I've had it in mind that you might be such a person."

"Where's Erasmus?" said Madelene.

"The ape? On his way back, I suppose."

"Back where?"

"Didn't it tell you? To the forests. Around the Baltic. The Swedish and Finnish forests. This one – Erasmus – was captured on that Danish island farthest to the east, the rocky island, what's it called again?"

"They must have had somewhere here where they could meet," said Madelene. "They may still be there. They may not have got out of London yet. I had an idea you would know where this place might be."

"Does it matter? Do you know what we have here?"

"She's in love with it." Beyond this room lay yet another. In the open doorway stood Adam, carrying a stack of files.

For the first time in a long while, perhaps for the very first time, Madelene saw the man to whom she had been married with perfect clarity. She saw that she had loved him for the unguarded vulnerability that shone out of him at that moment, to be extinguished the next moment and supplanted by that painstakingly cultivated indifference which had ruled out any possibility of her love enduring.

"The country is falling apart," said Andrea Burden. "I've spoken to Toby. The Government is to stand down tomorrow. There's a rumour going round that half the ministers are apes. A commission of inquiry is to be set up. Let's say, just for argument's sake, that there were a thousand apes. In high places. Their intelligence is, of course, not in dispute. The chaos they've left behind them will have to be cleared up. Steps will have to be taken to ensure that they don't come back. That they aren't still here. I have been offered the post of secretary to the commission. Adam is to be scientific consultant. The commission will be accorded legislative status. Provide an ad-hoc government. Ahead of us lies a time of cataclysmic upheaval. One thousand is a conservative estimate. Adam and I reckon it could be more like ten thousand. One hundred thousand is not out of the question. In Britain alone. But what about the rest of Europe! The New World! We have no idea of their breeding capacity, but what if, on a global scale what if there were . . . ?"

"Twelve. What if there were only twelve."

The heads of everyone in the room turned. One of the windows high up in the wall stood open. On the sill sat Erasmus. Cardinal numbers were still new to him. Wanting to make sure that he had been understood he held up first ten fingers, then two.

It was not the ape at which Andrea Burden stared. It was the figure its fingers were underlining.

"But that's impossible!" she exclaimed.

"Ten," the ape's fingers reiterated, "ten and two".

With an inhuman effort of will Andrea Burden reviewed her strategy.

"Nobody knows that," she said. "The confusion will still be tremendous. What about the other countries? Denmark? Sweden? Germany?"

The ape did not reply. Its face was empty of expression.

Everything fell quiet. No-one uttered a sound and yet above the rustling of the flames every one of those present could hear something, a sound not physical but mental: the sound of covert, far-reaching schemes coming crashing down.

Andrea Burden began to laugh, a maniacal laugh. Despite the shock to her system, despite the deeply problematic nature of the situation, she laughed, and her laughter was catching, catching as a respiratory infection. Bally started to chuckle, Johnny was giggling, Adam smiled – an uneasy smile but nonetheless a smile – and finally the ape's face cracked. Even the pyre of paper and paraffin seemed to be laughing along with them, an absurd mirth spread throughout that high-ceilinged room.

Only Madelene did not laugh.

"You let me down," she told the ape.

There is nothing so annoying as a spoilsport, sabotaging everyone else's fun, and Andrea Burden did try to stop her.

"Get out of the way," said Madelene.

The other woman moved aside. Madelene advanced on the ape.

"You used us," she said, "me and the others, like decoys you used us."

"I'm afraid there was no other way," said the ape.

"Through those road blocks, in front of the cameras, surrounded by hundreds of people. All because we thought we could help you."

"I had to have help to get in," said the ape. "People watch television. We wanted to say what we had to say on television."

Andrea Burden and Adam had moved back against the wall, Bally and Johnny had their backs pressed up against the door. The floor had been cleared for the first confrontation between Madelene and Erasmus the ape.

"You told me nothing. You left me to do all the worrying, all the agonizing alone," Madelene said.

"Among my people we say the plans that are seen through are the plans you keep to yourself."

The ape looked down from on high with an air of statuesque self-importance. But Madelene was close enough to discern the escalating panic behind the animal's half-shut eyelids.

"You've forgotten who you're talking to," she said. "Take a good look at me. Do you know who I am? I'm the woman you love."

The ape looked at her.

"I never regret anything," it said. "Where I come from we cannot have regrets. But if I had been capable of it I would have said I was sorry."

Erasmus could not edge away since, had he done so, he would have tumbled backwards out of the window. But he was now squeezed up against the window sash.

"I don't want an apology," said Madelene. "You don't have to say anything. What you have to do is to shut up. Keep your mouth shut for two minutes. So I know you've got the message. And if you don't, it's me who'll be heading off home to the forests. And you'll never see me again."

There was silence, for one minute, for two minutes, for three there was dead silence. Then Andrea Burden shifted, fidgeting, like someone trying to get comfortable on a baking hot sauna bench.

"The last pieces," she said, "the last pieces of the sky."

It was a small room. Once it had been a maid's room, now it served as a built-in strongroom, 32 feet square with ample headroom. The walls could not be seen for the yellow files arrayed on green enamelled shelves stretching from floor to ceiling.

"These are interesting times we live in," said Andrea Burden. "People are forming closer attachments to animals than ever before. Dogs and cats sleep in people's beds, get kissed on the mouth, stroked between the legs. The media are overrun with animals. Children's rooms are chock-a-block with them. It's extremely interesting."

There were only three of them in the strongroom: Madelene, Erasmus and Andrea Burden. Bally and Johnny and Adam had remained in the doorway.

"Everywhere you turn there are animals. When people die, when others inherit, coming between adults and children, for protection, in the garden, in the house, at sporting fixtures, in children's bed-rooms, in nursing homes, close by the people there are always animals, closer than ever before. And deep within human beings, in their minds, on the fringes of their consciences, their outlook on life, their angst and passion, animals abound. So they come to me. Researchers, politicians, the rich – they all come to me because they are all animal lovers. They come to me because I manage foundation funds, veterinary hospitals, dogs' homes. With an open mind I've managed them, taking no political sides, challenging no-one's conscience. To them I am public servant, lawyer, psychoanalyst, priest and the lady who holds the purse-strings. And above all else I am an animal lover, from their own class. It's in me they confide the story of the secret mistress's cat, the divorced husband's gun dog, the children's pets, the pets with which they got round the children, the snake he had her perform with for him, the watchdog he could no longer control, the animal that was witness to rape, breakdown, forgery, abuse. In a way, when they are sitting across from me I become that animal, I take on its characteristics, its devotion, its dependence, while at the same time I am understanding and I listen, like a human being. And so they start to talk, they talk and talk, they cannot stop, it comes pouring out of them, for twenty years it has been pouring out of them. And afterwards, once they have gone, I have made notes."

She slid her fingers over the files on the shelves.

"Five thousand cases. Five thousand sketches of the true anatomy of Britain's upper classes. The decisive factor, without which the New London Regent's Park Zoological Garden would never have become a reality. Without any pressure being brought to bear – I have not put pressure on a single person. I have, however, given them a hint, provided them with a glimpse of what they themselves, or their mother, or their cousin once happened to tell me. I've left them with a vague notion that a room such as this might exist. I've dropped the odd remark. With the investors. In Whitehall. How else do you think we managed to have the area exempted from the standard planning regulations, by bringing it under a development corporation? Getting that sort of planning permission would normally set you back millions of pounds. But this way they've met me halfway. And then I and others have been able to fit the last pieces into place."

"That's blackmail," said Madelene, "You're a terrorist."

Andrea Burden's eyes narrowed.

"British slaughterhouses murder 200,000 animals every day. The last wild animal populations of any size are in the process of being exterminated. My conscience is snow-white."

She stretched out her hands to Madelene and Erasmus.

"Come over to us," she said. "Right now. If the cataclysm doesn't strike today then it'll hit us tomorrow. Up to now we've been able to put the squeeze on a minority, an élite. But the élite count for nothing. Those in government do not wield power. I know, because I understand about power, it's my stock-in-trade. They merely administer it. It's not the rich who are destroying the world, they are too few and too insignificant for that. It is the common people who are devouring the Earth. It's petty greed, the greed of the little woman, the greed of the tiny tots, Joe Bloggs' piddling little car times twenty million in the United Kingdom, times one hundred and fifty million in the USA, times one hundred and fifty million in Europe. That's what we have to shout from the rooftops, that's what we have to put a bomb under. The new zoo is the detonator, you two could help us prime the explosive. Come, and let's start fitting in the pieces of blue sky."

Madelene shook her head. Andrea Burden looked at the ape.

"Where I come from," said Erasmus, "we're too . . . jumpy for anything that goes bang."

"You and your race will be wiped out," said Andrea Burden.

"I'll take that as it comes," said the ape.

It took Madelene's hand and they backed away – through the room, past the glowing embers in the steel container.

"You can't leave me," said Andrea Burden. "Not after the trust I've put in you both. We have need of support."

By her side stood Adam. Now with a rifle in his hands.

The ape stopped in its tracks and regarded the weapon.

"We have a saying," it said. "We say that on coming upon an enemy the first thing you have to do is try to make peace. If that fails, you should employ charm. And if that fails, you should resort to magic."

"And if that fails?" asked Andrea Burden.

"If that fails," said the ape, "you annihilate."

The room went quiet, very quiet, for one minute, for two, for three. Then Adam Burden put down his rifle. Madelene and the ape retreated towards the door. Adam followed them, unarmed, awkward. He stopped in front of the ape.

"I would like . . . to wish you good luck," he said.

Then he turned to Madelene.

"I have come to the conclusion . . . now . . . here . . . that it is best this way. It was never going to work out between you and me. I . . . couldn't have borne it. I need someone . . . sweeter."

Madelene laid her hand on his shoulder, a tiny gesture, but one imbued with great tenderness.

"And you will find her too," she said.

12

The last morning was a scorcher. The sun shone down on London as if through a burning glass and the city and its inhabitants awoke to this disagreeable light as though waking to the morning after an attempt to drink themselves to death. Uncertain as to whether the real world still existed, they proceeded to crawl out of their houses to find themselves – as one always does after an attack of delirium – faced with the painful choice of repeating those mistakes which would in the long run be the death of them or making an effort to stay sober.

Alongside Klein's Wharf Bally was taking in *The Ark*'s fenders. All that now bound him to London were two mooring lines which would shortly be cast off and hauled aboard. A few minutes from now he would be leaving the city and the traumatic events of the past two months behind him. He would never be back and he would never give another thought to what had taken place there. In fact he had already given up thinking. Only when he heard the sound of a car engine somewhere among the warehouses on the deserted dock and automatically stuck his hand through the hatch to release his shotgun and saw that it was bent as a horseshoe magnet did his mind cheat him and force him to think of the ape.

Johnny's truck drew up. Johnny, Madelene and Erasmus got out. Madelene and the ape shook Johnny by the hand, walked over to the quayside and *The Ark* and climbed on board.

Bally considered his useless weapon. He felt a throbbing in the – still swollen – side of his face. He realized that – sadly – strong-arm tactics were not an option here and instead he toyed with the idea of calling the River Police over his short-wave radio, of citing the law of piracy. For the first time since his boyhood he contemplated appealing to someone's better feelings.

Before he could make a move, while he was still standing there confused and quiescent, the ape reached out, took the crooked weapon from him, straightened it out – almost absentmindedly it seemed – and threw it overboard.

"We do hope we're not putting you to any trouble," it said. "We've brought our own food."

Bally glanced up. From the sleeping quarters at the back of the van emerged one ape, two apes, three, then three from the cab and another two from the sleeping quarters – seven apes, ten apes, eleven, all of them enormous, as big as Erasmus or bigger still, all wearing life-jackets, oilskins and sou'westers and carrying boxes and duffel bags.

"Now let me help you cast off those moorings," said Erasmus.

Even as Erasmus was coiling the mooring lines; as Bally, stiff as an automaton, put the vessel's engine into gear and swung away from the quay; as the eleven other apes spread out to bring *The Ark* back onto an even keel – at that very moment Madelene waved to London and to Johnny. And just as she raised both arms into the air she detected a movement which first-time mothers-to-be are not usually able to identify, at least not that early in the pregnancy, but which she instantly – quite definitely, beyond a shadow of a doubt – knew to be their baby, her and Erasmus' baby, rolling around, like a little fish still, in its ocean of amniotic fluid.

Erasmus came down from the foredeck and Madelene took his hand and gazed up at the sky.

"Those last pieces," she said. "It's not only blue sky. There's an angel there too."

"What is an angel?" asked the ape.

Madelene shook her head.

"That's something I've never been quite clear about," she said. "But for all we know it's one-third god, one-third animal, and one-third human."

FINIS

PETER HØEG'S BOOKS

The History of Danish Dreams

"Høeg has a touch of the Ancient Mariner about him . . . He lures you from the safe familiarity of your world into one you didn't think you wanted to know about"   JOHN SPURLING, *Sunday Times*

"It is nothing less than an examination of what it has meant to be a Dane in the twentieth century . . . Høeg's novel of greed, vice and ambition and self-deception in modern European society is a remarkable piece of work"   RUTH RENDELL, *Daily Telegraph*

"This is a vaultingly ambitious and hugely accomplished first novel . . . heralds a writer who combines narrative scope and imaginative zest to breathtaking effect"

PETER WHITTAKER, *New Statesman & Society*

"Buoyant, inventive, and very funny"

HELEN DUNMORE, *The Times*

"A beautifully written story from a fertile imagination"

CLARE BRISTOW, *Sunday Express*

"A delightful invention, a constant surprise"

J.D.F. JONES, *Financial Times*

Miss Smilla's Feeling for Snow

"A subtle novel, yet direct, clever, wistful, unforgettable"
RUTH RENDELL, *Daily Telegraph*

"Smilla Jaspersen is a wonderfully unique creation of snow and warmth and irony. She shimmers with intelligence"
MARTIN CRUZ SMITH

"A cracker, hard to put down, style of its own, a real find"
EDMUND WHITE

"On one level, both a whodunnit and a thriller – ingeniously, elaborately and satisfyingly plotted and with a breathless narrative pace. It is extremely hard to put this long novel down and the excitement it engenders spills over into your time away from it . . . Peter Høeg's novel is already making for classic status"
PAUL BINDING, *Independent*

"An Arctic tale worthy of Conrad"
JOHN WILLIAMS, *New Statesman*

"Høeg is a masterful writer, using a thriller-like plot as a means for investigating other, more profound matters . . . The novel is both melancholy and beautiful. It is also unputdownable"
NICHOLAS TRELAWNEY, *Mail on Sunday*

"One of the most unusual and enveloping novels I have read for some time . . . Smilla is a fully rounded, sensitive and appealing heroine, portrayed with greater depth and originality than the genre usually provides . . . extraordinarily evocative, atmospheric and poetic writing"
MARCEL BERLINS, *Sunday Times*

"The plot whirls with surprises and revelations. . This extraordinary novel . . . reveals some of the most memorable images of life at sea I have encountered. Here is *Moby Dick* without the metaphysical claptrap . . ."
ANDREW RIEMER, *Sydney Morning Herald*

Borderliners

"It exerts the same chill grip on the imagination as its predecessor *Miss Smilla's Feeling for Snow*, posing questions and withholding answers with the same disconcerting skill . . . The power of the novel lies in the awesome truthfulness of the child's voice"

SALLY LAIRD, *Observer*

"For all the simplicity, the tension builds like a pressure cooker . . . The pared-down, almost obsessively clinical language of *Borderliners* methodically works a fascinating web into which the reader is drawn . . . When the delinquent finds redemption, the book breaks your heart, not with a gush of emotion, but with a dry snap"

SARAH LONSDALE, *Literary Review*

"The sustained intensity and brilliance with which the lives of these 'dark and dubious children' are captured is overpowering"

JOHN MELMOTH, *Sunday Times*